Love's Thankful Heart

Featuring
Laura V. Hilton
Rachel J. Good
And Thomas Nye

Cover designed by Chautona Havig

Celebrate Lit Publishing
Visit our website at www.celebratelitpublishing.com

Printed in the United States of America

First Printing: November 2017
Celebrate Lit Publishing

ISBN-13: 978-0-9991451-2-8

Gingerbread Wishes

By Laura V. Hilton

Dear Reader,

Thank you for picking up this book. My story, Gingerbread Wishes, is set in Jamesport, Missouri, and is a spin-off from Christmas Admirer (available now from Whitaker House).

Becca is the sister of the hero in Christmas Admirer and Yost was introduced near the end of that book. And then there is the whole gingerbread thing which is explained in more detail in Christmas Admirer. Gingerbread Wishes is a novella and there isn't a whole lot of room. Early readers of Christmas Admirer fell in love with Yost and Becca and wanted to know their story, so when I was offered an opportunity to write a Thanksgiving novella, I was happy to do so.

I hope you enjoy Yost's and Becca's story!

Because of Him,

Laura V. Hilton

Chapter 1

Jamesport, Missouri

Nothing is going right.

Becca Troyer sighed and strode down the sidewalk of the town square, away from the ice cream shop. *Closed!* Although, the sign did say it was for a family emergency. Sure, it was autumn, but she really wanted a milkshake, especially the much-talked about pumpkin-spice flavor. It sounded *ser gut* when she heard people mention it. She'd left her friends at the farmer's market, after promising them milkshakes—her treat—and now she couldn't provide.

She should pray about the emergency, though, whatever it was. She shot a quick prayer heavenward and included a post-it-note about her bad attitude.

A sudden, brisk whirlwind blew her skirt up around her knees. She pressed her arms tight against her hips and legs to hold it down and hurried across the street. It was the last farmer's market of the season, and the winter squash and pumpkins that didn't sell today would need to be canned on Monday.

Most of the other farmers had already quit for the season. The birdhouses and fishing gear made by some wouldn't be needed until next year. Gardens had mostly stopped producing, which meant it was she and Gizelle Miller manning booths. Gizelle sold baked goods until they were gone or until her shift at the grocery store began. They'd both brought a couple friends, so they wouldn't be alone.

Becca's friends, Mellie and Erma, watched the antics of the fire department fundraiser behind them. A fireman called to the crowd to take a turn at plunging their chief from his perch into the frigid waters of the dunktank below. Watching them was more fun than paying attention to the *Englischer* family browsing through the abundant display of pumpkins, looking for the best ones for carving into Jack-o-lanterns.

Tourists grouped in the center of the park. Becca neared her booth just outside the throng of onlookers and stopped to rearrange a couple of pumpkins to fill empty spaces. When she straightened, the exaggerated movements performed by four mimes captured her attention. When had they arrived? It had to have been during her futile search for the evasive milkshakes. Large words painted on a piece of drywall said they would accept donations for the volunteer fire department.

Sammy Miller—Gizelle's cousin—manned the donation jar next to the sign. Becca didn't know the rest of the firefighters, but one wore Amish clothes—black pants, pine green shirt, suspenders, and a black hat. The white face paint hid his identity, but he was tall and thin. She didn't know who else volunteered for the fire department besides Sammy. After the fire that destroyed her home last year, she really appreciated their bravery.

The mime pretended to chase a silver balloon he really held onto by the knot. He held it out in front of him as if it were blowing away and ran after it in long exaggerated strides, his arms outstretched as if he could barely hang onto the runaway balloon. She smiled, watching his antics. Her youngest sister would've loved seeing this.

He neared Becca's stand and slammed to a stop, as if he'd run into an invisible wall. His blue eyes met hers, and he stared, palm flat, against the unseen building for long, countless seconds. Minutes. Maybe even hours. Heart-pounding awareness built until the world faded around her. Then, with exaggerated motions, he made a big show of himself being yanked backward to a red case. He crouched beside it, returned the balloon to its home, then retrieved something else before shutting the case.

With the emotional connection broken, Becca tried to shake off the strange bond with the mime. But the longing in his gaze…who was he? She frowned and turned to her friends. "The ice cream shop is closed due to a family emergency, so we can't get any milkshakes."

Neither responded. Instead, they giggled at something the mimes did. She sighed. Her "help" was no help at all.

The pumpkin-shopping family approached her, lugging three of the largest ones. "We'll take these. And what are those huge, bumpy, green things?" The mother pointed.

"Hubbard squash," Becca said.

"I've never seen squash so big." The *Englisch* woman wrinkled her nose as she handed Becca a twenty-dollar bill. "Donate the change to the fire department. Those mimes are so cute. Especially the Amish one. Are they all firefighters? I didn't know Amish were firefighters."

"They volunteer sometimes." She counted the change and held it out to the lady. "Do you want to put it in their donation jar?"

The woman waved her away. "Oh, no. We need to hurry. We're late for a pumpkin-carving party. Besides, that actor obviously likes you. Come on, kids. Let's go."

Right. No male had ever shown interest in her, and at this rate, she was destined to be alone for life. No milkshake and no *bu*. Would this day never end?

Becca turned to her starstruck—and *bu*-crazy—friends, totally sidetracked by the mimes. "I'm going to run this over to the donation jar. Be right back." She took a couple steps in that direction, but the Amish mime rushed over and fell to one knee in front of her. He held up a cheap ring, the kind found in glass gumball containers for a quarter.

Becca's face heated. She stumbled to a stop, staring at him. His eyes weren't as blue as she'd first thought. They were turquoise. Who did she know with turquoise-colored eyes? She scrambled to place them, because something about them was familiar. If only the mime paint wasn't so distracting. It was hard to think with everyone staring at her. He must be from a different district.

His gaze intensified and his lips quirked.

A spark of interest ignited in her heart.

The mime reached into a pocket and pulled out a folded piece of white construction paper and a red permanent marker. "I love you." He printed the words then flipped the page over. "Marry me."

Seriously? Her mouth gaped. Tears burned her eyes. If only someone loved her so much. But she wasn't even courted yet.

The mime reached for her hand. Sparks shot up her arm at his light touch. He slid the toy engagement ring on her finger and pretended to kiss the back of her hand. His breath was warm against her skin, and she shivered. He rose to his feet, still holding her hand, and made an exaggerated fist pump into the air, as if she'd said yes.

For a brief second, he gazed into her eyes. Then he winked, released her, and jogged away.

Leaving the ring, and a serious case of tingles around her heart.

"How romantic!" Mellie appeared beside her. "What Amish man is on the fire department—and not married?"

"Yet." Erma appeared on her other side. "I didn't know anyone courted you."

Becca clutched her ringed hand against her heart along with the fist-full of cash she still needed to drop into the donation jar. No one courted her. Usually, she got mercy rides home from Singings and frolics with Yost Miller. If he were there. Which used to be rare, but had become more frequent—to the point where she anticipated the bi-monthly rides. He'd never mentioned a word about the gingerbread *haus* she'd given him the previous Christmas. All the girls had foolishly made love potions on the spur of the moment—really a recipe for gingerbread—and given their baked treats to their hopeful boyfriends. Except her crush back then had turned her down in no uncertain terms, leaving her crying in her bedroom, and she'd passed her creation off to the first *bu* who crossed her path, regardless of his identity and whether she liked him or not. That *bu* happened to be Yost.

Sometimes, after one of the mercy rides home with him, she wished the gingerbread really *had* possessed magical abilities. That Yost really courted her. It was nothing, as *Mammi* had warned. Just a treat.

And it hadn't caught Yost's attention.

∞ ∞ ∞

Yost Miller hurried back to his fellow mimes—all friends and relatives from the fire station where they volunteered—thankful for the paint that rendered him unrecognizable to the general public. He also wore colored contacts, so people wouldn't think it was him. It was easier to be someone he wasn't when he couldn't be recognized as a *tall, pimple-faced, overly shy beanpole with glasses, Yost.* And thankfully, as a mime, he was allowed—encouraged—to play the fool. Especially since his heart was already an over-the-top fool for the beautiful Becca. He wished he was brave enough to come out and say it in person...except she didn't see him that way.

He wasn't sure what the Amish community as a whole thought of the activities, but he enjoyed them. And Sam's *daed*, a preacher who knew Yost was a volunteer firefighter, had never complained about him participating in the fundraising activities.

The gathered crowd cheered, and Yost glanced over at the dunking booth. The police chief had hit the target, drenching the fire chief. Good-natured jeers followed as both men taunted each other and the police chief bought more balls to throw at the target.

Yost glanced back to the farmer's market. The business there had dwindled, and his cousin Gizelle had begun packing up whatever she had left on her table. Usually, she donated her leftovers to the fire department. His stomach rumbled. Hopefully, she would today, too.

"We're calling it a day," one of the other mimes, an *Englischer* named Chance, whispered as he sidled close.

Yost nodded his acknowledgement. He'd go to the station, wash the heavy coat of white makeup off his face, and then, if Becca were still here at the park, he'd...what? Reveal his identity as the mime who'd given her a cheap gumball machine ring she'd never wear? Not only because Amish didn't wear jewelry, but also because it wasn't real. They weren't in love.

Or at least she wasn't.

She'd owned his heart for years, but he'd been too shy to approach her, too shy to ask to court her, and too ashamed of his pimply face and glasses.

He groaned. Why'd he have to be the *bu* with the weird name? The teacher had even asked, "How do you spell *Jhaast*?" when his family changed districts the year he'd turned fourteen.

Becca had been the one who told the teacher it was a derivative of Justus and eased the teasing. He hadn't asked how she'd known.

He'd started to fall in love that day.

He glanced back at her. She hoisted a pumpkin in her arms, the toy ring on her finger flashing in the sunlight.

Maybe he would reveal himself. The worst she could say was "*Nein*."

∞ ∞ ∞

Becca loaded a pumpkin in the back of the buggy, annoyance filling her as her girlfriends linked arms and abandoned her to go talk to several other Amish *youngies* gathered in the park. At least some of the garden produce sold, but she wished more had, not only to save work when canning but also today, when reloading the buggy.

She had to drop Erma off at her job as a part-time caretaker for an old lady who suffered from dementia and couldn't be left alone. Mellie would likely want to stay there and hang out with the others.

Becca didn't have that luxury. Her sister Lizzie would marry Daniel Zook next Thursday, and she needed to help with the wedding preparations they hadn't completed yet. Plus can innumerable pumpkins and winter squash on Monday. Thankfully, some of the excess canned goods would go with Lizzie to her new home, to feed them over the winter. But next year, she would lobby for her family to cut the size of their fall garden by half. This bounty was more ridiculous than a blessing.

She loaded the next pumpkin and cast another glance over her shoulder. Mellie and Erma laughed at something someone said. The mimes had disappeared, and the dunking tank stood abandoned. The soaked fire chief loudly joked with the chief of police as they walked toward the station.

She hoisted a third pumpkin. A fourth, then a fifth.

Hands, holding the sixth pumpkin, appeared in her peripheral vision. She turned.

Yost Miller grinned at her. "Hiya, Becca. Thought you could use some help."

"I'd be beyond grateful." Her arms ached, and she still had a dozen huge pumpkins to be loaded. She hadn't counted the squash yet.

He winked, his turquoise-colored eyes twinkling. He wasn't wearing his glasses. His face, filled with a bad case of acne last winter, had finally started to heal. Only a smattering of pimples were scattered across his cheeks. A smudge of white was near his hairline, as if he didn't get all the makeup washed off. She glanced at his pine green shirt. Blinked. It was *him.* Her heart rate increased. *I love you. Marry me.*

He couldn't mean it. It was part of his act. She tried to calm her heart, but she wished that just maybe part of it was real.

"I didn't know you're a firefighter." Or a mime, for that matter. Her voice cracked.

"My cousin Sam got me involved. Great way to give back to the community." He loaded the pumpkin, then adjusted his black hat.

"I didn't know your eyes were that shade of blue, either." She should've noticed before.

Yost chuckled. "They aren't. Colored contacts. Easier to fight fires without worrying about glasses under the facemask. I couldn't resist when I was offered colors. I wear my glasses at home and around others in the community so I don't offend people. Some people don't like worldly things and say contacts are vain."

"But they look *gut* on you." The unplanned words slipped out in a breathy whisper, followed by a furious blush.

Yost hesitated instead of immediately lifting another pumpkin. He glanced up at her. His cheeks pinked. "*Danki.*"

She looked at the ring on her finger, and her face warmed again as she remembered the words he'd printed. *I love you. Marry me.* She wouldn't embarrass him by bringing it up, but she needed to give him back the ring. She twisted it, pulled it off, and held it out. "I don't want to ruin your prop supply."

The pink flamed to red. "Keep it." He hoisted the pumpkin and put it beside the others in the buggy.

"The next time you need a ring, you won't have one, and—"

He turned and rested his finger against her lips.

She caught her breath.

"I won't need another one, Becca. I already proposed to my girl."

Chapter 2

I won't need another one, Becca. I already proposed to my girl. Yost couldn't believe those words had crossed his lips. Seemed the brave self-confidence required to be an anonymous mime had seeped into his not-so-brave and extremely self-conscious life.

Becca's brow furrowed as she frowned, still holding out the ring. Then she slid it onto her finger. "Okay then. If you're sure."

He was sure. Maybe. Well, pretty sure. He managed a nod.

She studied him a moment longer, obviously puzzled. Was she trying to remember who he'd taken home from Singings recently? Did it register that it'd only been her?

She abruptly turned and picked up a humongous winter squash from the parking lot, bouncing it in her arms a little as she tried to get a good grip.

Had the abrupt turn meant she rejected him? He turned for the last remaining pumpkin. "You have *gut* ground for squash."

"Too *gut*," Becca grumbled. "They never grew well at our old farm, so when we made our garden at our new home, I planted the usual amount of seeds. But they took off like wildfire. We're going to have rows and rows of canned pumpkin and winter squash in the basement. Do you think your *mamm* could use some?"

He tried to remember what *Mamm*'s pantry consisted of, but couldn't recall. He only retrieved what she told him to get, and only on the rare occasions he was inside when *Mamm* needed something. Usually, he was out in the fields working beside *Daed*, or taking cattle to auction once a week, and subsequently working his second job at the auction *haus*. "I think she probably could use some," he finally said.

Becca hoisted another squash. "I'll make sure to bring some by."

He tried to imagine how that would play out. Becca introducing herself as his fiancée—although, come to think of it, she hadn't accepted and had, in fact, offered him the toy ring back—and *Mamm* reacting...how? He'd turned twenty in March. Six months ago. She'd likely think he was too young since the average marrying age for men in their community was about twenty-five.

He grimaced. Might be best to wait until he knew for sure Becca agreed to be his girl before *Mamm* became privy to the information.

"Uh, how about you give me a ride home, and I'll take—um, buy—one each of the remaining pumpkins and squash. That way *Mamm* can fix it up the way she likes." Not that it would likely be different from how Becca's family fixed it, though he couldn't say for sure if it was or not. And maybe *Mamm* wouldn't appreciate the extra work.

"Okay." Becca brightened. "That'd be great."

"I love eating pumpkin seeds right out of the oven, too. This will give *Mamm* an excuse to fix some." Yost grinned.

"*Ach*, they are so *gut*! There's never enough of those to go around at my *haus*." She perked up as she glanced at the abundant pumpkins in her buggy. Did she realize more pumpkins meant more seeds?

"Maybe we should rethink my buying a pumpkin then." Yost scratched his face. His finger came away white from makeup he'd missed. He cringed. He couldn't make himself look any more foolish if he tried.

"That's not necessary. You're welcome to a pumpkin and a squash." Becca shook her head. "So, you need a ride home, really?"

"Well, I rode to town with my cousin, Sam. He was in a hurry to get home though, and I wanted to stay and help you out a little, so I told him I'd find my own ride."

"I need to take Erma to work and drop Mellie off at her *haus*."

He glanced around, looking for her friends. They were nowhere in sight. "*Ach*." So they wouldn't be alone once she located them, and they wouldn't have a chance to talk. Well, he'd take what he could get. "That's fine." Except, the news that he masqueraded as a mime would spread throughout the community. *Mamm* and *Daed* would possibly hear undiluted criticism and comments about how they'd allowed him to be pulled away from the faith.

Nothing could be further from the truth. He lifted the last squash and put it in the buggy as Becca slid her cash box underneath the seat.

Yost looked around again. Still no sign of her friends. "Where are Erma and Mellie?"

Becca backed out of the buggy and glanced around. "I don't know."

With the departure of the fire department, the onlookers—*Englisch* and Amish alike—had departed. The park appeared vacated. He gave it another glance, then turned and surveyed the area nearby.

No sign of them.

Becca frowned, reached into the buggy, and retrieved a cell phone. "It's my *brudder*'s," she explained without looking up. She pushed in a series of numbers or letters or something...and waited.

The phone chirped. She ran her finger over the screen, then huffed. "They found a ride with someone else. Wow. Really nice of them to let me know."

Yost nodded. Then shook his head, not sure of the correct response. All he knew was, it meant he and Becca would be alone.

That might or might not be a *gut* thing.

∞ ∞ ∞

Becca climbed into the buggy as Yost unhitched Benaiah's horse Peppermint Twist from the hitching pole. Then he got in next to her and took the reins. "I'll drive. At least as far as my *haus*. If it's okay."

She nodded and slid over a notch, increasing the Bible-width between them. And then adjusted the black bonnet covering her prayer *kapp*. It wouldn't do for Yost's intended to see him giving another girl a ride home.

I won't need another one, Becca. I already proposed to my girl.

Wow, that hurt. She hadn't known he courted anyone. And he'd proposed to the girl already? Who was she? He was *gut* at keeping his girl secret, because Becca hadn't had a clue. She tried to remember who he'd given a ride home from Singings lately, but when he was there, it'd only been her. Did his girl live in a different district?

No wonder he hadn't been affected by her gingerbread "love potion." He had somebody. Might've already been courting someone when Becca had given him the gingerbread *haus* last year.

Had he gotten down on one knee before this other girl as he did in front of her at the park today? Written her a note? Probably not. Surely he wouldn't have offered an Amish girl a gumball machine trinket at the real proposal.

Her throat tightened.

It seemed she was destined to fall for men who loved another. She pushed that thought away.

She would not cry. She'd hold herself together until she got home and hidden in the privacy of her bedroom. She. Would. Not...

Despite her firm talking to, tears burned her eyes. She twisted away from Yost so he wouldn't see. The horse walked down the main road through town, toward the countryside where she and her family lived. Yost's family lived there too, but on the far end of the horseshoe-shaped road.

"Are you okay?"

Shoot. He'd noticed? She swallowed. "Um..." She hated liars, but what else could she do?

"Are you bothered by all the canning you and your family have to do?"

An excuse not to answer. One that would be truthful. "I'm grateful, truly I am. That awful year when my parents died, we struggled to put meals on the table. The garden didn't grow right and hardly anything produced. My *brudder* Benaiah didn't bring home much money, and there were seven of us trying to survive on a pittance. I don't know how many meals were simply boiled cabbage or potatoes. I got so sick of cabbage soup. But *Gott* always provided something. Now we live in a season of plenty, and it's *wunderbaar*, but I wish He'd bless someone else with some of the bounty. I've never had a bumper crop of squash or pumpkins before. The pantry shelves are going to be so *orange*!"

Yost chuckled, his strong hands tightening around the reins as a car passed. "Have you tried selling some to the market?"

"*Jah*, they took all they thought they could handle."

"Hmm." He pursed his lips and his brow furrowed.

Becca knew that expression. It was the same one Benaiah and *Daadi* got when they needed to solve a problem. She sighed. "Don't worry about it. The Lord gives and the Lord takes away."

His expression eased with his smile. "Blessed be the name of the Lord." He tapped the reins against the edge of the buggy, then glanced at her. "Maybe He figures your family will need it with your sister Lizzie marrying soon. She'll be taking some canned goods with her, ain't so?"

Becca forced a return smile. "True. She will."Although she didn't know for sure if Lizzie would use it if she did take cans of food. She hated cooking and believed *Gott* invented convenience meals for a reason. The cans would probably collect dust in the pantry.

Yost passed her turn-off to go home. Her smile flipped upside down. "Wait..."

"Going to my *haus*, remember? I am buying a pumpkin and a squash."

Right. Now that he reminded her. Grasshoppers tickled her stomach. How would his *mamm* react to him bringing her home instead of whoever he courted? Though technically, the Troyer horse, buggy, and vegetables were hers. She was bringing *him* home. Except he was driving.

She swallowed hard as he turned into the drive.

His *mamm* sat on the porch, a basket overflowing with socks beside her. As Yost parked, she stood and laid the sock she was mending to the side. A cautious smile appeared as she approached.

"Becca had an abundance of squash and pumpkins, so I told her you'd take one of each off her hands." Yost handed Becca the reins and climbed out.

"You did, did you?" A small smile quirked, and the woman's eyes settled on Becca. Assessing. Measuring. Speculating.

Becca wasn't sure if the other woman was happy to get vegetables or not. It was hard to tell. Or maybe it was lost in the evaluation of the situation.

A twinkle appeared in her eyes as if she approved of his choice.

Becca glanced at Yost. He should explain before more misunderstandings developed.

A dimple formed. "One can never have too many pumpkins or squash." His *mamm* moved to the back of the buggy with Yost.

Becca swallowed her retort. Were they teasing her? If they didn't need any, why didn't they just say so?

Yost laughed. "Becca would disagree. But I'm sure she wouldn't mind if you want more than one each."

"*Ach*, may I?" A smile quirked on Yost's *Mamm's* lips.

That settled it. The woman was definitely laughing at her. Although just what was so funny was more than Becca could understand. She hopped out of the buggy, tripping over the wheel in her haste. She lunged forward and overcorrected, the landing jarring her entire body. She stumbled forward a step or two, her knees buckling.

Yost moved quickly, his hand gripping her arm just below the elbow. Steadying her. "Easy there."

Those confusing sparks shot through her again. She made the mistake of glancing up into his face and seeing those amazing colored eyes again that he'd winked as a mime...

Her breath shorted out. She puffed, trying to get a thimbleful of oxygen.

Yost's brow drew together. "Are you okay?" His hand stayed put. Her brain cells fried.

His *mamm* joined him, her arm going around Becca's shoulders. "Come on up to the porch and sit a while. I used to have spells like this when I was younger. I'll brew you a mug of red raspberry tea."

Huh? His *mamm* thought she was suffering from women's issues? Becca's face heated. But she couldn't find the words to explain. Nor did she want to insult the other woman by withdrawing Yost's offer of vegetables because of the undiluted sarcasm. Because really, it would be ever so helpful if she took a couple, few...*all* of them.

Yost released her and let his *mamm* help her up the steps. "How many do you want? I'll put them inside for you."

"Two of each is fine," his *mamm* said with a pointed look at Yost. "Maybe Becca will be kind enough to come over and help me can."

Ach, nein. Nein. Nein. Nein. Becca swallowed and tried to think of a polite way of saying *Danki*, but *nein*. Because really, she had enough canning to do without helping someone else. Not to mention finishing up preparations for Lizzie's wedding. Plus she didn't want Yost's *mamm* making any more untrue assumptions—like that Becca would be marrying her *sohn*. While she'd hoped to get to know his *mamm* before, knowing Yost was engaged to someone else made this whole situation more than awkward.

Yost nodded. "I'm sure she'll be happy to, *Mamm*." He hoisted a large pumpkin, muscles stretching and pulling against the fabric of his shirt, and carried it into the kitchen with his *mamm* close behind.

What? No, she wouldn't be happy to. But she supposed since his *mamm* was nice enough to take four of the things off her hands, the least she could do was to allow herself to be *volun-told* to help.

"So, how long has Yost been courting you?" The older woman handed Becca a steaming mug of tea, then settled into her chair, and picked up the sock. "I had no idea he was seeing anyone."

"He's not. I mean, well, he is, but not me. He's promised to..." She shouldn't have added the 'to,' because she had no idea who, but too late now. She looked down at the toy ring, still on her finger. The colored plastic caught the sunlight and flashed. She tried to hide it by adjusting the mug and taking a sip of the tea.

She should've taken it off before and slipped it into her pocket, even if it was nice to pretend that maybe Yost was serious and had just introduced her to his *mamm*. Surely a girl was entitled to a few dreams to keep her company during the cold and lonely winter nights. And if she had to pick a tale to tell, a gingerbread *haus*, mime, toy ring, turquoise eyes, and bonding while canning pumpkin might be hard to beat.

Yost came back through, tromped down the steps, lifted a large squash, and made the return trip.

His *mamm* sat in silence, the needle pulling yarn through the hole in the sock, weaving it closed. A smile played around her lips, and she frequently glanced at Becca.

"Two each enough?" Yost reappeared.

"That's fine," his *mamm* said, not looking up.

He nodded. Grabbed another squash and passed the two of them. He glanced at Becca, caught her gaze, and smiled.

She managed a wobbly one in return, woefully embarrassed to be this close to a dream and aware she was an imposter.

His *mamm* nodded when the door shut behind him again, and chuckled. "*Ach*, it's you, dear. Please call me Kristina. Or maybe *Mamm* Kristina."

∞ ∞ ∞

Yost helped Becca into the buggy, then dug into his pocket, and handed her the money for the vegetables. *Mamm* hovered by his elbow. She had only allowed him to manipulate her into buying what she didn't need because he had a school-*bu* crush on Becca. Hopefully she wouldn't think it was anything more, because she might get pushy and scare Becca off before he had a chance to let her know he meant every written word of his mimed proposal.

Although, judging by the probing glances she'd given both of them, she likely had them betrothed and ready to pass out wedding invitations.

"Let me know when you'd like to can, Kristina." Becca's voice sounded strained. Her cheeks were stained a pretty pink.

Mamm shrugged. "I'll send Yost to get you when I am. Though I'm thinking you'll be mighty busy with your sister's wedding in five days."

"I might be able to come Tuesday. We're canning on Monday. Though, if we get done in time..."

"I'll send Yost for you Tuesday *morgen*. Unless you are able to come Monday afternoon. And if you are, just come. I'll be home. You can stay for supper."

Yost glanced at *Mamm* and caught the knowing twinkle in her eyes. *Jah*. She knew. And even if she didn't, she'd be hard-pressed not to figure it out when he had trouble staying out of the kitchen when Becca was there.

Becca flicked the reins as she clicked her tongue, and Peppermint Twist started around the circle drive.

Mamm touched his hand. "I always did like that girl."

What could he say? "Me too." His smile grew wider.

Mamm pushed her glasses up her nose and peered at him. "You best go change. And wash that white stuff off your face. What will your *daed* say if he sees you like this?"

"He'll say *gut* for me stepping outside the box." He hoped. With a jaunty grin, he turned to go inside.

"Think Becca and her family might want to come for Thanksgiving?"

The words stopped him in his tracks. "Bit early to think of that, ain't so?"

Mamm waved her hand. "Don't want anyone else inviting them. We're going to move fast here, *bu*. Can't let that one get away."

Nein. Now that he'd—unintentionally—made his move, he had no intention to. He hadn't planned on it, but when he saw the ring, paper, and marker in the supply box, he couldn't help it.

He'd figure out the relationship thing as he went along.

Maybe.

Chapter 3

The trip with Yost had succeeded in adding one more thing to Becca's to-do-list. Make it two new things. Not only did she promise to help Kristina can the vegetables Yost had purchased, but with her proclamation of *It's you*, Becca needed to make a batch of gingerbread when she got home.

Just to ensure that it truly was her. Just in case it really was a love potion.

Or to see if Yost refused it as...*Ugh! Nein.* She wouldn't think of *that* rejection.

Mammi's warning about gingerbread being only a treat played and replayed in her mind, even as she decided to check the pantry to make sure they had all the ingredients needed for gingerbread cookies.

Though, why bother to check? They would have all the ingredients needed. Benaiah made a good income these days, though he spent endless hours out in his glassblowing shop, while his *frau* of almost a year, Susanna, kept up with the shopping, the *haus*-work, the...everything. As if she'd stepped into *Mamm's* place and kept the *haus* running, single-handedly. Even *Mammi* had relaxed back into her role as *grossmammi* instead of trying to keep up with the *haus* and manage five *kinner*.

It was nice. Almost normal. Except Becca answered to a woman who was only a few years older than she.

When Becca drove in, Susanna leaned over the edge of the porch, her face pale. She straightened, one hand resting on her midsection as Becca climbed out. "You're home early." Her voice sounded strangled.

"Not really." Becca eyed her sister-in-law with concern and shook her head. "The activities at the park ended, and it is after lunch, ain't so? Everyone cleared out."

"I thought since you'd taken friends, you'd be gone awhile."

Becca shrugged. Rolled her eyes. No point in expressing her irritation at her *friends* to Susanna. She might as well have gone by herself for all the help they were. "I didn't do very well selling squash and pumpkins today. So we'll have canning to do Monday. I figured I'd get a head start by washing jars today. Unless you have something else you need me to do since you're sick."

Susanna shook her head. "*Nein. Nix.* Just a few minutes ago, we got a call on Benaiah's business phone from Kristina Miller, inviting us to Thanksgiving dinner. Isn't that odd? I told her I'd need to talk to Benaiah about it, because I usually host dinner for our families."

Yost's *mamm* called? About Thanksgiving? Already? She'd just left there fifteen minutes ago. Did this mean Kristina's "it's you" was the truth, after all? Becca's heart pounded. Her face burned. To hide it, she abruptly turned and started unloading pumpkins from the back. "Odd. *Jah.*" Her voice sounded breathy to her own ears. Hopefully Susanna didn't notice, because Becca would like to keep these wishes and dreams to herself for a little bit, especially if there was nothing to them.

"Kristina also said you'd be helping her with canning on Tuesday. It's really nice of you to volunteer, but you know we have so much to do with Lizzie's wedding."

"I was *volunteered.* Yost took two each of the hubbard squash and pumpkins, and since it was plain as anything he had coerced his *mamm* into buying them, it seemed as if I needed to help. Don't worry. It'll all get done. It always does." The final words were more for herself than for Susanna because, truthfully, she was a bit overwhelmed, too. More than a bit. Yet she was excited at the possibilities, especially since she planned to mix up gingerbread cookies, too.

That, mixed with the confusing events from today—the handwritten marriage proposal, the finger resting against her lips—made her shiver. The comment about him proposing to his girl. The plastic ring now nestled in her pocket followed by his *mamm*'s proclamation that it was *her.* Was it really?

Then an invitation to Yost's *haus* for Thanksgiving dinner?

Her heart thudded.

"*Ach.* Yost." Susanna nodded as if it all made sense. "You'll want to make cookies, for sure." A twinkle appeared in her eyes, and teasing filled her voice.

Gingerbread. Becca heard the words as clearly as if they'd been spoken. Had Susanna read her mind? She nodded, though *Mammi's* warnings replayed again just as clearly as if she'd said it. *It's just a treat. Not a magical love potion.*

Mammi was right. It was. Although Susanna had married Benaiah last December mere days after he proposed, and Lizzie would soon wed Daniel Zook. Both men had received spur-of-the-moment gifts of gingerbread houses. Becca couldn't help but wish that her fairytale, wish upon a star, and subject of every daydream would come true, too. A man who loved her the way *Daadi* loved *Mammi.* The way Benaiah loved Susanna.

Then again, she hadn't exactly taken time to pray about the relationship, except for a *Please, Gott, please, let Yost notice me.*

An *if it is Your will* would definitely be in order. Or maybe *not my will, but Yours be done,* just to keep *Gott* happy, because she really hoped Yost was *Gott*'s will for her.

The wind changed direction, blowing smoke from the wood fire in the shop their direction, mixed with an odor of manure from the barn and the earthy aroma of the compost pile.

Susanna gagged. Choked. And leaned over the railing again, heaving.

Becca wrinkled her nose. What was wrong with her? Hopefully, it wasn't the flu. "Are you okay? Can I help you inside? Or get you a drink of water?"

Susanna shook her head. "*Nein*."

With a shrug, Becca moved the squash and pumpkins to the kitchen floor, then drove the buggy into the barn, and took Peppermint Twist to the pasture.

She'd start with washing jars for their overabundance of squash, and then she'd mix up a batch of gingerbread so the dough could chill *over-nacht*. Or until the wee hours of Monday *morgen*, because she couldn't bake cookies on the Lord's day.

∞ ∞ ∞

Church services were at Yost's *haus* on Sunday. He trailed *Daed* through the barn Sunday *morgen*, knocking down the spider webs that'd been spun *over-nacht* and brushing off the benches.

Expectancy bubbled inside Yost, making him jittery. Becca would be there. Even if he didn't have a chance to do more than gaze at her during the *morgen*, he could pass her a note asking to take her home after the Singing—maybe when all the single men lined up outside the barn doors, hoping to catch the eye of their special girl as she walked past. Some of the men had passed notes before, but Yost had never found the courage. Maybe today, he would.

"Guess we're as ready as we're going to be." *Daed* stopped at the back bench and adjusted the box that held copies of the *Ausbund*, which he would hand out as people came in.

Yost opened the doors wide as the first buggy pulled in and parked. He hadn't had breakfast yet, but maybe he had time to run inside and grab a quick bite. *Mamm* had made some sort of sweet rolls. He didn't know what they were called, but they had a fruit filling and cream cheese icing drizzled over them. His stomach rumbled.

He brushed his hands together and went out to greet the first arrivals—his brother Amos and his small family. Yost picked up his young nephew Rudolf and swung him around. The *bu* giggled and snagged Yost's glasses, half ripping off his ear. He rescued his glasses, put the toddler on the ground, then turned to his *brudder*. "Here for breakfast?"

Amos clapped him on the shoulder. "Do you need to ask? When *Mamm* told my *frau* what she'd put on the menu for breakfast, Regina told her we'd be here."

"Come on in!" *Mamm* came to the door. "I have them warming in the oven."

"We need to eat fast, so we can help with parking." *Daed* caught Yost's eye.

Yost nodded, another bubble of excitement building. He couldn't wait to see her.

The large buggy containing Becca's family was among the last to arrive. Yost helped Benaiah find a parking spot, then assisted *die Großeltern* out of the buggy. *Daadi* Micah recently had hip surgery after an unfortunate series of falls during the past year, and he still used a cane for support.

"Hiya, Yost." Becca climbed out after *Mammi* Wren. Her face flushed as her gaze briefly met his, then skittered away.

"Hey, Becca." He resisted the urge to wipe his sweaty palms on his pants. With his interest revealed to her—and *Mamm*—he wasn't sure how the day would play out. Would *Mamm* corner her during the noon meal, attempting to get to know her better? Or would she wait until they canned either Monday evening or Tuesday? Undoubtedly, it would be sometime soon.

He swallowed, falling into step beside Becca as they led the rest of her family toward the barn. "May I give you a ride home from Singing to-*nacht*?" He lowered his voice, hoping no one would hear.

She glanced at him and nodded, her face turning a becoming shade of pink. “Not a mercy ride this time?”

Huh? It’d never been a mercy ride, whatever that was. He’d never heard the term before, but he could figure it out. His brow furrowed, and he stared at her. “What?”

She flicked her fingers as if shooing the question away, but shrugged. “You know. When you gave me a ride home because no one else wanted to.”

He sucked in a quick breath. Was that what she thought? “*Nein*. It was never like that.”

She hesitated a second. Glanced at him.

It took him a while to work up his courage to ask her each week. A few times he’d been afraid some other guy would, because he’d seen them approach her. A glare and a stiffening on his part usually let the other guy know Becca was taken—whether she knew it or not.

Maybe someday he’d tell her.

∞ ∞ ∞

Becca found a seat with the other unmarried women, on the opposite side of the barn from the men. Her sister Lizzie was on the end of the bench, and her younger sister Jackie on her other side. The two younger girls sat with Susanna and *Mammi*. A rustling followed as the single young men came in. They took up the back rows on the other side of the aisle. Becca twisted around to find Yost.

Lizzie jabbed her elbow into Becca’s side. “Sit still. You know better.”

Becca glared at Lizzie. As if she’d been any better when Daniel Zook first noticed her. But now they planned to wed, Lizzie sat demurely, hands folded in her lap, staring straight ahead as if Daniel’s *mamm* watched to see if she was as devout as she should be.

Maybe Becca should take a lesson from her sister. Instead she glanced around again. Yost’s eyes met hers, then he quickly looked away.

Lizzie stuck her elbow in Becca's ribs again.

But it was almost worth it.

Yost liked her! And he truly had deliberately asked to take her home...long before it could be interpreted as a mercy ride and despite the fact he said he had already proposed to his girl. She could still picture his turquoise eyes above a red-markered sign.

She sneaked a glance his direction again, but this time the man sitting next to Yost met her eyes. He didn't look away.

Instead, he winked.

Chapter 4

Yost clenched his fists, but quickly released them and gripped the edge of the bench to keep from swinging at Menno Schwartz. He was a player, and likely had gone out with every unmarried woman in the community at least once.

He'd hoped Becca was immune, but judging by the fierce red staining her cheeks, maybe not. He sighed. He couldn't compete with Menno, either in looks or personality. Menno had a charismatic personality, and people automatically followed his lead. Someone plain like Yost couldn't begin to overcome those natural advantages.

On the other hand, Becca had already agreed to let him take her home to-*nacht*. She'd honor her commitment, ain't so?

His breath lodged in his throat, and his heart ached. He studied her, but she'd shifted slightly away from him...from them. Maybe in rejection of Menno. Did he dare hope?

Menno snickered, as if he'd read Yost's thoughts and mocked them.

Yost bowed his head as the first preacher stepped up to the pulpit and opened his Bible. *Lord, help me to focus on You and Your words instead of on Becca and whether or not Menno will make a play for her.*

It seemed obvious he would.

Movement of Menno's arm caught Yost's attention. A paper airplane soared toward the women's side of the barn. Immature, but guaranteed to get attention, negative or otherwise. The plane hit Becca just above her ear and fell to her shoulder, then lower.

Yost had to admire Menno's aim.

Someone giggled. A sound quickly shushed.

Becca picked up the airplane, turned, and drew back her arm, sending it flying back. One of the preachers had come in late, and he caught it mid-flight and cast a frowning glare toward Yost, Menno, and then Becca.

Yost wanted to sink into the floor. Especially when the shame and hurt in Becca's eyes focused on him.

∞ ∞ ∞

Becca slumped, her face burning. She'd known better than to retaliate by throwing the paper airplane back, but she'd reacted automatically. And now...now...

Beside her, her younger sister Jackie held her hand tightly over her mouth. Her eyes widened, shocked. Lizzie pursed her lips, her cheeks flaming so red it was almost scary. Becca would hear about her shameful behavior this afternoon—and not only from her sisters.

Who'd thrown the paper airplane at her? Yost? Or Menno? Both sat innocently when the preacher glared. What she knew of the two men suggested it'd been Menno. He'd always been the one who acted out, but Yost's neck was red, his cheeks blotchy.

She shifted away from them again, forcing her attention on the preacher who read from somewhere in the Bible.

"'*You crown this year with Your bounty; Your wagon tracks overflow with abundance.*' Psalms 65:22." Preacher David gazed around the room. "As Thanksgiving approaches, many of us are thinking about the Lord's bounty this year. Gardens have produced bumper crops, and the women have kept busy canning and preserving fruits and vegetables all summer and well into the fall. As your pantry shelves buckle under the weight, let's not forget the needy in our community. The widows, the poor, and the strangers. *Gott* says in Luke 6:38, '*Give, and it will be given to you. Good measure, pressed down, shaken together, running over, will be put into your lap. For with the measure you use, it will be measured back to you.'*"

That'd be something Becca could do with the winter squash and pumpkin she'd put up tomorrow. She could take a few jars over to a group of elderly ladies who lived alone, and maybe some to the new mothers who didn't have time to put in a garden this year. Of course, there was always the box set up in the corner of the store for donations to the needy. It made her feel better about the overabundance from their garden. She'd probably need to ask Susanna before giving the food away.

Surprisingly, Preacher David hadn't mentioned the verse about caring for angels unawares. Or maybe he had, but she missed it.

Whatever the case, giving some of the abundance away would be better than making numerous batches of pumpkin soup.

On the other hand, it sounded *gut*. Maybe when she worked on canning tomorrow, she'd start a kettle of soup.

Preacher David continued. "'*Bring the full tithe into the storehouse, that there be food in my house. And thereby put me to the test, says the Lord of hosts, if I will not open the windows of heaven for you and pour down for you a blessing until there is no more need.*' Malachi 3:10."

It seemed *Gott* had plenty to say about the overwhelming amount of canning she'd had to do as a result of the overproducing garden. It *was* a blessing. And she should give as *Gott* had given to them.

What if someone had thought of them the horrible year after her parents died? She'd have welcomed a day of squash to interrupt the endless kettles of cabbage soup. Thoughts of the soggy, tasteless concoction turned her insides. If she never ate it again, she wouldn't complain.

Becca dipped her head. *Lord, help me to be thankful. You have been so gut to us. Even during that terrible, nicht, beyond-awful year. Please let me know who I can give some of the extras to so we can be a blessing as so many were to us after the fire.*

∞ ∞ ∞

When the service was over, Yost followed the rest of the young men out. Preacher Samuel, the one who'd caught the airplane, took Yost by the arm as he walked past. "Meet me in the back stall. Now."

Yost swallowed hard and went where he was directed. Menno was already waiting in the stall, his body in a casual *I didn't do anything wrong* stance.

On the other hand, Yost was consumed with shame, even though he hadn't been the one to make the paper airplane or fly it. He was guilty by association, however, and the preachers probably weren't sure which one of them had sent it soaring. Unless someone had actually seen it.

If they had, they wouldn't have summoned Yost to the stall.

Maybe they wouldn't have been caught if Becca hadn't sent it flying back. She'd get scolded, as well. He hated it. If she thought he'd thrown the plane, their relationship would be over before it began.

His stomach hurt.

Steps marched toward the stall.

Yost swallowed the bile rising in his throat. This was ridiculous. He hadn't done anything wrong.

The stall door creaked open.

The three preachers stopped in a solid line in front of Menno and Yost. They wore identical black pants, black vests, black hats, white shirts, and stern expressions. The only differences were eye and hair colors.

Yost swallowed. Hard.

Denying the charges before they were made would only serve to make him look guilty, but he probably already did.

He wiped his damp palms on his pants, then looked down at his scuffed shoes.

"You may go, Yost," Preacher David said. Since he'd been the schoolteacher in Jamesport for a time, he likely had the most experience deciding who was truly guilty and who was only ashamed of being a suspect. Of course, he'd been the one standing behind the pulpit at the time of the incident, too. "We'll find you if we need to talk more."

More? He probably meant if Menno offered a convincing enough argument about his innocence.

Yost nodded, and without looking at Menno, headed out the door. Relief didn't follow though. Menno had enough experience lying. He'd find a way to get out of it and blame Yost.

The women had set the food on the table, but since the preachers and the old people with health concerns were supposed to eat first, only the elderly had gone through the line.

Yost didn't see Becca.

Come to think of it, he didn't see any of her family. Had they left?

He dashed outside. Their buggy was gone. A rock sank to the bottom of his stomach.

Would she be back for the Singing that evening?

Chapter 5

Becca stirred the kettle of simmering pumpkin soup, then pulled a loaf of crusty bread out of the oven, and set it to cool on the counter. The jars of canned pumpkins and squash stood in neat rows on the table while she waited for them to seal.

Susanna still suffered from her mysterious ailment. They'd ended up leaving church before lunch yesterday because of it. She'd sat at the table sipping the ginger ale Benaiah had brought home and nibbling saltine crackers while Becca and *Mammi* worked on canning winter squash.

Ginger ale and saltines? Could it be? She should've guessed earlier.

Excitement washed through her, but until someone told her, she shouldn't make assumptions. Focus on work. Becca wiped her hands and checked the clock hanging on the wall. She needed to go to Kristina Miller's *haus* and help them get ready to can tomorrow, unless Kristina had worked on it today. If she hadn't, Becca would start the process.

Too bad they had to leave yesterday before she could confirm their plans.

First she needed to let someone know where she was going. Both *Mammi* and Susanna had disappeared.

She found *Mammi* in the living room, sitting next to Susanna and clutching both of Susanna's hands. The two talked in low voices.

Becca cleared her throat as she hovered in the doorway. "Sorry for interrupting, but I'm heading to Kristina Miller's to help. I should be home by supper, but the soup is simmering." The airplane incident probably disqualified her from eating supper with Yost's family.

Susanna's eyes were watery. "*Danki*, Becca. I don't know what I'd have done without you today. I feel so awful. Tell Kristina we'd love to accept her invitation for Thanksgiving. There's no way I can handle it this year."

"I'll do that." If they were still welcome. "I hope you feel better soon."

"*Mammi* Wren says three months, give or take a week or two. And she tells me it's all worth it. It's the sign of a healthy *boppli*."

Susanna *was* having a *boppli*. It'd be nice to have a *boppli* around. "*Ach*! How *wunderbaar*!" Becca crossed the room and hugged her gently.

"Don't tell anyone, okay?" Susanna cautioned. "I don't want anyone excited and then if something bad happens..."

"I won't." Becca assured her. "Hopefully *Mammi's* right and the *boppli* will be healthy." She backed away. "I'll see you in a few hours."

"Say hi to Yost for me." Susanna's expression held a hint of impishness.

Becca's cheeks heated. She swung around, detoured back to the kitchen to grab the cookies, then crossed the yard to the barn. After hitching Peppermint Twist to the buggy, she left for Yost's *haus*.

Her stomach churned, and she wished for a few bites of Susanna's crackers.

After her misbehavior at church yesterday, making a public spectacle of herself, she wasn't sure what her welcome would be like. Would his family scold her as hers had? Would Kristina turn her away at the door? Probably not, since she had to can four large members of the squash family.

However, Yost might have something to say about withdrawing his offer to...What?

Take her home from Singing.

Last *nacht*.

Becca cringed.

She'd been too ashamed to go. Too embarrassed by her behavior. Too afraid of what Yost might say, and she'd ended up breaking their date in the process.

She swallowed hard as she pulled into Yost's driveway. His *mamm* rose from her seat in the rocker, holding a bunch of recipe cards in one hand.

"Hiya, Kristina." Becca forced the words past the lump in her throat as she climbed out of the buggy.

"*Gut* afternoon, Becca. I wasn't sure if I'd see you today. I was afraid you were sick after your family left so quickly yesterday."

"Not sick." Just embarrassed. Should she wait until Kristina brought up Thanksgiving before she accepted? Becca looped the reins on the hitching pole. Maybe she should apologize to Yost, too. She swallowed. "Where—"

"I thought we'd make pumpkin butter today. My daughter-in-law Regina told me that canning pumpkins and winter squash isn't recommended." Kristina flapped the recipe cards toward Becca. "I told her I've been doing it for years with no problem and I'm not going to stop now."

Becca retrieved the gingerbread cookies she'd baked earlier that *morgen* and approached the porch. Hopefully, the cookies would be more than a peace offering to get her through the door after her disgraceful behavior yesterday.

"I didn't know it wasn't recommended." She was pretty sure *Mamm* had canned the vegetables when she was alive. And *Mammi* hadn't said anything about it as she cut squash into cubes.

"Stuff and nonsense. That's all." Kristina tucked the cards in her apron pocket. "*Ach*, you brought cookies. *Danki*. They look *gut*. Want a mug of tea before we get started? I just brewed some peppermint leaves."

Becca glanced around. "Maybe I should find Yost first, to tell him where I was yesterday." And offer him a cookie. They were gingerbread, after all.

"I'll get you some tea. And a slice of apple pie. I daresay Yost will be in as soon as he notices your buggy. No sense in looking for him when he can come to you." Kristina opened the kitchen door. "Besides, he'd likely enjoy a piece of pie while watching you work."

Becca shivered. She'd probably be all thumbs if Yost did sit there and watch her.

She glanced around, scanning the fields and the open door of the barn, but didn't see any sign of Yost or his *daed*. Kristina was likely right. He'd come to the *haus* eventually. And when he did, she'd apologize for not showing up for their date.

She followed Kristina into the kitchen. She'd been busy. The counter was full of freshly washed jars. She'd baked the squash and pumpkin to make them easier to scoop out of the shells, and they were cooling on cookie sheets on the table. A large kettle sat beside the stove in preparation for the filled jars.

Kristina dished out two slices of apple pie and set them on the table. "Have a seat, dear." She turned and poured a mug of tea and brought it over.

Becca hovered by the table, not sure where to sit.

Kristina waved a hand at the table. "Anywhere is fine. Sit." She sat at the foot of the table.

After another hesitation, Becca set the plate of cookies in the center of the table and took the seat next to her.

Kristina slid a plate closer to her. "I called and invited your family for Thanksgiving dinner. I hope you'll be able to join us. I'm really excited about getting to know you better."

"Susanna mentioned it. She said to tell you we'd love to join your family. *Danki* for the invitation." It was *gut* to know it still stood, after her behavior.

Kristina smiled. "So glad to hear it. I figured with her in the family way..."

Becca gave her a sharp look.

"*Ach*, honey, it's obvious to us old married ladies. She has a glow about her. And we all know the first trimester is pretty miserable. With the history of miscarriage in her family, she's wise to keep it quiet." Kristina lifted her fork. "Now tell me about you."

Becca squirmed. Was she supposed to start with the obvious? "Um. I have four sisters and one brother and—"

"I know your family, dear. We live in the same district, and I spend time with your *mammi* Wren, Susanna, and your sister Lizzie at quiltings, ain't so? I also was *gut* friends with your *mamm* when she was alive. I want to know about *you*. When did Yost start courting you?"

Becca stared at Kristina, struggling to find a *gut* way to answer—truthfully, because Yost wasn't courting her. At least, she thought he wasn't. She'd believed the rides he gave her home were mercy rides, offered because no one else had asked. She hadn't had an inkling Yost might like her until he wrote those five words on the paper at the park. *I love you. Marry me*. He'd been in costume though—as a mime. The note had been accompanied with a gumball machine ring...

Becca slumped.

It was all an act—despite Kristina's belief that Yost was courting her.

∞ ∞ ∞

Yost stepped out of the barn, cuddling a cat close. The tabby had purred and made awkward figure eights around his ankles, keeping him company the whole time he'd been sitting on an upturned bucket and bottle-feeding a newborn calf the mother cow had rejected.

He startled when a horse nickered a few steps away from him. His hands tightened around the cat. The feline yowled and clawed its way free.

Peppermint Twist. The horse's presence meant Becca was here. In the *haus*. With *Mamm*.

He swiped a hand over his chin, then realized too late it was grimy. He probably stank of hard work and...Well. It'd be safe to assume he needed a shower before he saw her. Before he apologized for Menno's behavior getting her into trouble. Before he told her he hoped her absence at Singing hadn't been because of him.

A quick shower. So she wouldn't leave before he came down.

Though, hadn't *Mamm* said she'd invite her for supper?

He wouldn't take any chances.

He hurried around to the front of the *haus*, left his barn boots on the porch, and snuck in the living room as quietly as he could. He ran upstairs and shut the bathroom door behind him, yanking his shirt off.

Mamm yelled, "Who's there? Yost? That you?"

His response stuck in his voice box.

And *Mamm* yelled again, "Jacob, that you?"

That question wasn't directed for him, so Yost didn't bother attempting to answer. Instead he turned the water on in the shower. Full blast. Full heat.

Maybe it'd help cool the flame burning in his cheeks.

Afterward, he ran downstairs and toward the silent kitchen, hoping he wasn't too late. No conversation. *No...*

He stumbled to a stop in the doorway and forced himself to breathe. Becca stood at the stove, stirring something in a kettle. *Mamm* hummed at the table, a large spoon in hand as she scooped cooked squash out of the shell.

She looked up. "Took you longer than I expected." Her glance rose to his still damp hair. And she smirked.

Jah. Well. So much for cooling his heated cheeks. They flamed again. Hotter this time.

Becca turned, a becoming blush coloring her pretty face. Strands of honey blond hair escaped her *kapp*. "Yost, I...I need to talk to you for a moment." She wouldn't meet his gaze.

His heart folded in on itself. "Sure. Can you take a walk?"

She gave the bubbling concoction another twirl with the wooden spoon. "Kristina, I'll be right back. This should be fine for a minute."

"Take your time, dear. I can stir." Kristina laid the spoon to the side of the squash she'd been working on. "Take this shell to the compost pile on your way out, Yost."

He nodded. "*Ach*, cookies." He snagged a couple in one hand, the discarded part of the squash in the other.

Becca opened the door for him and followed him out to the compost pile, then fell into step beside him as he headed toward the road.

Yost took a bite of a cookie. "Did you make these? They're *ser gut*. I think gingerbread is my favorite." Or at least it had been since last year when the gingerbread challenge swept through the district. He'd been amazed, awed, and astonished he'd been blessed by one—and from the girl who'd held his heart for as long as he could remember.

He'd also been too scared to follow through with the implied message. Because what if he read too much into the gift?

Maybe she asked to talk to him now because she wanted to reject him. Privately. It was probably why she hadn't shown up for the Singing. It was easier to say "*Jah*" and be a no-show than it was to face the shame of being seen with a man who was a beanpole with acne and glasses.

His throat hurt.

He was tempted to make it easier on her, to cast her aside and hurt her before she could inflict the pain on him. But...

Nein.

It wouldn't be honest. Even if she didn't give a relationship with him a chance, he still loved her.

He swiped his hand over his chin, forgetting about the cookies. They crumpled against his skin, falling like snowflakes against his clean shirt and to the ground. Gingerbread wishes. That was all it'd been. All it'd ever be.

He sighed.

She moved a bit closer, but still didn't look at him. "I'm sorry I missed the Singing last *nacht*. Susanna was sick, and I felt bad leaving her."

Her sister Lizzie was there. He tried to find something to say, but couldn't get a sound past the lump closing up his throat.

"That's not the whole reason though." She pulled in a breath, her chest rising and falling. "I was embarrassed..."

To be seen with him. *Jah*, he got that. Didn't mean he liked it. He dusted the cookie crumbs off his hands. His version of the Biblical advice of brushing the dust off the sandals, moving on, not looking back.

Or would he be like Lot's wife, forever turned into a pillar of salt because he couldn't let go of the past and embrace the unknown future?

"...after the paper airplane. I don't know what got into me, throwing it back like a child. I'm a grown woman. I know better. I embarrassed my family, I embarrassed you, and I completely understand if you don't want to see me again."

He scratched his neck, the unexpected words seeping into the cracked surface of his heart and lodging fast. She turned the rejecting over to him? Because she didn't want to be the one to break his heart?

Didn't she know he couldn't do it? He loved her.

∞ ∞ ∞

Becca trudged beside Yost, waiting for confirmation of her stupidity. Instead, his fingers brushed hers. He moved a shade closer. And this time, he grasped them, pulling her to a stop.

She turned to face him. He stared down at her, his face half-shadowed by his hat, hiding the expression in his light grayish-blue eyes. A muscle worked in his jaw.

Still, he didn't speak. Instead his hands rose, trembling, as he brushed his thumbs over her cheeks. Softly. Tenderly. So sweetly that tears sprang to her eyes and pooled on her lashes.

"Becca..." His voice was hoarse. He cleared his throat, his gaze dropping to her upturned lips.

She leaned toward him. Couldn't help it because *jah*, she wanted his kiss.

He sucked in air, his hands cupping the sides of her face. His head dipped toward hers.

The clip-clop of horse hooves broke into the charged air.

Yost released her and stepped back.

The moment hitched a ride on the back of the buggy as it hurried on its way.

Chapter 6

I'm sorry. I shouldn't have tried to take advantage of you. Words Yost should've said instead of dipping his head and shuffling his feet in the dirt road, as if he were a bashful school *bu*. Just before he could force the words past the lump of disappointment, the buggy stopped at the next drive, backed up several feet, and Menno emerged.

He jogged up to them, trampling Yost's lagging self-confidence into the dirt with every step he took. "Hey, Becca. Just the person I'm looking for. Glad I happened upon you." He didn't bother to glance at Yost. "I'm thinking of getting a group together to go canoeing. Interested?"

A delightful blush appeared on Becca's face. Figured Menno would be the one to put it there.

Yost bit his lip. With Thanksgiving next week, it wasn't exactly canoeing season. He did enjoy going during the summer though.

"My family has a few canoes in the fishing shed by our stocked pond."

Becca hesitated, but interest glimmered in her blue eyes. Yost tried to decipher whether it was interest in the canoeing or in Menno. His stomach ached.

"It's been warm. Indian summer, my *daed* said. I think it'd be fun. Maybe this coming weekend?" Menno shifted so his back was to Yost. Excluding him.

It hurt. He pulled in a breath. *Say nein, Becca.*

"It would be. I love canoeing. You want to go, Yost?" She sounded eager. Excited.

At least she was inviting him. "*Jah*, sure." And he'd try to get a canoe with Becca, though it wouldn't exactly be romantic floating on the pond with Menno.

"Cool. You can invite someone, Yost." He shifted. "*Ach*, looks like my horse is in a hurry. He's leaving without me. Becca, you'll be with me."

She caught her breath in a gasp and frowned.

"We're going to have so much fun. Gotta run." With a wink, he turned and jogged back to his moving buggy.

A muscle jumped in Yost's jaw. Had Menno seen him attempting to kiss Becca and decided to make his move because of that? Or had he heard about the proposal at the park and decided then to win Becca away?

Yost turned toward the direction they'd come. He needed to get away from Menno before he chased after the horse and told the guy to leave his girl alone. Not only did Menno bully his way into a date with Becca, but he also interrupted what could have been a very sweet kiss.

He needed to escape before he grabbed her and kissed any thoughts of Menno right out of her head. Unfortunately, that was something only the bold mime would do. He needed to escape with a bit of dignity intact. "I guess you need to get back to canning with *Mamm*, and I need to go to work. I'm helping someone harvest honey this afternoon. A late fall harvest, but they had an illness and didn't get it done." A bit curt, but...

His chest tightened. He shifted his gaze to her, hoping she'd do something to encourage his interest.

Becca bit her lip and glanced back the direction the buggy had gone. She sighed, then nodded. "I do need to help your *mamm* and get home. Lots to do yet."

Yost's heart shattered. He'd forego the pie he'd been looking forward to and the pleasure of watching Becca work while he ate. With his current mood, he wouldn't be very *gut* company. Maybe he'd grab a couple gingerbread cookies to go.

She had made them for him. Not for Menno. That cheered him some. And she had leaned toward him as if welcoming his kiss.

Still, he needed to retreat, regroup, and spend time in prayer instead of mulling over how Menno was making a play for the one girl Yost had loved, did love, and wanted to love for eternity.

∞ ∞ ∞

The week marched on, with little time for rest. Becca helped Kristina finish the canning and assisted Lizzie and *Mammi* with wedding preparations. Now, three days after the almost-kiss, she sat at a long table set up for the bride and groom and their attendants, rearranging food on her plate. She'd been paired with Menno. Lizzie had always liked him, and her new husband, Daniel Zook, was Menno's best friend. "Wouldn't it be nice if you married my husband's best friend?" Lizzie had whispered to her last *nacht* as they lay beside each other in their double bed for the last time.

Becca had sighed. *Menno? I don't think so.* She deliberately didn't look at where he sat on the other side of Daniel. She needed to figure out how to get out of the canoeing invitation for the day after tomorrow. Or at least set it up so Yost would be her partner. Not Menno. She never should've accepted, since her heart was set on Yost. She shoved a piece of meat to the side of her plate.

It was still warm for mid-November, temperatures in the seventies. But the leaves had begun to change: vivid yellows, oranges, and fiery reds, mixed with the duller and not so pretty rusty-browns. Lizzie had pots of coral-colored chrysanthemums displayed on the long table set up for the bride, groom, and their side-sitters. She planned to plant them in her garden at her new home.

It seemed so strange that Lizzie was married now and leaving their home. Or she would leave tomorrow. As per tradition, the bride and the groom were spending their first *nacht* at the bride's home, so they could help to clean up after the wedding. Then they would leave on their honeymoon—an actual trip—to some place. Daniel wanted to surprise Lizzie. She and Lizzie had giggled about it being a romantic destination. Maybe even Niagara Falls.

That was where Becca wanted to go, if she got a honeymoon trip.

It didn't do any *gut* to think on it, though. She wasn't engaged or even courting. It seemed that if Yost was serious, he would've made some effort to see her since she'd apologized for her airplane throwing behavior...and he'd almost kissed her.

He hadn't. Not even so much as a hand-written letter. Had her spontaneous accepting of Menno's canoeing scared him off? She needed to tell them both she'd changed her mind.

She scanned the room—Yost wasn't at the wedding. She'd hoped the wedding might give him a few ideas. That he'd want to be her date to the Singing that evening.

Though, to be fair, two days ago, she'd heard about a call for the volunteer firefighters to help battle an out-of-control blaze in another state. Yost and his cousin Sammy were both missing. She spied Sammy's *frau*, Abigail, sitting in the crowd, her two children beside her, the littlest one asleep in a stroller.

If only Becca could remember where the fire was. Tennessee, maybe? Or was it Georgia? Benaiah had mentioned it last *nacht* at dinner, but she hadn't paid much attention since she and Lizzie were talking about final wedding preparations. She hadn't thought Yost would be with them. Maybe because she'd figured he'd put priority on her. Foolish, especially considering she hadn't broken the date with Menno. Yet.

She needed to do that now. She got up, walked behind the bride and groom and tapped Menno on the shoulder.

He glanced up. Smiled. "Hey, Becca. Excited about canoeing Saturday. It's just going to be us though. I'll have my *mamm* pack a picnic."

"I can't go. I didn't mean to encourage you. I'm...seeing...Yost."

Menno snorted. "Don't worry about Yost. He understands the way things are."

The way things are? Becca shook her head. "*Nein.* I'm not going with you." She turned on her heel and stalked back to her seat.

Pray for them.

The command came out of nowhere, and with such clarity, Becca jumped, almost expecting to see the speaker standing nearby. She glanced over her shoulder. Nobody was, of course, except the wedding party. They were too busy eating the food the women had spent long hours preparing—roast chicken with bread stuffing, mashed potatoes, gravy, creamed celery, coleslaw, applesauce, cherry pie, donuts, fruit salad, tapioca pudding, bread, butter and jelly.

The conversation at the tables spread around the living room, dining room, and kitchen reaching almost thunderclap level. Becca couldn't hear herself think, much less a voice from someone who wasn't there.

Pray for them.

The command was repeated with enough force that she immediately complied. Bowing her head, she closed her eyes. *Ach, Lord...*How could she pray when she didn't know what about? Or how? Or even why? *I don't know what the problem is, but You do. I'm worried about Yost and Sammy. Take care of them, and help me pray as I should.*

Yost and Sammy? Her breath hitched. Despite her prayer, peace eluded her. She opened her eyes anyway, and scanned the room, looking for Yost's *mamm.*

From the other side of the living room, Kristina stared at her, her eyes wide.

∞ ∞ ∞

The week hadn't gone exactly as Yost expected. When he went to harvest honey on Monday afternoon, he hadn't expected the fire chief to call and tell him about the need for volunteer firefighters in Tennessee. He'd taken time to grab only what he needed, then his ride—another volunteer firefighter named Viktor—came to take Yost on the long drive. His cousin Sam had already been picked up. They'd driven through the *nacht*. Sam's license was still valid, so he took a turn behind the wheel, helping them to arrive in time to catch a couple hours of sleep before they needed to relieve the team already out there.

Days later, he still stood in the Tennessee portion of the Appalachian Trail, fighting a wildfire that'd gone on too long, done too much damage, and left people homeless. More houses were being evacuated as he and his assigned team cleared away everything that might catch fire. They'd been armed with rakes to clear leaves, blowers to eliminate the small stuff, and chainsaws to cut up dead trees. Someone was supposed to follow along with the water truck and soak the ground. The awaited vehicle and moisture didn't come. Instead, thick, black, heavy smoke choked the sky. Despite the handkerchief tied over his nose and mouth, it was hard to breathe. And hot. Ever so hot. He reached for his canteen and took a swig of water to soothe his sore, parched throat. He coughed and his eyes burned. Fingers of unease crept up his back, and he shuddered. It seemed as if the roar of the fire had increased since his arrival hours earlier, but it might be his imagination.

The team leader, Mick, called on the radio to find out why the water truck was delayed.

Sweat beaded on Yost's forehead. His vision blurred.

Mick's radio crackled to life, the static nearly drowning out the voice. Mick stiffened and his jaw worked. Then he looked around. "Boys, grab your equipment and let's go. The fire turned. We've gotta get out of here. Now."

Yost wiped the sweat from his eyes. Smoke and salty moisture irritated his contacts. He blinked, but it didn't help. They burned so bad he couldn't see.

"Run!"

Yost ran blindly toward Mick and the vehicle on the road a mile beyond him. His feet tangled in something, propelling him forward. His head slammed into something hard.

Gott, help.

The world went black.

Chapter 7

Despite the ongoing wedding festivities, fear blanketed Becca, thick and heavy. The weight of it threatened to cut off her oxygen.

Fear. She should pray for the firefighters to get the blaze they battled under control. Her stomach knotted. She wished she could somehow magically fix the problem. There was nothing she could do about the situation, whatever it was, except pray. She still didn't know what to say. Had *Gott* even heard the prayer she floundered through a short time earlier? *Gott, help...*

A chime caught her attention. She glanced toward the sound. Preacher Samuel pulled a cell phone from his pocket and checked something. He rose from his seat, his skin paling beneath his tan. Becca caught her breath. He was Fireman Sammy's *daed.* He met someone's gaze, gave a slight motion of his head, then without warning or words, several men—not all of them preachers—stood and left the room.

Kristina looked after the men, half-rose, then plopped back down. She bumped the table with her elbow, sloshing her water.

Becca wanted to go, too. She *had* to know what was wrong, but she couldn't think of a *gut* excuse to leave the meal and follow the men outside.

Did she really need one? She could pretend to check on the overflow crowd who sat at picnic tables outside. It was part of her job to make sure everyone got enough to eat and drink.

She leaned close to Lizzie. "I'll be back."

Lizzie acknowledged her with a slight nod, but her attention was focused—as it should be—on whatever Daniel said.

Becca scurried outside, glanced around the crowd of people eating at picnic tables, and...There. They were going into Benaiah's glass shop. Except Benaiah wasn't with them. If he had been, she might've been able to come up with a reason why she *had* to speak with her brother. Now Becca couldn't think of a *gut* excuse to trail after the men.

She hesitated a long moment, then took a few steps in that direction. The gnarled hand of an elderly spinster caught her arm. Becca forced her attention away from the closed shop and to Zelda.

Becca pasted a smile on her face. Before she could form polite words, Zelda patted her arm. "Go to them. Don't be shy. We're all concerned."

Huh? But Becca nodded. She had permission, such as it was, and she'd use it if anyone dared question the sudden appearance of an uninvited *maidel* to the impromptu meeting certain men were having. *Zelda said to go...Jah,* as if the words of an eccentric old woman would make them accept her presence any quicker. Either that or the strange *Pray for them* command she heard twice along with the feeling of fear. Either story would place her in the same crazy-lady status as Zelda, but it would be worth it to get information about Yost.

She hurried across the yard and burst into the room. Preacher Samuel quieted and looked up from the cell phone he held, his eyes focusing on her. The other men's gazes shot to her too, wearing matching expressions: Serious. Concerned. Alarmed. And something else she couldn't identify. Curiosity and shock at her daring behavior, maybe?

"May I help you, Becca?" Preacher Samuel's eyebrows rose.

Becca hesitated. Swallowed. "Zelda said..." *Nein.* She couldn't blame this on Zelda. She had to tell the truth, no matter what. "I just have this hunch."

Preacher Samuel glanced around the room at the group of men, then nodded. Without a word, he came nearer and handed her his phone. "It's a text. From my *sohn*, Sam."

Becca's throat clogged. She couldn't breathe. She stared at the preacher,
waiting...

"It's okay, Becca. *Gott* has them in His hands. Go ahead and read the message."

She glanced down.

Fire turned. Man down. Can't find Yost. Team leader sent

me to look. Pray hard.

Her lips parted, Becca sucked in a breath and froze. *Nein. Not Yost. Ach, Gott! Help!* She read the message over and over before finally moving on to the reply under it.

Gathering men to pray. Keep us updated.

Preacher Samuel studied her, then drew in a long, deep breath. "There's no need to alarm everyone, but as I told Sam, we're going to pray." He motioned toward the phone. "You might want to consider finding a quiet place to pray, too. You could invite a trusted woman or two."

How could she, without inciting panic?

"*Danki* for letting me know." Her voice cracked.

"You have need." Preacher Samuel retrieved his phone and keyed something in. Another reply to Sammy, probably.

She had *need*? What exactly *did* the preachers see from the front of the church meetings? Her squirming around to peek at Yost? Him, looking at her? Becca frowned, but took the excuse to leave. She'd go up to her room to pray. That, and to ponder what Preacher Samuel might have meant. No one would bother her there.

She hurried as fast as she could through the maze of picnic tables.

"Hold on a second there, Becca. These old legs don't move so fast anymore."

Becca paused and glanced over her shoulder. Zelda hustled along, cane thumping, behind her. Praying upstairs wouldn't be an option since Zelda clearly couldn't handle the long flight, and two women, including one who didn't live there, couldn't slip past the audience as easily as one. She could use the *dawdihaus*, though. Both *Mammi* and *Daadi* were eating and visiting with family and friends. Probably more visiting than eating. She changed direction and headed toward the outside door to the *dawdihaus*.

The main *haus* door opened, and Kristina peeked out. "Everything all right? Never mind. Don't answer that." She shut the door behind her, her expression tight. "It's Yost, ain't so? I'll come, too. Where two or more are gathered in His name, there He is in the midst of them."

How did Kristina know these things? Did she get hunches, too?

Never mind *asking* a trusted woman or two. Seemed *Gott* provided before she even asked.

The fear was still heavy, but a bit of confidence grew from knowing there was a circle of men and women praying, too. The same *Gott* who told her to pray and then sent women to join her held Yost in His hands.

"Don't worry, girls," Zelda said. "We'll pray until we know."

Know what? Yost was safe? *Gott* heard? Or Lord forbid, Yost went Home?

Becca's heart hitched.

Gott, please save him.

∞ ∞ ∞

Yost woke with an oxygen mask strapped to his face, fresh clean air flowing into his lungs. An ambulance siren wailed. He turned his head to the side. He was in the back of a vehicle—the ambulance, no doubt—flying too fast over the potholes in the roads. Seemed they hit every one of them.

A blurry figure that might be a man sat beside him. He leaned forward. "You're awake."

Obviously. Yost yanked at the oxygen mask, but the man reached to stop him.

"Leave it. You inhaled quite a lot of smoke."

Yost's head hurt, his hands burned. He raised them and squinted in the dim interior of the ambulance. Whatever he'd fallen on had scraped them.

"You're lucky they were able to rescue you. Heard the fire was licking at the guy's heels as he carried you out of the forest," the EMT said.

It wasn't luck. It was *Gott.*

He'd tell the man so, but his throat burned so badly he didn't want to talk.

"We're taking you to the hospital. They'll make sure you're fine. Scraped your face up, but good. Hands, too."

Yost grimaced. That was all he needed. Something to make him even less attractive. Acne, glasses, *and* scars...He turned his head away.

He stared at the wall of the ambulance. Except it was moving. Swaying. A wave of colors and...Wait.

Man looks at the outward appearance, but I look at the heart.

He blinked at the words appearing next to him. His eyes obviously still bothered him. Probably needed to take the contacts out, sooner rather than later. Either that, or *Gott* had renewed His habit of writing on the wall.

The other man didn't say anything about the words. Because maybe they weren't there. Or were a mirage. A somewhat familiar sense of peace accompanied the words.

Gott looks at the heart.

Could He help Becca look at the heart so she could see the man he could be instead of the mess he was?

He slid his hand over his pocket. His wallet? *Jah*, it was there. He relished the feel of it against his fingers for a second. Not that the contents were many. Money. His identification card. And the piece of paper he'd written on over a week ago—*I love you. Marry me.*

Would they send him home early due to his klutziness? Or would he be able to stay and fight? He'd rather go home a wounded hero, not hanging his head in shame because he tripped when running blind.

Nothing would drive Becca into Menno's arms faster than Yost coming home a failure.

Although if he came home a hero…maybe she'd accept his proposal. Such as it was.

Pride. All pride. Yost sighed.

At least waiting for an overworked doctor to see him in a hospital emergency room would give him plenty of time to pray. He needed to thank *Gott* for saving his life first, before he asked for Becca's love again.

∞ ∞ ∞

Becca collapsed to her knees in front of the living room chair. She bowed her head, her palms flattened against her eyes. Despite her closed eyelids and the additional pressure, tears seeped out. She hadn't even told Kristina or Zelda what the problem was, but somehow they seemed to know.

Yost. The man she loved.

Gott, take care of him. Help them to find him. Help him to be okay.

I am the Gott who sees you. And I see him. I am holding him in the palm of My hand.

Peace filled her.

Danki, Lord.

A series of verses from Psalms came to mind.

Lord, you have examined me and know all about me. You know when I sit down and when I get up. You know my thoughts before I think them. You know where I go and where I lie down. You know all about me…Gott, examine me and know my heart; test me and know my anxious thoughts. See if there is any bad thing in me. Lead me on the road to everlasting life.

The door opened and Becca looked up.

Preacher Samuel held up his phone. "He's been found. Alive."

Chapter 8

A week later, Yost grabbed his backpack and climbed out of the backseat of Viktor's truck by the mailbox. It was Thanksgiving Day, and his parents' drive was crowded with buggies. His brothers and their families, no doubt.

"*Danki,* Vik." His voice was still scratchy from all the smoke, but he'd been treated and released from the hospital, able to return to fight the fires. His scrapes had mostly healed, too.

Viktor had already dropped Sam off. He lifted a hand in a wave and drove off, no doubt in a hurry to get home to his own family.

Yost trudged down the dirt driveway toward the *haus*. Smells of a feast permeated the air. His stomach rumbled. Tears burned his eyes. The first time he'd been away from his family, from his home, from *her* for an extended time.

They'd been taken care of in Tennessee, with churches and other businesses stepping forward to feed the firefighters, but it was nothing like a home-cooked meal, surrounded by loved ones.

There was an extra buggy in the yard—the big one Benaiah Troyer used for his large family. Yost's heart pounded. That likely meant Becca had come after all. He hadn't been sure, since they hadn't seen each other, hadn't talked since the almost-kiss in the dirt road the day Menno had interrupted them, ten days ago.

Had Menno been quick to step in to stake his claim during Yost's absence? Or had he lost interest when Yost wasn't there to provide a challenge?

Men's voices came from the barn, laughing, joking, telling tall tales no doubt. The usual routine. It meant Thanksgiving dinner hadn't been served yet.

A smile touched his lips as he set his backpack on the porch. He'd go to the barn and join the men. Going in would be too much of a temptation in so many ways, especially if Becca was there. A hug and tears from *Mamm*. The cooking food, some sitting out and ready for him to snatch a nibble of—though he was supposed to fast and pray until the meal was served. Plus Becca, moving around his kitchen, her skirt swirling around her legs, her...her...He closed his eyes.

Best to keep his distance until he had food to occupy his hands and lips.

The kitchen door opened as he started to move away.

A gasp.

"Yost?" The question was whispered.

He turned, hesitantly. How would she react to all his healing scrapes? Becca stood there, her hand over her mouth. He forced a smile. "Bec—"

With a cry, she flew down the steps and launched herself into his arms.

He couldn't help but wrap his arms around her, savoring the feel of her body next to his for the first time...

He almost groaned as she pressed herself closer against him, her arms going around his neck. And she clung.

He tightened his grip, pulling her closer.

"*Ach*, I missed you," she whispered.

His lips crept up in a smile. He pulled away, his hands sliding from her back to her waist, slowly forcing himself to release her, one tiny step at a time. "Bec—"

"Don't ever leave me like that again." She pressed herself against him again, her arms tightening on his neck. Her tear-filled eyes stared into his. "You look so *gut*."

Gut? She didn't care how he looked? Or she was willing to ignore all his healing scrapes and glasses. Maybe he should ignore them, too.

He quivered. Drew in a much-needed breath. He'd lost the ability to breathe twice in the last week, but he'd take this cause every day.

And then wonder of wonders, she kissed him!

She. Kissed. Him.

He stiffened in shock for a brief second, felt her hesitate, then start to move away.

Nein.

He tugged her back, instinct and desire taking over. "Becca..." He cupped her face in his hands, leaned in, and took control.

He didn't know, and didn't care, how long they stood there kissing, but eventually chuckles, cat-calls, and giggling broke in. Yost slowly pulled away.

Becca's face flamed red, but he caught her hand in his...as he had that day at the park. A burst of confidence filled him. The same as it had then. Before it was the contacts and face paint that gave him boldness, but now with her obvious feelings for him and *Gott*'s hand in his surviving the fire, he could be bold without the props.

He dropped down to one knee in front of her. In front of their families. In front of *Gott*. He pulled out his wallet. Fumbling with his free hand, he opened it, and pulled out the paper that started it all. Shook it out, and held it up.

I love you.

Marry me.

She whimpered. "*Jah*!"

He barely had time to rise before she was back in his arms.

He crushed her into him, the page crinkling between them.

Gingerbread wishes, an answered prayer, and a dream come true.

The end

Thanksgiving Strangers

By Rachel J. Good

Dedication

To a wonderful friend who helps me brainstorm and encourages me,
and to my Amish friends who bring great joy into my life.

Author's Note

I hope you enjoy Faithe and Crist's story. I've included several characters who appear in other novels. Sarah and Jakob's love story is told in Gift from Above, (Book 3 in the Sisters & Friends series), and Ada and Nathan can be found in The Amish Teacher's Gift (Book 1 in the Love & Promises series).

The idea for Crist's brother, Ethan, came to me after I toured an Amish center for special needs children, and our guide was a teenager in a wheelchair. He was so cheerful and upbeat that I had to make him a character in my next book.

I also mention Survivors in Action (http://survivorsinaction.org). If you, or anyone you know, are being abused or stalked, the website has great information. Also, an easy-to-read book about abuse, stalking, and cyberstalking is Cyber Self-Defense by Alexis Moore and Laurie J. Edwards.

I pray Crist and Faithe's story will bless all who read it, especially those who have doubted God after tragedy has devastated their lives and those who question why God allows bad things to happen to good people.

Chapter One

The frigid air sliced through Crist Petersheim's thrift shop parka, sweatshirt, and old flannel shirt. He could barely feel his fingers and toes. If he didn't get inside soon, he'd risk frostbite. The weather in Lancaster was so unpredictable in November. Some years it stayed brisk and chilly through early December, but this year, the falling October leaves were frosted every morning, and a few inches of snow had fallen already as the weeks edged closer to Thanksgiving.

Mounds of slush lined the curbs, and Crist picked his way along the icy sidewalks, his mood as gray as the overcast skies above. Snowflakes drifted down, dusting him with small white spots that reminded him of showers of dandruff. *Great.* Just what he needed to put him in the holiday spirit this Thanksgiving week. For Christmas he could say, *Bah, humbug!* But what did you say about Thanksgiving when your spirits were lower than a snail's belly?

He was tired of trudging up and down this street to stay warm and keep an eye on the pharmacy across the street. His attention was so focused on the activity outside the drugstore, he jumped when bells jangled nearby. He barely avoided a collision with the glass door of a restaurant. A couple emerged holding hands, too busy staring at each other to notice him. Maybe he should add *Bah, love!* to his list.

He didn't want to, though, because deep inside he wanted to believe in love's magic, in its power to transcend time and space to connect two hearts forever. But love was for others, not for him. He had no time or opportunity for fanciful notions like that.

The aroma of coffee drifted out through the open door. He jingled the change in his pocket, hoping he'd have enough to cover the bill. If not, he could warm up for a short while at least. He shuffled inside the small homey restaurant, making sure his scuffed, too-large shoes didn't trip him up on the threshold.

His practiced eyes scanned the window booths for an empty seat. The third one down had a good view of the pharmacy. He scuttled past the full tables scattered around the center of the room and slouched his six-foot frame as low as possible on the worn maroon leather bench, keeping his head below the top of the booth. The fewer people who saw him, the better. He picked up a menu and opened it to hide his face. Setting it down as a barrier, he ducked behind it. His fingers and toes burned as they thawed, and he removed his cracked and peeling gloves to rub his hands together briskly, generating heat that he applied to his icy face.

A cup and saucer clattered down on the table. Crist lowered the menu as a cheerful girl with a smile like sunshine tilted a glass coffee pot. At the sight of the *kapp* on her head, a ball of tension knotted in his stomach, making him sick. *Faithe Beiler*, her name tag said.

Of all the restaurants in the area, he had to walk into this one. All the servers were wearing Amish clothing. He hadn't realized the restaurant was Amish-owned. If he had, he'd have walked right past. Could his day get any worse?

Crist waved a hand to stop her from pouring the coffee. "Wait. How much is the coffee?"

"It's free," she said eagerly, "so don't worry about that. Whenever it's cold outside, anyone's welcome to come in here to warm up and have coffee and a meal on the house."

Crist passed his hand over the stubble covering his chin. The pity in her eyes made it clear she thought he needed a free meal. He couldn't blame her. With his bloodshot eyes from lack of sleep, rumpled clothes, and disheveled appearance, he must look a wreck.

The meal part was tempting, though. The aroma of frying bacon hung heavy in the air and combined with the maple scent from the pitcher on the table. How long had it been since he'd had a good home-cooked meal?

"I'm happy to pay," he said gruffly, glancing quickly at the menu to find the cheapest item. He had enough change for an egg on the à la carte menu. "I'll take one fried egg."

"Would you like a dippy egg?"

He hadn't had dippy eggs for years. Not since *Mamm*...He cleared his throat. "Yes, please."

"I'll be right back with your egg. Would you like anything else?"

He shook his head. "No, that will be all." In truth, though, there were plenty of things he'd like, but most of them she couldn't give him. He wouldn't mind more of her sweet smiles, but he couldn't take a chance on being sidetracked.

After she left, he stood his menu at an angle so it blocked others from viewing his face and then returned to staring out the window. The narrow city street had rows of brick businesses sitting side by side, but he was only interested in the drug store. He'd been watching the patterns at the pharmacy for weeks, and he hoped he hadn't missed anything important while he'd been distracted by the waitress.

Hmm...That was the third time in the past two days that bearded man had entered. Crist pulled out his small black notebook, flipped through a few pages, and jotted down the time the man walked through the door. He timed how long the man stayed inside and noted he had a large pharmacy bag when he exited.

Crist was slipping his notebook and pen back in his pocket when the girl headed toward his table with a breakfast platter loaded with toast, hash browns, and two eggs. His stomach growled, and he wished he had more change for a meal like that.

Faithe whisked his menu out of the way and set the plate in front of him. He grabbed for the menu before she could put it back in the holder on the table.

"Privacy?" she asked, as if she understood his need to hide from the world.

"Yes," he muttered, and she returned it to the place where he'd had it. He motioned to the plate she'd set down. "I'm afraid there's been a mistake. I ordered a dippy egg."

Her melodious laugh stirred a longing deep inside for connection and closeness. He struggled to concentrate on her words rather than the loneliness and emptiness within.

"You looked hungry," she said. "And it's freezing outside. A hearty breakfast can keep you warm longer."

"But I didn't plan to pay for a full meal this morning." Or most mornings.

"I did say we offer complimentary meals on cold winter days. Feel free to pay only for one fried egg. Or leaving nothing at all is fine too, if you'd like to save money for a meal later in the day."

"Bring me the bill for the egg then." He didn't appreciate being treated like a charity case, even though he might look like one.

For a second, he glimpsed a flash of hurt in her eyes and regretted his brusqueness. He shouldn't have snapped at her. Most likely she only worked there and was following restaurant policy. No need to take his frustration out on her.

"I'm sorry," he said. "I didn't mean to sound so ungracious. It's only that I like to pay for what I eat, and I hadn't budgeted for a full meal."

"I understand. I just felt God was leading me to bring you a full plate today. So you can thank Him for the meal."

The knots in his gut yanked so tightly he wanted to clutch his stomach. The G-word always made him sick. He'd definitely made a mistake in coming in here.

Faithe continued. "Everything we have comes from God, and He's blessed us with so much, we like to pass along some of those blessings to others." She waved a hand toward the crowded restaurant.

If everything that came his way was from God, Crist wanted nothing to do with Him. All he'd had were hardships and sorrows.

Faithe stood there as if waiting for a reply. A reply he couldn't give. His faith may have wavered, but that didn't mean he wanted to destroy hers. Her sweetness and innocence made him hope she'd never have any trials to test her beliefs.

"Thank you," he said, wishing his words hadn't come out so gruffly.

Faithe took no offense. Again, she smiled. "I'm sure God appreciates your thanks."

He hadn't intended his thanks for anyone other than her. Certainly not God.

Throughout their talk, he'd kept one eye peeled for unusual activity at the pharmacy, but the steady stream of customers seemed to be going about their normal business. Nothing out of the ordinary had happened. After she left, he concentrated on the building more closely, hoping to forget the conversation they'd just had.

Faithe swished past his table several times waiting on other customers, but she always flashed him a gentle smile. She was sweet, so sweet she made his teeth hurt. That's what one of his buddies used to say. A buddy who was no longer around.

The next time she passed, she laid the bill on the table along with a cream-colored envelope imprinted with a cornucopia. A semicircle of letters curled around the picture: *O, give thanks to God.*

"What's this?" Crist demanded.

"Open it and you'll see."

Crist had no intention of opening an envelope with those words on it, but he didn't want to hurt her feelings, so he pulled on his gloves and tucked it in his jacket pocket.

A movement outside the window caught his eye. He made a mental note of a teenager with tattoos up both sides of his face and across his forehead. Crist checked the time. He'd write it down when he got outside. He'd seen that teen before, but he'd need to flip thru the pages to document the last time the kid had gone into the store.

Too bad he couldn't sit in here all day and stay warm. He had a great view, but he couldn't take up a table for the price of one egg, and he had a promise to keep. He sighed and stood, then reached into his pocket and pulled out a handful of coins.

He counted out his change and felt around in his pockets for more, but found no stray coins. He'd thought he had more than that. After he paid for the egg, he only had enough to leave a ten-cent tip. The waitress had gone above and beyond with the service and the extra food, and all he'd given her in return was such a paltry tip. It was embarrassing. He'd have to find a way to make up for it.

Crist hurried to the door so he wouldn't have to see her face when she picked up his bill. Reluctantly, he turned up his collar and braced for the frigid weather outside.

Behind him, a handful of coins jingled. "Hey, thanks," Faithe said as she headed to the register with his check. She acted as if he'd given her a huge tip. What was up with that girl?

He didn't have time to think about it. Tattoo boy was exiting the pharmacy. Crist slouched against the brick wall beside the restaurant, his eyes half-closed as if he were tipsy, and watched the boy get in a waiting car.

After the car disappeared around the corner, he pulled out his notebook and recorded the information, including the car's make, model, and license plate number. Then he staggered down the street and crawled into an old maroon Impala that had more rust than paint. Although it guzzled gas, the backseat was roomy enough to stretch out his legs and get some decent sleep. Living out of a car was the pits.

After hours of freezing with little to show for it, Crist was ready to sleep, but first he had to find a safe spot where he wouldn't get arrested. Last night he'd found a fleet of company cars at the back of a deserted parking lot. Patrol cars circled the main parking lot, but not the secondary storage area, so he managed to get decent sleep despite waking chilled to the bone several times during the night. He'd turned on the engine and prayed no security guards would spot the clouds of exhaust billowing from his vehicle or hear the roar and rattle from the loose muffler. He fought to stay awake to avoid carbon monoxide poisoning, but even with those disadvantages, it was better than sleeping on the street. Although he had to admit, if you got a spot over a heating grate, the sidewalk wasn't so bad. But he tried to leave the grates for the elderly and ill.

Crist alternated between running the engine briefly for the heater, striding up and down the street to warm his muscles, and shivering in the cold. When he was outside, he dodged the slush sprayed up by the constant stream of traffic. Yet inside the car, even with a quilt wrapped around him, his teeth chattered.

On his final brisk walk of the late afternoon, an argument began in front of the drugstore. With the honking horns and car engines, Crist couldn't hear the words. He rushed along the sidewalk to get a better view and smacked into a bearded man with a hoodie, running in the opposite direction. His notebook and pen went flying. While Crist struggled to his feet, the man bent over to retrieve his notebook and pen. When he turned, he held them out, and as soon as Crist took them, the man dashed off.

Although Crist had missed most of the altercation, from what he could hear, a wife or girlfriend was berating her husband for spending too much time with his buddies instead of her. Deciding the scene wasn't notebook-worthy, Crist tucked the small black book into his pocket and returned to the car.

To turn on the heater, he pushed lightly on the gas pedal a few times before cranking the engine. The motor made a whirring noise as if it wouldn't turn over, but then the engine caught. It idled roughly for a few minutes, and he jiggled the gas pedal slightly to keep it from shutting off. White clouds of smoke belched from the tailpipe, looking even more ominous against the darkening skies. As soon as the heater had warmed the car, he turned off the engine. He couldn't afford to waste gas.

Crist looked longingly at the restaurant as lunchtime passed and his stomach grumbled. He wanted to go in to warm up, but he didn't want Faithe to offer to feed him again. She'd been gracious about his stingy tip, but the minute he left, she'd probably gossiped about him to the rest of the staff.

The afternoon inched by, and he only noticed two more repeat customers. One was an elderly lady with a walker, who appeared to need prescriptions pretty badly, but he wouldn't rule out anyone. The other was a thirty-something woman. She'd entered three Mondays in a row.

A white van with a plumbing logo pulled into the curb a few spaces behind Crist, his signal to leave. He checked his watch. Yup, exactly on time. He didn't even need a watch. He only had to wait for that van to function like an alarm bell. It always arrived at precisely 5:30.

Crist got out of the car to stretch his legs, his hands tucked deep in his jacket for warmth. As he passed the truck, he slid on a patch of ice. He jerked his hands out of his pocket, pinwheeling his arms to keep his balance, and his notebook went flying through the air and landed at the plumber's feet. The man bent down, scooped up the book, dusted it off on the side of his coat, and handed it to Crist.

"Thanks," Crist said, sliding the small black book in his pocket.

The man stooped and picked up a soggy cream envelope. "Looks like you lost this too." He gave Crist a quizzical look.

The envelope was too wet to put in his pocket, so Crist pinched it between his gloved thumb and forefinger and held it out, away from his body. He'd pitch it in the nearest trash can. He waited until the man entered the apartment building a few doors down before heading to the bin on the corner. As he held it over the wire metal basket, Faithe's face appeared before him. After the meager tip he'd given her that morning, he owed her big time. The least he could do was open the card and read it, even if it was something about God.

The paper shredded when he pulled on the flap, and he tossed the soggy bits in the bin. The damp cardboard inside remained intact.

Nowhere to go for Thanksgiving? the outside asked. Inside it said, *Come and join us for our annual family meal. Yes, you're part of our family too*. Below that, it listed the date and time. The last line indicated there was no charge, but attendees could bring a dessert or side dish to share if they so desired.

How could a restaurant stay in business giving away so much free food? Crist shook his head. It was a nice idea, but he worried it was foolish.

He crumpled the invitation and prepared to toss it after the envelope scraps, but something held him back. Instead, he smoothed it out and took out his notebook to place it inside. When he opened the cover, the pages were blank.

He riffled through the whole notebook.

Every page was empty.

Chapter Two

Faithe's heart went out to the man who'd headed out the door earlier. The Bible talked about the widow's mite, and she suspected that man had dug into his pockets and given all that he had. It was the greatest tip she'd ever received. What a kind soul he must be. That act of kindness warmed her all day.

She only hoped she hadn't offended him by giving him more than he'd ordered. It was hard to know when being generous might wound someone's pride. She had felt God nudging her, though, so she prayed she'd done the right thing.

The restaurant was busy, and she had little time to wonder. She bustled around serving meals to the regulars and issuing Thanksgiving invitations to anyone who looked lost, lonely, or homeless. She'd started this tradition several years ago, and now many in their Amish community came to join them for Thanksgiving Day dessert after they had dinner with their families. All of her extended family members who didn't live locally came from out of state to be together that day too. Faithe loved having everyone in one place. As the invitation indicated, everyone was a part of the family.

It cost a lot to host the meal, but Faithe believed it was worth every penny. Without *Daed* around for the past three years, money had been tight, but she'd found that the more she gave to others, the more blessings flowed back to her. She didn't give to get a reward, but she'd discovered firsthand that God did bless cheerful givers. She'd had trouble convincing *Mamm* to do it that first year after *Daed* left, but now *Mamm* was as enthusiastic as Faithe.

The Thanksgiving feast had done so much for the community. It had reunited estranged family members, healed broken hearts, comforted the grieving, provided jobs for the needy, and even ignited romances. She couldn't wait to see how this year's meal would touch lives. Faithe pictured the homeless man from that morning. She hadn't been able to get him off her mind. Would he come? Perhaps she could introduce him to some of the men from her church. One of them might be able to give him a job.

She was still thinking about him the next morning when he strode through the door and headed for the same table he'd occupied the day before. Once again, he set up the menu as a barrier between himself and the other diners, and spent a lot of time staring out the window. Although he seemed like a nice person, she wondered if he was hiding out from the police.

She picked up the coffee pot and headed over to take his order.

"I want what I ordered yesterday," he informed her. "One dippy egg. Nothing else, and"—he placed his hand over the cup on the table—"no coffee."

"Yes, um..." She waited, hoping he'd supply his name. They were on a first name basis with all their regular customers. He'd been here twice now, so maybe he'd also be a repeat customer.

He stared at her warily, as if uncertain whether to trust her. Was he just shy, or did he have another reason for not sharing his name? Maybe she'd violated his privacy.

"I'm sorry," Faithe said. "I wasn't trying to pry. We're just friendly around here, so we like to know how to address our customers."

"*Sir* is fine."

"That feels so cold and formal," Faithe burst out and then wished she'd held her tongue. "But if that's what you prefer..." She hoped he'd contradict that, but he didn't.

His solemn look indicated he didn't plan to tell her anything else. She ached inside that this man had put up such a barrier around himself that he didn't even feel comfortable sharing his name.

"Very well, sir," she said. "I'll be right back with your egg. One dippy egg with no sides."

"Perfect." His smile revealed gleaming white teeth and nearly took her breath away. He'd be quite handsome if he cleaned up a bit.

Faithe returned his smile and hurried off to place his order. Then she circulated around to her tables, refilling hot coffee or topping off beverage glasses. From time to time, she peeked over at "Sir" to be sure he hadn't changed his mind about coffee, but he was either engrossed in staring out the window or jotting notes in his small black book.

She served two tables before his egg came up. As soon as it did, she hurried it to his table. "Here you are, sir. Exactly what you ordered. If you need anything else, just let me know, sir."

"It's Crist." When she looked at him blankly, he repeated, "My name is Crist."

"Oh, right." She gave him a broad smile. "Please let me know if you need anything, Crist." She walked away from the table with a bounce in her step. From the way he acted, he'd shared a deep dark secret with her.

Interesting, though, he had an Amish name. He definitely didn't look Amish, and yesterday he'd seemed uncomfortable whenever she brought up God. Perhaps an *Englisch* parent had copied the name.

As she flitted around the restaurant, Faithe handed out invitations and discussed the upcoming Thanksgiving dinner with her customers. Crist was still there when she stopped at the table beside his booth. Again, the menu hid his face from the view of seated customers.

"Ready for your check, Jakob?" Faithe picked up the empty plates and balanced the stack on her arm. "Or would you like a refill on coffee?"

"Much as I'd like another cup, I should get Sarah and the baby home. It's icy weather."

Faithe handed him the bill, and he pulled out cash and set it on the table. He turned to his wife. "Ready, Sarah?"

She gazed at him lovingly before bundling up the baby. Then she turned to Faithe. "How are your Thanksgiving plans coming along? Anything I can do to help?"

Faithe, her arms loaded with dishes, smiled at Sarah. "One of your snitz pies would be *wunderbar*."

Jakob picked up the diaper bag and took Sarah's arm. "Do you need help with the pickups?"

The dishes were growing heavy on Faithe's arms, but she needed to secure more rides for the elderly and lonely who lived in the community. "Yes, I do need pickups. If you stop at the cash register, I have several lists made up. You can take your choice." Faithe sighed. "Most of the *Englisch* drivers are celebrating the holidays with their families, so I'm short one or two car drivers."

"I can make an extra buggy run." Jakob followed her toward the kitchen area.

To prevent him from following her through the door, she pointed to the small stack of orange papers beside the register. "I'll let you know if I need more, but I usually get quite a few buggy offers. My main concern is the people who live in the remote areas. I really need some cars to fetch them."

Jakob and Sarah headed for the papers she'd indicated.

"Let me just take these into the kitchen"—Faithe tipped her chin toward the plates on her arms—"and then I'll go over the lists with you."

She bumped her hip against the swinging door to open it, took the dishes to the busboy, and reemerged to find Sarah and Jakob discussing the lists, their heads close together.

Sarah pointed to three papers spread before her. "Jakob and I can pick up these two people on our way. Then after he drops me off, he'll go back to do this list."

Jakob held up the third list. "I'd also be happy to do this one."

Faithe beamed at them. "Thank you so much. That would be such a big help."

After she said good-bye, she hurried to refill beverages, take orders from customers who had entered, and check on the ones who were eating. When she passed Crist's table, he held out a hand to stop her. Assuming he wanted his bill, she reached into her apron pocket for her pad.

"I overheard you mention you needed cars to pick up people for your Thanksgiving dinner. I'm happy to help."

Faithe gaped at him. "You have a car?"

"Surprising, isn't it?"

She blushed. "I'm sorry. I didn't mean that the way it sounded." She bumbled on, trying to cover her mistake. "It's just that..."

"That bums like me don't usually have cars." A touch of bitterness oozed into his words. "Just because people are poor doesn't mean they don't have feelings. Or a sense of pride."

"I'm so sorry." She hadn't meant to hurt him or to prejudge him. She tried so hard not to do that. "If you have a car and are willing to pick people up, that would be a Godsend."

He winced, and once again Faithe had the impression he disliked talking about God. Her heart went out to him. What had he been through in life that caused him to block God out of his life? How lonely and desperate he must be without a strong faith to carry him through his trials.

"My car's not the greatest. To be honest, it's a rust bucket, but it runs. It's also warm and roomy."

"That doesn't matter," she hastened to assure him. "No one's going to care what the car looks like. If you're sure you don't mind?"

"I wouldn't have offered if I did."

"True." Everything she said seemed to rub him the wrong way. Or maybe he was prickly because she'd insulted him by assuming he didn't have a car. "I'll go get a list for you."

Faithe scurried to the cash register and selected a cream-colored paper. She didn't know how much money he had for gas, so she chose a list where all the pickups were close together.

When she handed him the paper with the names and addresses, he glanced at it and blanched.

"Is everything all right?" she asked.

He rubbed his forehead. "Fine, fine." He hesitated a few seconds before adding, "If you don't get enough volunteers with cars, let me know, and I'll do another round of pickups for you."

"That's so generous of you." Faithe had been impressed with his ten-cent tip yesterday, and today his generosity overwhelmed her. He barely had enough money to pay for a meal, but he'd volunteered to help others. "The restaurant is happy to pay for gas."

"I can manage," he said stiffly.

She'd offended him again, though she hadn't meant to. "I didn't mean..." What had she meant? "I'm sorry. I wasn't trying to imply..." Her words tangled up again. How did she correct this blunder? "The restaurant always offers to pay for gas, but we're grateful when volunteers donate that as well as their time. So thank you."

His brisk nod didn't reveal whether or not she'd succeeded in smoothing things over. Faithe sought his eyes, hoping to gauge his reaction, but when their gazes met, she sucked in a breath. Staring into his gray eyes threw her completely off balance. The rest of the room faded into the background. She forgot her job, the customers, the waiting orders...

He broke the connection and turned to stare out the window. Faithe was still free-falling, and reality hit with a thud. She had to pull herself together. "Thank you, Crist."

His head jerked back when she said his name. A wary look crossed his face. Had he forgotten he'd told her his name? It seemed so, but then the tension in his shoulders relaxed, and he even managed a half-hearted smile. "You're welcome, Faithe."

Now it was her turn to be startled, until she realized she had a name tag on. She laughed. "It's nice to be on a first-name basis with our regular customers."

He flinched, and the teasing in his eyes when he said her name disappeared, to be replaced by a blank stare. With a chilly smile, he returned to staring out the window.

She'd stepped on a landmine again, but had no idea what she'd said to detonate it. Had she been overly friendly and made him feel uncomfortable? Or did he not appreciate being called a regular customer? Maybe he thought she subtly was pressuring him to keep coming back?

"Would you like anything else, or should I bring your check?" she asked, hoping to get their association back to businesslike terms. Perhaps he'd sensed her attraction and was signaling his disinterest. He needn't worry. She had no intention of having a relationship with an *Englischer*.

His wan smile seemed to almost be an apology. "The check, please."

"I'll be right back."

She hustled to prepare his check, took a trayful of orders to her large round table of young mothers, and bantered with them for a while. She asked after other family members, inquired about everyone's children in the local public schools, and listened to the mothers lament about the upcoming half-day of school and the long weekend for Thanksgiving vacation. It seemed as if these *Englisch* mothers would rather be without their children than with them. As soon as Faithe could slip away, she stopped at Crist's table.

Setting down the check, she said, "Thanks again for agreeing to do pickups for the Thanksgiving dinner." She stopped before she added *Crist*, in case that was what had bothered him before. "I'm, um, we're glad you'll be coming for the meal."

Again, Crist appeared taken aback. "Oh, I hadn't planned on coming to that. I usually spend the day with my brother."

"He's welcome to join us, too."

Crist shook his head. "I don't think..."

He heaved a sigh, one that conveyed a world of hurt and made Faithe long to reach out to him. She wanted to say *I'm sorry*, but she didn't even know what she was sorry for. That he carried such heavy burdens, perhaps.

Crist's attention wandered to the view outside the window again, and Faithe was curious what held his interest out there. He seemed mesmerized by it. She wondered if he'd ended the conversation, but then he turned in her direction. His gaze, though, was fixed on something far, far away. "Ethan's, um, not normal."

Faithe had no idea what he meant by that. Was his brother not 100%? That's what it sounded like, but she couldn't be sure. Other families brought their children with special needs, and Faithe didn't want to exclude anyone, so she said, "Everyone is welcome, including your brother. If he wants to come, that is."

"He'd probably love it, but I'm not sure others would be as appreciative of having him."

"I think you'll be surprised by how accepting everyone is. And it's Thanksgiving, so full stomachs and grateful hearts usually make people quite expansive." Faithe wanted to ask more about his brother, but she didn't want to pry.

"We'll see." Crist stood and reached into his jeans pocket.

Faithe didn't want to embarrass him as he counted out his change again, so she turned and rushed toward the kitchen to pick up orders. As she passed one of her tables, a man held out his coffee cup.

"Refill, please."

"Oh, I'm so sorry." Faithe's cheeks burned. She tried never to let customers' cups run dry. Spending too much time with one customer meant all the others went without items they needed. She grabbed the coffee pot and made a quick round to top off everyone's mugs. "I'll be right back with your tea," she promised several Amish women in a booth.

When she reached the kitchen, orders for three tables were waiting. How long had she been chatting? Now she'd have to race to catch up.

She slid two tables' orders onto one tray and rushed from the kitchen and down the aisle, almost colliding with Crist. He reached out a hand to steady the shaking tray.

"Careful there," he said.

His deep voice and caring expression did strange things to Faithe's insides. She didn't dare look into his eyes again, so she focused on the hands holding the tray and discovered one more thing to puzzle over. His clean, neatly manicured hands didn't match his scruffy appearance.

Once she had a better grip on the tray, Faithe tried to squeeze over so he could pass, but the aisle was too narrow to make enough room.

"That's all right," he said. "I can wait."

Feeling self-conscious, Faithe set down plates for the two customers near her. Then she moved around the table, aware of Crist's gaze following her every move. He could fit past now, but he didn't move. What was he waiting for?

∞ ∞ ∞

Crist's mind warned him to get out of here—fast. But his body refused to cooperate. He enjoyed listening to Faithe's pleasant voice. She was chatting with the customers at the table, and he'd have to brush past her, so he waited.

"Yes," she said in answer to a question from one of the ladies, "I still have more invitations to give out. Tonight and tomorrow after work, I'll head out into the streets around here and closer to downtown, where the homeless hang out, to hand those out."

Crist's gut clenched. Didn't she know how dangerous that was?

The man across the table must have had a similar reaction. He frowned. "Faithe, that's much too dangerous. Surely your *mamm* won't let you do that."

Crist bent and fiddled with his shoe so he'd have an excuse to hear her answer.

As perky as ever, Faithe asked, "Don't you believe God protects us wherever we go, and that whatever happens is His will?"

"Of course, but there's no need to be foolish." The man's stern tone revealed his worry for her safety.

A worry Crist shared. Faithe's cheerful response made it clear that she wouldn't let fear or caution deter her from doing God's work. He needed to find a way to convince her otherwise, but right now he needed to get out of here before she discovered the tip and decided it was a mistake. Besides, he was missing important observations across the street.

∞ ∞ ∞

Faithe continued setting meals in front of customers, but she noted when Crist walked by, almost brushing her, and when he stopped to tie his shoe. Then the bells on the door jangled, signaling he'd left the restaurant. Was it odd to feel disappointed when he walked out the door?

Faithe bustled around, trying to catch up with all the orders she'd missed while she'd chatted with Crist. She didn't want any of the customers to feel neglected and tried to make everyone feel special. Many of the regular customers wanted to talk about the Thanksgiving meal, but in most cases, she responded briefly and kept circulating.

Leah Stoltzfus touched Faithe's arm as she passed. "I need to get a list from you so I can do Thanksgiving pickups."

"I'll be right back." Faithe grabbed the first orange paper on the stack and handed it to Leah. "Here you go. Thanks so much." Why did thanking Leah bring up Crist's face? As if her thoughts had conjured him up, Crist appeared outside the window, hunched over against the wind, his hands deep inside his pockets. He looked frozen as he stomped along the snow-dusted sidewalks. Faithe wished she could invite him in to warm up, but he'd probably rebuff her suggestion.

"Are you all right?" Leah asked. "You seem so distracted today."

Faithe turned her attention away from the window. Crist was just disappearing from sight anyway. "I'm mostly tired and worried about all the details of the Thanksgiving meal." And about whether Crist would show up with his brother.

After she finished her conversation with Leah, *Mamm* beckoned her, and Faithe scurried over to see what she wanted.

Mamm's normally cheerful expression held a hint of sternness. "*Dochder*, we need to spend an equal amount of time with all of our customers, so nobody feels neglected."

"I was trying to..."

Mamm interrupted her. "I wasn't talking about Leah." Her eyebrows rose slightly as she motioned with her head toward the still-empty table where Crist had sat. "The *Englischer* may be attractive and charming," *Mamm* continued, "but with the small amount he ordered, it didn't appear he needed the excessive attention you showered on him."

"*Mamm*." Faithe's tone was sharper than she'd intended, and she softened it before continuing, "He offered to drive some people to our Thanksgiving dinner. Otherwise I wouldn't have spent so much time talking with him." Was that really true? And had that been the only thing they'd talked about? "Oh, and he seemed uncertain about bringing his brother, so I was trying to reassure him his brother was welcome."

"I see." *Mamm*'s tone and expression indicated she saw a lot more than Faithe had mentioned.

And, as usual, *Mamm* was probably right. Gazing into those gray eyes, she'd lost all sense of time and place. "I'll be more mindful of that in the future."

"I know you will." *Mamm*'s gentle smile took the sting from her rebuke and made Faithe eager to obey her. "You still haven't cleared that table yet, and we have customers waiting to be seated." *Mamm* indicated Crist's table.

"I'm so sorry." Faithe grabbed a rag and hurried over to clean it.

On the table a small stack of bills lay atop the receipt. Curious, Faithe counted and pocketed the money. He'd left a tip three times more than the cost of the egg. Perhaps he'd been trying to cover yesterday's bill.

Maybe he'd counted wrong. Or didn't know how to count. Or... some of the street people gambled. Often they were down on their luck and needed the free breakfasts. Occasionally they were flush and threw their money around, treated others to meals, and left generous tips. Faithe disliked thinking Crist might be addicted to gambling. He didn't seem the type, and she'd made snap judgments about him before, so she hesitated to come to any conclusions without proof. She only hoped he hadn't done anything illegal to get the money.

Chapter Three

Crist left the restaurant, his mind in a whirl. Being around Faithe did that to him. He had to be careful. Staring into her eyes had been electrifying. If he hadn't broken that connection...

A limousine pulled in front of the pharmacy across the street. Crist kept an eye on it and noted the license plate number as he hurried toward his car. Seeing a limo in this rundown neighborhood was unusual, and the dark-tinted windows made it even more odd. He'd seen an occasional wedding or two, and once he'd seen a whole group of teens headed to prom, but those limos were white. The windows were clear, with the passengers clearly visible in the back, or in the case of the kids, the windows were down, and a few had their heads out the window, yelling.

Crist got into his car and pulled out the notebook—the blank notebook from yesterday—and jotted down the information. After he'd visited his brother last night, he'd spent time recording all the information he could recall. Then he'd tossed and turned for much of last night, puzzling over the theft of the notebook. Someone was worried enough about his notes to not only steal them, but to substitute a similar small black book. Why not just steal the book? Maybe so he wouldn't be alarmed enough to chase them down or note what they looked like and report the theft?

He tried to figure out when it happened. Had the argument outside the pharmacy been a setup to distract him? The runner who'd collided with him had handed him his notebook. He had his back turned when he picked up the notebook.

Or was it the plumber? When the plumber dusted off the notebook on his coat, he could easily have substituted a new one from his pocket. But why? Were they just curious what he was writing? Or did they have a more sinister motive? If so, why didn't they get rid of him instead of taking the book?

Other than the limo, Crist noted no unusual activity or repeat customers that morning, which gave him plenty of time to think about Faithe. He wished he hadn't been so testy with her about the car, but she'd touched a nerve. Not so much for him, but for so many of the others he'd met on the streets. Each person had a different story, and most of them had lived fascinating lives. Yet so often mainstream society dismissed them, ignored them, averted their eyes when they walked past. Passersby often pulled their coats around them more tightly and skirted around the street dwellers as if afraid of being contaminated, making him want to shout, *Hey, that's a human being you just passed, not a tree stump or a trash can.*

After a while, you came to expect it, but it never stopped hurting. If Crist had one goal in life, it was to convince the world to treat everyone with dignity and respect, whatever their outward appearance, mental abilities, or lifestyle choices. Whether they chose to live on the streets or had to out of necessity, did that make them less worthy of being treated as fellow human beings?

He sighed. He'd better not get started on his mental tirade. He still hadn't found a way to spread his message about loving everyone, but he'd noticed the people least likely to embrace his ideas were those who called themselves Christians. It was sad to think they didn't follow the teachings of the Bible. The Amish, with their emphasis on humility and not putting themselves above others, should be the ones who most exemplified those teachings. Yet even Faithe, who appeared to be one of the most loving people he'd ever met, seemed to judge by outward appearances. She'd automatically made assumptions about him just because of how he looked.

And speaking of judging, Crist had to laugh. What had he been doing this whole time but judging those who judged others? He'd been smugly self-righteous at their expense. Evidently, he had a lot to learn, too.

Cold seeped into his bones even with the quilt wrapped around his legs, and he turned on the car heater to warm up. He'd parked where he couldn't see into the restaurant window because he didn't need that distraction. Earlier this week, if anyone had told him he'd be more interested in watching an Amish girl than in taking notes, he'd have laughed at them. Unfortunately, that wasn't the case anymore. He had to find a way to get his mind off her, but first he needed to come up with a plan to protect her tonight and tomorrow. He couldn't let her wander the streets alone at night.

Crist's legs cramped. He had to get out and walk, but before he did, he slipped the notebook under the car seat. He wasn't taking any more chances with losing the information.

It felt good to stretch his legs, but he had to hunch himself against the bitter wind. He kept his eyes averted the first few times he passed the restaurant as he jog-walked up and down the block to stay warmer, but the temptation to see Faithe grew stronger each time he went by the window.

Finally, he couldn't resist and slowed his pace to a stroll. Faithe, her face glowing, talked animatedly to a customer. As he passed, she glanced up, and their eyes met. Once again, her gaze lit a spark inside of him. A spark he'd thought was dead and cold and lifeless.

She seemed as mesmerized by him as he was with her, and her customers turned to stare at what had caught her attention. As much as he didn't want to, Crist turned his head and walked past briskly. He'd been foolish to do that because now Faithe and her eyes filled his thoughts, distracting him, and he'd revealed his interest in her. He couldn't afford the complication of a woman in his life right now. He was in no position to date.

Date? Where did that crazy idea come from? He wouldn't date Faithe in a million years. She was Amish. And even if he did want to date her—which he definitely did not—she'd never date him. She could only date someone of her faith, and he certainly didn't qualify.

But that didn't mean he could tamp down the urge to protect her. He'd do the same for any person in distress, man or woman. Faithe was too naïve to understand the dangers of the streets at night. He wished he could convince her to let him hand out the invitations, but he suspected she preferred the personal touch.

The afternoon slid by rapidly, filled with thoughts of Faithe. Little of interest attracted his attention at the drugstore. When the plumber's van pulled to the curb behind him, it was time to go. He debated about confronting the plumber about his notebook, but he didn't want to stir up trouble. If they'd gotten what they wanted, he hoped they'd leave him alone. On the other hand, if they found something in his notebook that looking incriminating, would they come back?

He didn't have time to dwell on that possibility. His brother would be waiting. Crist pulled out into rush hour traffic and headed across town. When he pulled in front of the group home, Ethan sat by the window watching for him. Crist waved, and Ethan smiled, his head bobbing up and down slightly in his usual greeting.

Crist picked his way carefully around icy patches on the sidewalk, rang the bell, and waited for the buzz and click that signaled the door had unlocked. He pushed open the door, hung his jacket on one of the hooks, and plugged in his cell phone. Sophie had given him permission to charge his phone whenever he visited, so he used an outlet near the front door. Then he hurried into the living room where Ethan waited.

His brother smiled and said, as he always did, "You come."

Crist set a hand on Ethan's shoulder and gave it a light squeeze. "Time for dinner?"

Ethan's head moved up and down slightly. "Pork chops."

"That sounds delicious." Crist put his hands on the wheelchair handles. "Want me to push, or do you want to do it?"

"Do it myself," Ethan said, so Crist stepped back and followed Ethan as he maneuvered his wheelchair to the group dining room.

When the aides had assisted everyone to a place around the large wooden dining table, the houseparents for the group home, Sophie and Joe, asked everyone to bow their heads. They allowed time for silent prayer. Crist kept his head bowed and eyes closed out of politeness, but his jaw clenched until they all said "Amen" aloud.

Crist wondered if Ethan remembered prayers around the family table, if he mentally recited words when he bowed his head, or if his mind remained blank when he followed the houseparents' directions.

During the meal, Crist cut Ethan's meat, helped spoon applesauce and mashed potatoes into his brother's mouth, and conversed with Ethan's housemates. Ethan grunted and contributed to the discussion as much as he could. Dessert proved to be a challenge. Crist struggled to spoon vanilla ice cream into Ethan's mouth before it melted into a puddle, but much of the liquid dribbled down Ethan's chin. For some reason, Ethan had difficulties with liquids or soft foods.

"Have Ethan tell you what he did today," Sophie suggested.

The ice cream melted even more as Ethan, his eyes shining, struggled to say, "Learn computer."

Sophie beamed as much as Ethan. "The adaptive devices we ordered finally came in. He can manipulate the mouse and type using simple finger movements. It also follows voice commands. He did really well."

Crist laid a hand on his brother's shoulder and looked him in the eye. "Good work, buddy. I'm proud of you."

Ethan beamed at the praise and gave his usual small shoulder bounce. Then Crist went around the table listening to each person's accomplishments and congratulating them. All of Ethan's housemates had become like family. Crist wondered if Ethan would be lonely when the two of them managed to get out on their own together.

After dinner, Crist helped his brother get ready for bed. The staff were willing to do that, but Crist preferred to handle it himself. He missed his brother during the day, so he wanted to spend as much time as possible with Ethan while he was there. Once Ethan had completed his nighttime routine, Crist pushed the wheelchair to the bed.

Then came the hardest part of the day, the time Crist always dreaded. He hated to leave Ethan for the night, and he tensed, waiting for the question his brother always asked.

Ethan looked up at him with trusting eyes and an eager expression. "Go home tomorrow?"

Crist's throat tightened. Every night before bed, Ethan asked the same question, and every time, Crist had to give the same answer. "Not yet buddy, but soon." His heart ached at the disappointment in Ethan's eyes.

Crist swallowed hard. "But I do have a surprise for you."

His brother looked up eagerly, and Crist told him about Faithe planning the Thanksgiving dinner for everyone. "She invited you to come. Would you like to go?"

Crist had no need to ask that question because his brother's eyes shone and his shoulders bounced slightly as he flapped his hands. Those small movements were Ethan's usual way to convey excitement.

"OK, then, I'll take you on Thursday. Today is Tuesday." Crist went over to the large wall calendar where he marked off days for his brother. "I'll cross off today." He put an "X" through Tuesday. "I'll come tomorrow." He pointed to Wednesday. "And then Thursday will be Thanksgiving." He wrote *dinner* in that block.

Ethan stared at the calendar blankly, so Crist repeated the information. Then he crossed the room and squatted in front of his brother so he could look directly into Ethan's eyes. "Do you understand?" Crist held up two fingers. "In two days we'll go to the dinner. One. Two."

His brother nodded, but Ethan's eyes didn't reflect a spark of understanding. Tomorrow his brother would ask about the dinner, expecting to go right away—if he even remembered the conversation. Sometimes Ethan remembered things and kept asking about them doggedly. Other times he had no recollection of events or conversations. Memories with strong emotional associations seemed to be easier for him to remember.

"Remember Thanksgiving with *Mamm* and *Daed*?" Crist asked him. "The turkey? Gravy? Filling?"

At the last word, Ethan smiled. Filling had been one of his favorite foods. Crist smiled. So Ethan did recollect some of the past holidays.

"In two days—one, two—we'll have Thanksgiving dinner with filling," Crist told him.

"Two days," Ethan repeated. He lifted his thumb and index finger. "One, two."

Crist had no way of knowing whether Ethan actually understood, or if he was parroting the words he'd heard, but Crist smiled at his brother. "That's right. Two days. What will we do in two days?"

"Filling," Ethan responded.

"You got it, buddy." Crist praised his brother, but he ached inside as he tucked him into bed and held his hand as Ethan mumbled an unintelligible bedtime prayer. Ethan had kept his faith despite all that had happened to him, although Crist had no way of knowing how much his brother understood and how much was ingrained habit.

As Crist stood and turned off the lights, he railed at the accident that had taken Ethan's strong, healthy body and intelligent mind, and left behind this stranger with little control over his own body—one who struggled to talk and understand. If people wanted to know why Crist no longer believed in God, the answer was lying right here in this bed.

Chapter Four

Faithe walked briskly down the street outside the restaurant, her hand filled with envelopes. She'd head to the park where a lot of homeless people slept. *Dear Lord, please make me a blessing to those I meet tonight. Lead me to the people You want me to help.*

As she crossed the street, shuffling footsteps followed her. She sped up a bit, but so did whoever was behind her. Then she slowed down to see if the person would pass, but they seemed to keep whatever pace she kept. Faithe glanced over her shoulder but didn't see anyone. She prayed that if it was God's will, He would protect her. Then she relaxed and trusted that whatever happened was God's plan for her life.

She shivered in the frigid air and worried about the people who slept on the streets at night. She entered the dark park and made the rounds of benches and bushes. Many of the people who slept there had quilts or sleeping bags now because she'd coordinated a group of women from several Amish communities to make them, but even those were little protection against the icy weather. Some had covered themselves with layers of plastic, old newspapers, and leaves to give them insulation.

Faithe knew many of the regulars. She also fed quite a few of them or at least gave them free coffee in the morning. Those who knew her readily accepted the invitations. Some of the others took them warily. Two new people picked up their belongings and ran away. Perhaps they thought she planned to kick them out of the park. That made her sad. She hadn't meant to scare them.

From there, she crossed to the street on the other side of the park. During the day, even when the weather was nippy, people usually sat on white plastic chairs on their row house porches, but tonight every chair was empty. Faith walked up and down the stairs, putting envelopes in mailboxes. Except for the loud rumbling engines and cars shaking from blasting rap music, which passed in a steady stream, the streets were deserted.

Walking briskly past a boarded-up warehouse, Faithe hurried to the next block. Soon after she crossed the narrow street to the next block, the shuffling began again. Someone definitely was following her. She glanced over her shoulder, and twice she thought a shadowy figure disappeared into the alleyways between buildings.

Once again she whispered a prayer for safety as she handed out the invitations to two men sharing a heating grate on the sidewalk outside a store secured with metal bars. She headed toward an old apartment building and pulled open the heavy door. Several people sprawled on the cement under the stairs. They had a little more protection from the elements. She handed invitations to each one.

Her toes had turned into icicles from being outside in this weather, so she could only imagine what it was like to sleep out here all night. She longed to find a way to get housing for all these people. The city shelters were already too full.

Motorcycle engines roared in the distance as she exited the apartments. The motors grew louder, their revving drowning out the sounds of passing cars and the hum of traffic in the distance. As they thundered through the red light and screeched around the corner, hands reached out and grabbed her from behind. A man clamped one hand over her mouth and dragged her into the alleyway.

Fingers over her mouth muffled her scream.

"Hush," he ordered, his whisper harsh, and his lips so close to her ear his breath puffed against her cheek. "Stay still. You don't want them to know you're here."

He pushed her down behind a row of overflowing trash cans. The stench of rotting food sickened her. Faithe tried to wriggle loose from his grasp, but he only held on tighter. He pulled her close to his body and wrapped her in his coat. She was shivering from the cold and from the scare.

"Don't struggle. I won't hurt you." His low, gravelly voice sent waves of fear crashing through her.

Enveloped in the darkness of his coat and pressed against his muscular chest by his strong grip, Faithe had no idea what this man intended to do. She prayed for God's protection, but most of all for the man who held her so tightly. *Please, God, meet the deepest needs of his heart, and help him to know Your peace, Lord.*

Peace descended over her, along with the assurance that God was in control and would work this situation to His glory. Silently she repeated the verse from Psalms, *In God have I put my trust: I will not be afraid what man can do unto me.*

Behind her, the man's chest rose and fell in an unsteady rhythm, revealing his fear. The backfires of motorcycles drowned out the pounding of his heart, a syncopated thumping that reflected her own heart. The riders revved their engines, an ominous sound. They circled the area near the alley, weaving onto the sidewalk, buzzing past the buildings, but none turned into the alley.

After ten minutes that seemed like an eternity, they zoomed off. As the sound faded into the distance, the man gripping her spoke. "Stay here for awhile. They may be trying to flush us out."

Faithe wondered if the man was mentally unstable. Some of the street people had been released from state institutions due to lack of funding. Some saw and heard things that weren't there; others walked along muttering to themselves. This man found motorcycles menacing, so menacing he dragged strangers into an alley and hid. So far he hadn't hurt her, but would he turn violent?

His grasp loosened slightly now that the motorcycles had passed. With a swift twist, she broke free of the hands that imprisoned her. She stumbled to her feet. She'd caught him off guard, and he fumbled with his coat, trying to grab her.

"No, don't go," he insisted. "It's not safe yet." He stood and started after her.

Faithe dodged the arms reaching out for her, but after crouching for so long, her feet were numb and she was unsteady. She tripped and almost fell. He caught her, trapping her in his arms again.

The motorcycles droned, coming nearer, and the man's voice held fear as he said, "I told you they'd be back. Get down."

Once again, the stink of decaying food overpowered her before he wrapped her in his coat and yanked her down behind the rows of garbage cans. He held her tightly as the motorcycles swooped down the street. They repeated their circling, but for a shorter time.

When the cycles left, he lifted her to her feet. "Let's get you to safety."

Faithe wanted to get to safety, but not with him. She let her muscles go limp, hoping if she appeared pliable, he'd relax his hold. It worked. The second his grip slackened slightly, she wrenched away from him and raced toward the restaurant. As long as he didn't have a gun, she could barricade herself in the restaurant until he left.

All her farm work and hurrying around the restaurant, combined with the rush of adrenaline flooding her body, made her swift on her feet. She quickly outdistanced him. Soon his footsteps faded in the distance, but Faithe didn't slow until she reached the restaurant door.

Her breath was coming in gasps, but she blew out a long sigh. She was safe. As she turned the key in the lock, footsteps sounded behind her.

"Good. You made it safely," the man said behind her.

Her hands shaking, she yanked the door open and slipped inside, worried she'd be no match for his strength if he pushed on the door.

"I didn't mean to scare you. I took a shortcut to make sure you were all right."

Faithe started to slam the door, readying to lean her full weight against it, but he didn't touch the door. He only stood there while she clicked the lock into place.

As he stepped back out of the shadows, the bright overhead light illuminated his face.

Crist?

For a few moments, he stared at the door with forlorn eyes, then he turned and strode off.

Faithe leaned her forehead against the chilly glass.

Had Crist been following her through the park and down the streets? He'd come into the restaurant twice in the past few days. Was he a stalker?

∞ ∞ ∞

Instead of heading to his car, Crist wound his way back through the maze of dark alleys. As he chased Faithe, he'd noticed a van parked behind the pharmacy and boxes being unloaded. It might be a routine delivery, but if it was, why were they doing it in the dark? He'd been so busy observing the front of the building until it closed at 5:30 every evening, it never occurred to him he might have been watching the wrong side.

He made his way down the alley, grateful for dark clothes that blended into the shadows. He walked as silently as he could in his oversized shoes. Usually he shuffled, but tonight he picked up his foot, careful not to lose his shoe. Then he set it down a short distance in front of him, first probing the ground with his toe for gravel or broken glass that might crunch when he stepped on it. His progress was painstakingly slow, but he didn't want to alert anyone to his presence.

A motor turned over. They were leaving. Figuring no one could hear him over the car engine, he hurried the rest of the way to the pharmacy's service entrance. Two men stood in the shadows on each side of the small parking area, their eyes scanning the buildings and alleys. Security guards? Or were they protecting a drug shipment?

The back door of the cargo van slammed, and a man rounded the vehicle. The younger pharmacist. Another man accompanied him. Crist noted his height and build. It was a bit too dark to see any distinguishing features, but when the man climbed into the driver's seat, the van light clicked on, revealing a swarthy complexion, a bulbous nose, shaved head, and shaggy black eyebrows that almost met in the middle. The smoke from his cigar wafted toward Crist, choking him.

Crist lifted his jacket to cover his mouth and nose, but the smoke irritated his eyes and nose. He gulped and swallowed, trying not to cough and give himself away. One of the guards paced toward him. Had he seen his movements? The man slid his hand into his pocket, and Crist didn't wait to find out.

He pretended to stumble and weave his way to the nearest apartment building. Pulling out a ring of keys, he jangled them and stabbed one in the direction of the door, missing the lock entirely. Swaying on his feet, he looked stupidly at the key ring, selected another key, and tried to insert it sideways.

The eyes bored into his back. Crist hoped his performance was convincing enough. Making sure his hood was pulled well forward, he dipped his head to avoid any light from windows shining on his face. Then he shook the keys, stared at them as if puzzled, and sank onto the stoop. He alternated between hiccupping and singing slurred snatches of songs. The guard studied him, but to Crist's relief, the man pivoted and returned to the van. To be safe, Crist remained slumped on the stoop for a long while after the van pulled away, even though his whole body was shivering. By the time he stood, his toes were so brittle with cold, they felt as if they could snap off. He could barely hobble to his car. Even if the guards were still watching, he probably appeared far from sober.

When he reached the car, he turned on the engine, but cold air blasted from the vents. He idled for a while, waiting for heat. The freezing air changed to lukewarm before it turned hot. Warmth seeped into his frozen limbs, penetrating his bones. His face, toes, and fingers burned and stung as they thawed.

After the car reached a sauna temperature and he was practically sweating in his coat, he flicked off the heater, hoping the car would hold the warmth for a while. He leaned back and closed his eyes, but couldn't let himself go to sleep because he'd soon need to move his vehicle.

By taking that shortcut tonight, he'd stumbled on a new possibility. He'd been so busy watching the drugstore entrance, he'd never thought to check the service entrance. The information he'd been jotting in his notebook might be valuable, but the people he'd been observing at the front of the store were likely much smaller sources than this nighttime delivery. He had no idea how he'd manage to watch the rear door. He couldn't park in the loading area, and the nearby alley was too narrow for a car.

He regretted not getting the license plate number and vehicle model, but they were out of view with the van facing toward him. The shape of the van reminded him of the plumber's vehicle. Was there any connection between them?

Crist's thoughts moved on to the reason he'd cut through the alley in the first place. Faithe. Holding her in the dark alley had done strange things to his heart. Yes, it had been banging against his chest at the thought of what that gang might do to her, but her softness in his arms had stirred a long-buried wish for a home and family. A longing he had to erase because it could never come true.

Chapter Five

Despite the excitement of the previous night, Faithe arrived at the restaurant early. She unlocked the door and picked up the small bundles of *Englisch* newspapers on the sidewalk. After letting herself in, she snipped the ties on each bundle and arranged the newspapers in the rack near the cash register. *Mamm* ordered several local and national papers for their customers.

She picked up the last stack, and her hands stopped before placing them in the wire rack. Splashed across the front page of the local paper was a photo of blurred motorcycles under the heading, *Motorcycle Gang Strikes Again*. Was that the same gang that had buzzed around the alley last night when Crist had held her?

She read the article, sickened by their vandalism. They'd defaced several buildings not far from here. Even worse, they'd surrounded an old man, beaten him, and stolen his wallet. The man was in intensive care. The article made it sound like even the police were afraid of this gang.

So Crist hadn't been paranoid. Living on the streets, he must have heard about or possibly even seen some of the previous incidents the paper mentioned. The gang had beaten and robbed people, smashed windows, broken into stores, sprayed graffiti on buildings, and terrorized neighborhoods.

Faithe unlocked the service door for the cooks and started the coffee pots. She did a quick check to be sure all the booths, tables, and chairs had been cleaned, and all the condiment trays were filled. Each table was set with silverware wrapped in a napkin. By the time she lifted the blinds, the servers had arrived. While they donned aprons, she flipped the sign to OPEN.

On cold days, a line often stretched down the block. People streamed in for free coffee. Faithe's heart went out to one family dressed in ragged clothes. The mother clutched the hands of a young boy and girl about the same age as her cousin Nathan. She couldn't let them go hungry.

Faithe seated them in a booth. "I can bring hot milk for the little ones." The mother gazed up at her with gratitude, then tears filled her eyes as Faithe handed her a menu and said, "Breakfast is on the house."

"Thank you so much," the mother said without opening the menu. "We'll each have one egg."

"I'll be right back with your beverages." As soon as she was out of eyesight, Faithe scribbled additional items on the order pad, asked for two warm milks, and poured a cup of coffee.

When she set the drinks on the table, she noticed fading bruises on the woman's neck and one side of her face. Should she say something? She debated with herself as she served coffee after coffee. The regulars usually didn't come in during the first half hour or so the restaurant was open because it was so crowded. Although the tables were filled, street people stood around, warming themselves and drinking coffee.

When the family's breakfast arrived from the kitchen, Faithe set plates filled with scrambled eggs, sausage, hash browns, and toast in front of the children and their mother.

"This is too much," she protested.

"I felt God nudging me to do it, so consider it a gift from Him."

Tears ran down the woman's face. "I've been praying for a miracle, and this is it."

Faithe hesitated to interfere in people's personal lives, but this woman looked like she needed help. "If you need a place to stay, I can recommend a local women's shelter."

"Been there. Too full for three more. We're heading farther south, where it's warmer"—she glanced around warily—"and safer."

"I see." So Faithe had been right about the bruises.

"I have a sister in Maryland. We can stay with her for awhile before we move on."

"I'll be praying for you." Faithe glanced up to see a man slide into a booth. Crist. Maybe she should get someone else to wait on that table. Especially if he was stalking her. She was so focused on Crist, she barely heard the woman's quiet *thank you.*

"You're welcome." She hurried over, grabbed a coffee pot, and made her rounds, refilling cups, the whole while murmuring prayers for the small family. Then she added one for courage to face Crist.

Her steps faltered as she approached his table, and she avoided his eyes. Pasting a welcoming smile on her face, she set a cup in front of him and poured his coffee with shaking hands.

"Faithe?"

His deep voice made her so nervous, she slopped coffee over the rim. She babbled to fill the silence. "I'm so sorry. I can get you another cup. I didn't mean..."

"It's all right," he said. He used the same tone she and *Mamm* used to gentle a skittish horse. "I didn't mean to frighten you last night. When I overheard you planned to deliver invitations on the street, I worried about your safety and followed you."

So it *had* been him shuffling behind her. And there was no doubt it had been him who grabbed her from behind and pulled her into the alley.

"The motorcycle gang makes a circuit through different neighborhoods starting at that time of night and going through to the wee hours of the morning. They prey on people who are alone. I didn't want anything to happen to you."

Faithe tried to wrap her mind around what he was saying. He'd been there to protect her? Not to stalk her or hurt her? After being so frightened of Crist last night, she was still a bit unsure if she could trust him. Perhaps, though, God had sent Crist as an answer to her prayers. "I prayed God would protect me, if it was His will, and He did."

Crist's face darkened. "You mean if something terrible had happened to you, it would have been God's will?"

"We don't always know the reason for tragedies and pain, but yes, I would have accepted any outcome as God's will for my life."

"I don't buy that," he growled. "If God is supposed to love and care for us, why would he allow innocent people to suffer?"

"I don't know God's plan or purpose. I just trust that everything is His will, so it will all work out for good in the end."

Crist shook his head. "No, it doesn't. Not always."

The bitterness in his voice made Faithe want to reach out and ease whatever burdens he was carrying. Maybe he blamed God for his life on the streets. *Lord, please help me to find a way to show him your love.*

∞ ∞ ∞

Once again, Faithe's unshakable belief in God's goodness bothered Crist. She'd probably never had anything devastating happen in her life. Maybe if he hadn't been there last night to rescue her from the motorcycle gang and she'd been in the hospital in intensive care along with that poor old man, she'd understand what he'd already discovered. It was better not to trust anyone. Not even God.

As usual, Crist slouched and hid behind the menu. He kept his gaze on the pharmacy, but he'd lost interest in the front. He needed to find a way to keep an eye on the service entrance. Did they have daytime deliveries too? He also had to find a way to track down that white cargo van—an almost impossible task with no unique visible markings and no license plate number.

He'd planned to do a little checking this morning, long before the pharmacy opened, to see if he could find a vantage point that allowed him to see the back doors. But he'd woken with a start to discover the car was freezing inside and he was running late. He rushed to the YMCA, skipped his usual weight training and exercise routine, and hurried through his morning shower. He reached the group home a few minutes late. Everyone but Ethan sat around the table.

"He insisted on waiting for you," Sophie said.

"I'm sorry I'm late." Crist shrugged out of his coat and greeted his brother, who beamed at him.

But then a slight frown creased Ethan's brow. "You not come?"

"You worried I wouldn't come?" Crist asked him.

Ethan moved his head a small fraction to the right, then the left.

"So you knew I'd come, huh?" His brother managed a slight nod with a shoulder bounce. "So the houseparents—" Crist stopped and corrected himself. "I mean, Sophie and Joe thought I wasn't coming, but you did?"

After Ethan's second head and shoulder bounce, Crist grasped the wheelchair handles without asking Ethan if he wanted to propel himself. His brother wouldn't like him taking charge like this, but he didn't want to disrupt the schedule. Some of Ethan's housemates got upset at even the slightest change in the schedule. They likely were agitated already. He didn't want to add to their distress.

Sophie smiled at them and, as soon as they'd prayed, she passed the oatmeal in their direction. Crist tied on Ethan's extra-large plastic bib with the rigid pocket to catch spills. Then he fixed the oatmeal the way Ethan had preferred it as a little boy—with maple syrup and applesauce. Sophie always shook her head when Crist stirred those ingredients into Ethan's oatmeal, but she provided them, ever since Crist had explained his brother's favorite recipe. Back before the tragedy, that had been Crist's favorite way to eat oatmeal too. Now he ate it with brown sugar and raisins.

Crist's stomach growled at the scent of the tart apple and sugary maple as he slid the bite between his brother's lips. His brother tried to swallow, but most of the spoonful slid back out. Frustration built inside Crist until he wanted to slam his fist into his palm. Not at his brother's struggles to eat, but because of the indignities Ethan endured.

It was so unfair that his brother still retained much of his intelligence, but he couldn't take care of his bodily needs, communicate his thoughts, or express his feelings except through limited facial expressions and shoulder movements.

Several of Ethan's housemates shoveled in their own food, but both Sophie and Joe helped the young men sitting next to them.

Sophie smiled at Crist. "Thanks for doing this. It helps us a lot. We appreciate your dedication. Some of these guys are lucky to see their families once a month or even less."

Joe wiped Martin's face with a napkin, then turned to Crist. "Ethan counts on you every day for breakfast and dinner. Today, he refused to believe you might not show up."

"I wish I could come at lunch too, but I can't take time off then." He might miss something important. Although, with this new information, he might need to change his hours.

After feeding and cleaning up his brother, Crist dressed Ethan in the clothes his brother insisted on wearing. The hardest part was attaching the suspenders in the back because Ethan couldn't lean forward, so Crist had to scoot him forward in the wheelchair, being careful not to move him too far so he wouldn't tip or tumble out, yet far enough for Crist to reach his hand and arm behind his brother's back. After he slid Ethan back in the chair and strapped him in, Crist breathed out a sigh. Saying good-bye always was hard. Facing Ethan's pleading eyes and answering his question *Go home?* was painful.

The faint aroma of oatmeal lingered as Crist headed to the restaurant. Ordinarily, he skipped breakfast to save the money. He only planned to have coffee, but when Faithe bustled up to his restaurant table and asked if he was ready to order, he asked for a bowl of oatmeal.

He watched her weave around tables, patting people's shoulders, refilling water glasses and coffee cups, chatting with customers. Her face alight, she scurried back and forth balancing trays filled with plates. He admired her deft movements as she set each plate on the table and spoke to each person. Sympathy in her eyes, she spent a lot of time chatting with one woman and her two small children, staying until their depressed faces turned hopeful and excited. He'd never seen anyone spread so much happiness everywhere she went or enjoy a job as much as she did.

Crist's heart longed for the peace and joy she had.

∞ ∞ ∞

As Faithe passed the table where the mother and two children sat, she refilled the woman's coffee cup and gathered the children's mugs. "I usually ask all our customers' names, but you don't have to tell me your real name if you'd rather not."

The woman lowered her eyes and ducked her head. "You can call me Molly."

Faithe's heart felt burdened for this woman. "You said you were heading for Maryland?"

"Maybe." Molly sounded uncertain, or perhaps evasive.

"I'm not trying to pry, but I wondered if you needed a place to stay. You're welcome to stay at our home if you'd like. It may not have all the amenities you're used to, like electricity, but you'd be warm and dry. If you don't mind riding in our carriage, that is."

The little girl who'd been bent over her plate kept her head lowered, but in a voice barely above a whisper, she asked, "A carriage? Like Cinderella?"

Faithe smiled. “It’s not fancy like that. Maybe you’ve heard it called a buggy?”

Molly caught her daughter’s eye and motioned with her hand. The little girl nodded and sat up straight, but she glanced around uneasily. She looked so frightened, Faithe wanted to wrap her arms around the child and comfort her.

“Buggies are those black boxlike things we saw,” Molly said. “The ones pulled by horses.”

The girl’s eyes shone. “Is yours pulled by horses?”

“Yes, it is,” Faith said.

Although the little boy looked up at her with round eyes, he also hunched into himself, like a turtle about to pull its head into its shell.

“The children would love a ride.” Eagerness shone in Molly’s eyes but was quickly masked by fear. She shook her head. “We’d better not. I don’t want to endanger you or your family.”

Faithe had been right about the bruises. “We follow God’s leading. I feel very strongly that this is something God wants me to do.”

When the woman started to shake her head, Faithe gestured toward her children. “If not for yourself, at least protect your children.”

“You don’t understand what you’re asking.”

Faithe set a hand on Molly’s shoulder, and Molly flinched. “I’m sorry. I should have thought.” She set her hand on the table. “From time to time, we’ve sheltered women for Survivors in Action, an organization that helps people who are in abusive relationships or being stalked. I don’t know your situation, but if you need their help, I can contact them for you.”

“He’s too dangerous. I don’t want to involve anyone else.”

“You should be safe with us. Our community won’t mention your whereabouts to anyone. Why don’t you stay a few days to rest before you continue on your way?” Faithe could also use those few days to find her a ride to Maryland.

“Thank you, but I can’t afford to pay you.”

"There's no need. If it bothers you to accept this help, you can pass it along by assisting someone else later on."

"I'd gladly do that," Molly said, "but—"

Faithe interrupted her before she could make any more excuses. "Tomorrow is Thanksgiving, and the children should have a special meal." She pulled an invitation from her pocket.

"What's this?" Molly opened the envelope, and tears filled her eyes. "You're a true angel, aren't you?"

Faithe shook her head. "No, I'm not. I just try to follow God's leading."

Molly ducked her head and murmured, "It's been so long since I've had much to do with God. I used to believe. I read my Bible, prayed, and attended church every Sunday. My husband didn't like that and forbid it. With the way he treated me, I started to doubt God."

God seemed to be bringing doubters to Faithe's attention today. First Crist, now Molly. She sent up a quick prayer for wisdom and the right way to convey it. "I've found I need God the most when life is difficult."

Molly's eyes brimmed with tears. "Since we"—she glanced over her shoulder at the other patrons and lowered her voice—"left, I've been praying more. And God seems to be answering my prayers."

Faithe nodded. "I'd never have made it through the rough times in life without prayer." Faithe glanced toward the man barricading himself from the world with a menu and a gruff exterior. If only she could convince Crist that God had answers to all his difficulties.

Chapter Six

Mamm stood waiting for Faithe. "*Dochder...*"

"I know, *Mamm.* I'm spending too much time talking to Molly, but she's running from an abusive husband. I don't want her and the children sleeping outdoors in this weather."

"Of course not. The poor things."

"I invited them to spend a few days with us," Faithe said. "She has relatives in Maryland, so I'm hoping to find someone to drive her there."

Mamm studied Molly and the children with sympathetic eyes. "I see. But they can't stay here all day."

"Yes, I know. I'm hoping *Mammi*'s still here. I thought the children might enjoy playing with Nathan."

"That's a fine idea." *Mamm* loaded plates from her order and hurried toward a table of businessmen headed downtown to work.

One of Faithe's orders was up, but she rushed into the kitchen. *Mammi* had wrapped her black cape around her and was tying on her black bonnet to protect herself from the cold.

"*Mammi,*" Faithe called. "I need to talk to you, please."

Mammi turned and waited as Faithe dodged kitchen staff to reach the other side of the room.

"Thanks for making all the pies this morning," Faithe told her. *Mammi* came in at five every morning to do the baking for the day. Many of their regular customers frequently stopped by just for her desserts.

"I'm happy to help. It gives me a chance to be around people while Nathan's in school and Josiah's working."

"If you're looking for company, I have some for you." Faithe launched into Molly's story, and after she finished, she said, "I thought if they could go home with you, I'd come by to get them after the restaurant closes tonight." They closed early on Wednesday evenings so their Mennonite and Baptist workers could attend prayer meetings.

"That would be fine. Ada sent a note home that the children would have a half day today, so Nathan will be back from school at lunchtime. The children can play together."

"I'll go get them." Faithe crossed the room and swished through the swinging doors to gather the meals for two of her tables. Crist's oatmeal was also ready, but she'd come back for that and the toppings.

Although she disliked keeping *Mammi* waiting, she stopped to speak to each of the customers as she set their plates in front of them. *Mammi* would understand. Then she took three orders and refilled beverages before returning for the oatmeal. After clipping the orders up for the kitchen staff, she took Crist's bowl in one hand and the topping caddy in the other, and headed for his table.

∞ ∞ ∞

When Faithe set the oatmeal in front of him, Crist inhaled the warm, steamy aroma, but what caught his attention was the metal turntable she placed on the table. It held little bowls of raisins, brown sugar, and nuts as well as a small dish of applesauce and a pitcher of maple syrup.

Crist squeezed his eyes shut for a minute. In an Amish-owned restaurant, he should have expected it, but being faced with the two toppings *Mamm* always stirred into their oatmeal for the second time that morning proved to be too much.

He struggled to hold back his sadness. All his siblings sitting around the table. Ethan, young and lively, upsetting his glass of milk or telling jokes. A sharp, swift pain shot through Crist, and he gasped.

"Are you all right?"

Crist opened his eyes to find Faithe hovering over him, a worried expression on her face. He waved a hand as nonchalantly as he could. "I'm fine."

She didn't look convinced. "Are you sure?"

"The oatmeal brought back a childhood memory." He concentrated on the toppings to avoid looking at her. "It's been years since I had applesauce and syrup on my oatmeal. I guess it's time to try it again."

Faithe smiled. "I hope it brings good memories." As she flitted off, he stared after her. What would life be like if his faith were as strong as hers? Would he move through life with the same joy? What would happen if he released the bitterness and trusted God the way she did?

Crist shook his head. *Impossible.*

As he stirred his oatmeal and the maple-apple scent tickled his nose, his *mamm*'s face floated in front of him, and her words sounded in his ear. *God sends many signs to remind us of His presence.*

Did a bowl of oatmeal count as a sign?

Crist wasn't sure he wanted to be reminded of God's presence. He'd never stopped believing in God's existence. For him, nothing else made sense. Only a superior being could have created the natural beauty of this world. But he found it too hard to believe God loved and cared about him or about his brother.

Each bite Crist put in his mouth brought both pleasure and pain. The sweetness on his tongue reminded him of the past, of the way things used to be when he was young and innocent. When his family had been together. When he'd believed everything he'd been taught. But each swallow left his mouth as empty as his life.

Across the room, Faithe ushered a woman and two children through the door to the kitchen. They hadn't paid at the cash register, and no bill or money lay on the table. Another free meal? How many did she give out in a day?

Crist scraped the bottom of the oatmeal bowl. He could set some money on the table and leave, but he wanted to see her again. Remembering her smile helped warm him in the icy weather.

He also wanted to discuss her plans for tonight. He hoped to talk her out of distributing invitations. Perhaps after last night she'd realize how dangerous it was, but he needed to be sure she'd skip giving out the rest.

Faithe returned with another tray full of plates, so he waited until she'd made the rounds of tables to signal her. She headed straight for him, but got sidetracked several times along the way. She caught his eye and held up one finger, urging him to wait. He nodded to let her know he was in no hurry. In fact, it was a pleasure to watch her animated face as she conversed with the customers as she passed. He should be checking out the window, but Faithe mesmerized him.

When she finally reached him, she gave him the same dazzling smile she'd given the others, but it seemed to hold extra special caring. He hoped he wasn't reading more into it than he should. Reminding himself he had no time for attraction, he cooled the longing rising in him for closeness—for a relationship, for a woman who would share his life. If he were ever lucky enough to reach that point, he'd want his wife to be just like Faithe, with her sweet disposition, her loving nature, her gentle spirit, her outgoing personality... Crist stopped his mental list. Yes, he'd like a wife exactly like her, except not Amish.

Faithe tilted her head to one side with a questioning look, and Crist's cheeks heated. He'd been staring at her, lost in thought. He averted his eyes.

"Would you like more coffee?" She sounded as flustered as he was.

Crist struggled to get his mind back to ordinary things and to speak in a normal voice. "No, thanks."

"Your check then?"

"Yes. Yes, please." He needed to get out of here before he made a fool of himself. If he hadn't already.

She headed for the cash register and rang him up. By the time she returned, he'd managed to compose himself enough to have a conversation. Their fingers brushed when she handed him the bill, and everything he'd planned to say flew out of his mind. She'd already turned to leave before he stuttered out, "Wait."

Faithe pivoted to face him. "Yes?"

"Are you planning to hand out more invitations tonight?" When she nodded, he said, "It's too dangerous out there. You heard what happened last night, right? That could have been you." He needed to stop rambling and get to the point. "I could hand them out for you."

Faithe hesitated. "I like to do it myself, but thank you for offering."

"Look, I know some of the dangers of the streets at night. If you won't let me do it, at least let me walk with you or behind you for protection." When she started to protest, he held up a hand. "A few days ago, you said you felt led to feed me breakfast. Today I feel led to watch out for your safety." He was pretty sure God wasn't the one leading him, though.

Faithe must have sensed the same thing because she studied him with a suspicious look in her eyes. "I'll pray about it."

Crist nodded. That was her polite way of saying *no*, but Crist planned to show up anyway. He stood as she headed for the kitchen, paid his bill and left a large tip, and then meandered past the woman's table, which was still uncleared, and dropped some bills onto the table when no one was looking. He was glad he'd gotten the extra cash. The only problem was, it would cut into the money he was trying to save for Ethan, and who knew when he'd be able to replace it.

∞ ∞ ∞

As Faithe served her tables, cleared away dishes the busboys hadn't yet removed, took orders, and chatted with customers at each table, Crist's offer remained on her mind. She shivered recalling the mind-numbing fear she'd felt when he'd dragged her into the back alley, one hand over her mouth to muffle her screams. Had he really done that to protect her? Or had he used that as an excuse later? Maybe he'd chickened out and intended to try again tonight.

Even if his suggestion was completely honorable, being around him was much too dangerous. When they made eye contact, she struggled to tear her gaze from his. Last night she'd dreamed of being held against his muscled chest and had woken this morning filled with guilt. He wasn't Amish, and even if he were, she shouldn't be thinking of him like that.

She did need to pick up Molly and the children tonight, though. If Crist handed out the invitations, she could take Molly to her house and get the little ones bathed and settled down for the night at a decent hour. Maybe God had sent him to help her. She'd promised to pray about it. It was time she did that rather than fretting about things.

She rounded the corner to clip up two more orders. Stepping aside so she wasn't in anyone's way, she bowed her head. *Dear Lord, I don't know whether I should trust Crist. If you've sent him to help me, please calm my fears and give me a sense of peace about the correct decision.*

Faithe still had not felt any clear direction as they closed the restaurant for the night, but she hadn't seen Crist again. Usually he walked up and down the sidewalk during the day. She'd identified his huge, old-fashioned maroon car yesterday, and it hadn't been parked on the street today. Faithe breathed a sigh of relief. That must be God's answer to prayer.

The phone in the office rang when Faithe was shutting the blinds and flipping the sign to CLOSED. *Mamm* went into the office to answer it. The staff had cleaned the kitchen and mopped and swept the floors. Faithe dismissed them and finished a few final tasks while waiting for *Mamm*.

It wasn't like *Mamm* to spend this much time on the phone. Her mother disliked using a phone; she only kept one for the business. Faithe headed for the office but stopped before turning the knob. Sobs issued from behind the closed door. *Mamm*? Why would she be crying?

Faithe stood there, uncertain whether she'd be intruding, but longing to comfort her mother. She tapped at the door.

"Faithe?" *Mamm*'s shaky voice was so faint Faithe barely heard her.

"It's me. Is it all right to come in?"

"Yes, if everyone's gone home."

"They have." Faithe pushed open the door to see *Mamm*'s face streaked with tears. "What's wrong?"

Mamm motioned to the chair. "I'm not sure how to tell you this."

Faithe sat where *Mamm* indicated, her nerves buzzing at her mother's ominous tone.

Chapter Seven

As Crist fed Ethan dinner that evening, he turned to Joe. "I'll need to leave right after dinner tonight. I don't like to ask you to do extra work, but could you put Ethan to bed?"

Joe's eyebrows shot up. "You have a date or something?"

"No, no, nothing like that." Although he wished he did. "I'm helping out a friend."

Sophie frowned at her husband. "Don't tease the poor boy. We'd be happy to put Ethan to bed. It's our job."

"Boy?" Joe spluttered. "He's almost our age, and he's old enough to be married."

"That may be." Sophie's voice was firm. "But it's not our business to pry into his personal life."

Crist caught Sophie's eye. "Thanks for taking care of Ethan." He hoped she also realized he was thanking her for not prying. After dinner he had trouble explaining the change of plans to Ethan.

When Crist said, "I have to help a friend," a flicker of understanding flashed in Ethan's eyes. Crist wasn't sure if Ethan responded to the word *help* or *friend*, but his brother stopped his protesting noises.

After a quick good-bye, Crist pocketed his cell phone and hurried off, hoping he wouldn't arrive too late. The sign on the door had been flipped to closed by the time he arrived at the restaurant, but the blinds hadn't been lowered, and a few lights still shone inside. He peered through a window. The restaurant appeared empty. Crist tugged on the door to check that it was secure, and to his surprise, it jiggled. They hadn't locked it.

He'd have to coach Faithe on basic safety practices. Leaving the door unlocked and the blinds up was asking for trouble. This time of night, when gang members roamed the streets, it could be dangerous. She was making herself an easy target for druggies, criminals, and the motorcycle gang.

He eased the door open so the bells wouldn't jangle and startle whoever remained in the restaurant. Then he held it so it drifted closed smoothly. He stood by the door, but heard only silence. No clang of pots and pans being washed, no rattle of dishes, no sounds of human voices. The kitchen was pitch black. An uneasy roiling began in his stomach. Had something happened to them?

He tiptoed toward the light source in the hallway beyond the kitchen. Murmuring came from behind the heavy oak door. He moved closer, trying to make out the words, to assure himself she was safe.

"What can we do?" That strained voice sounded like Faithe's.

"I'm going to wait here until the accountant calls back. He wants to consult with a lawyer about our rights. I told him we wouldn't sue."

"Of course not," Faithe agreed.

"I know it's rather late to suggest this, but maybe we should cancel the Thanksgiving dinner tomorrow. That would save some money."

"No, *Mamm*, I can't do that."

The anguish in Faithe's voice made Crist wish he could hold and comfort her.

"But it always costs several thousand dollars."

"We've already accepted the deliveries of the food. We can't return it."

"I'm aware of that, but rather than using it all up tomorrow, we could keep the bags of flour and sugar, the frozen foods, and the canned goods for our regular customers. We wouldn't need to buy as many supplies over the next few months."

"What about all the people who show up here tomorrow expecting a meal? We just let them go hungry?"

"Oh, Faithe..."

"Don't cry, *Mamm*, please. I can get a job as a waitress. I'll do whatever we need to do to replace the money he embezzled."

Crist was torn between listening to see if he could help and guilt over eavesdropping on a private conversation.

Between sobs, her mother replied, "The money you'd get…as a waitress…will barely pay…the interest."

"Why don't we pray about it?" Faithe suggested.

Her mother sniffled. "Yes, that's what we should have done when we first got the news." She sounded stronger, surer.

A rustling came from behind the door, and then Faithe prayed, "Dear Lord, we don't know what to do, so we're turning all this over to You. We love this restaurant, and it's been our livelihood, but if it's Your will, we'll give it up." A low cry followed that tore at Crist heart.

She resumed in a tear-choked voice. "Lord, we have all these people coming tomorrow to be fed. I can't believe You'd want us to turn away the hungry, but show us what to do. We're open to Your leading. Help us to show Your love and forgiveness to Mr. Mason." Her words wavered as she added a final sentence. "And please bring *Daed* back to the faith. In Jesus name, Amen."

Crist had no idea who Mr. Mason was, but if he needed forgiveness, he must be the embezzler. Crist's anger bubbled up at the thought of some unknown man destroying Faithe's life. He tamped down the same fury whenever he thought of the stranger who'd ruined his own life.

"*Mamm*, my heart's telling me God wants us to step out in faith. I planned to give out more invitations, and I'm still going to do that. We have enough food to feed anyone who comes tomorrow. We'll just have to trust God for our own needs after that."

Faith's words not only penetrated the door, they penetrated Crist's soul. She had no money, possibly no business or job, yet she thought only of others. And through it all, she kept her belief in God. When he'd been faced with loss, he'd retreated into himself and rebuffed the world, caring only about his own hurt and that of his brother. And unlike her, he'd totally abandoned his faith.

∞ ∞ ∞

Her heart heavy, Faith moved toward the door. "Don't stay too late," she said to *Mamm*. She was relieved to see the deep worry lines in *Mamm*'s face had smoothed out.

"I won't. I'll head home right after the phone call." She spread out the ledgers and bank statements, flipped to a clean sheet on the notepad in front of her, and then met Faithe's eyes. "I feel at peace about the decision."

"I'm so glad. I didn't want to go against your wishes." Faithe started toward the door, but stopped to listen. Had she heard scuffling outside the office? Her pulse racing, she hesitated to move forward and turn the knob.

"Is something wrong?" *Mamm* asked.

Not wanting to alarm *Mamm*, she shook her head, twisted the knob, and opened the door. Nothing outside the door. She glanced both ways as she exited. The kitchen light was off, so she turned it on. The bright light temporarily blinded her eyes, but once they adjusted, she scanned the room to find everything in its proper place. The bells on the front door jingled lightly. Sometimes strong winds made the door rattle and shook the bells. The brightness of the kitchen made it hard to see into the dark restaurant beyond.

She flicked off the overhead light. A shadowy figure stood outside the door, shrouded in a dark coat with a hood pulled tight to shade his face. He grasped the handle of the door. The door she'd left unlocked.

He shook the door, and Faithe froze in place, her heart hammering. What would someone want at this time of night? Maybe he'd confused their hours. Most evenings they stayed open later. With a prayer for courage, she approached the door and pulled it open.

She released her pent-up breath when she realized who it was. "Crist?" She hadn't expected him to come.

He frowned. "You didn't recognize me, and you opened the door?"

Icy wind whistled through the opening. Faithe pulled the glass door open wider. "Come in. You must be freezing out there." A thought niggled in the back of her mind. Had he tried to scare her? He'd frightened her last night and tonight. Could she trust him?

"I came to see if you wanted me to pass out the invitations." From his overly friendly smile and the way he avoided her eyes, Crist appeared guilty.

That added to Faithe's sense of unease. She'd prayed God would direct her decision about this. Was this gut feeling God's answer? She didn't want to go out on the streets to deliver the envelopes if he accompanied her or followed her.

"I'd appreciate it," she said. "Let me get them." Afraid to turn her back on him, she felt on the counter behind her for the stack.

"They're on the other side of the cash register." His eyes revealed his hurt. "If you want to move behind the counter so you're safe, I could pick them up. Unless you don't want me near the cash register."

Faithe hadn't meant to reveal her mistrust. "I'm sorry. I'm still nervous after last night."

"I understand." Yet his words still carried a trace of hurt. "I would never harm you or anyone."

She wanted to believe him and to make amends, so she turned around, picked up the envelopes, and walked over to him, her arms outstretched. She didn't flinch when he took them from her. "If you could give them out along Main Street and around the bus station, I'd be grateful."

"Will do," he said. "I'll also pick up the people on the list tomorrow."

"That's such a help. I can't thank you enough."

"It's nothing." He took a step toward her, but then pivoted and headed toward the door. "Will you be all right getting home? I could—" He shook his head. "Never mind."

Had he been about to offer to see her home? "I'll be fine," she assured him.

"If you go now, the motorcycle gang won't be out yet," he said as he opened the door.

A blast of icy wind knifed through her, making her shiver. She had to warn *Mamm* about the gang.

"You really should put down the blinds and lock the door as soon as you close. Anyone could walk in from off the street. Like me." The door swung shut behind him.

Faithe hurriedly locked the door and closed everything down for the night. After cautioning *Mamm*, she let herself out the back door and entered the outbuilding they'd added in back for their horses. She fed both horses, then hitched hers to the buggy, and took off for *Mammi*'s house.

When she arrived, *Mammi* greeted her at the door. "You're rather late. The little ones were exhausted and barely made it through dinner. Molly bathed them, and we put them to bed. She's in the shower now. I've already fixed her a bed because she looked so exhausted."

Faithe glanced at the battery-powered clock on the wall. "I didn't realize how late it was." Talking to *Mamm* and then Crist had taken more time than she'd thought.

"Did you have dinner?" *Mammi* bustled over to the refrigerator. "I'll heat up the meatloaf and mashed potatoes."

"You don't have to do that."

Mammi ignored her, and a short while later, she set a plate in front of Faithe. "You feed everyone else, but you need to remember to eat."

After being on her feet all day, it felt good to sit down and have someone fix food for her. "Thanks, *Mammi*, this is delicious."

Faithe didn't mention the money troubles. She didn't want to upset *Mammi*. She chatted about other things after dinner, but soon stood. "With the amount of work we need to do tomorrow, we all should be in bed." They'd be at the restaurant around five to start roasting turkeys.

Driving home on the back roads, Faithe tried to relax and enjoy the stars dotting the sky overhead, but worries crept in. She believed God would provide for their needs, and she had a deep assurance He wanted her to feed the hungry. Not only tomorrow, but also every day the way she had been.

The nagging concern bothering her was Crist. She hoped he'd given out her invitations. She wasn't quite sure what to think of him. He scared her, but she wasn't sure if she was afraid he'd harm her or if she was more afraid of her attraction to him.

∞ ∞ ∞

As Crist handed out the Thanksgiving invitations, a man sidled up next to him. "Hey, I seen you with Faithe from the restaurant last night. Remember me? I'm Burt."

Crist tried not to wince at the putrid breath from Burt's decaying teeth. Burt often slept on the sidewalk grate near the restaurant, but hearing him say Faithe's name put Crist on alert.

"Some man's looking for her. He looks like bad news, and he's packing."

A man with a gun was coming after Faithe? That didn't make sense. Some of the men in the park had delusions or DTs, but Burt sounded sober and serious. And extremely worried.

"You sure?" Crist asked.

Burt nodded. "Heard him outside the bank and supermarket. He asked everybody where she lived. I went to the restaurant to warn her, but it's Wednesday, so it closed early."

"Why is he interested in her?"

"He ain't. He jest wants his wife and kids back."

Crist was puzzled. What did this man with a gun and his family have to do with Faithe? "I don't get it."

"Word is, Faithe's letting some woman with two kids stay at her house."

The woman from the restaurant this morning had two children, and Faithe had escorted her into the kitchen. That part of Burt's story rang true. "So her husband's coming after her?"

He nodded. "With a gun."

Faithe would be in danger too, if she came between the woman and her angry husband. The gun and the fact his wife had run away added up to domestic violence. He had to warn Faithe.

"Listen, can you do me a favor and hand these out? I'd better let Faithe know."

"Sure, man. We don't want nothing to happen to her."

"Do you know where she lives?" Crist had no idea.

"Barney looked her up on the internet at the library once. He bet me Amish addresses would be on there. I lost." Burt gave Crist the address.

Cutting through back alleys, Crist jogged to his car. He'd almost turned down the alley behind the pharmacy when he spotted the white van again. He was dying for a look at the license plate, but if a gunman was after Faithe, saving her life was more important.

He reached his car and fretted over the time it took to warm up. If Faithe was as careless about locking her door at home as she was at the restaurant...

Imagining possible scenarios, Crist panicked. He floored the gas pedal, but the car's top speed barely reached the posted speed limit. That had never mattered before, but tonight it could be a matter of life and death.

Chapter Eight

Crist hadn't been out of the city in ages. His nighttime world consisted of bright lights from headlights, streetlights, and flashing neon signs and clashing noises—the constant roar of traffic, honking cars, music blasting, and screaming sirens. After he left the city limits, the world around him soon became dark and still. No streetlights illuminated the back roads, and most farmhouse windows were dark. Farmers went to bed early, and Amish farms had no electricity.

As he got closer to Faithe's, the night grew even blacker. No light shone anywhere, except for one lone light bobbing inside a window, probably someone using a battery-powered light to head to bed. The only sound shattering the silence was his noisy clunker of a car.

Just before he reached Faithe's house, he turned off the engine and drifted in neutral alongside the road by the stubbly cornfields and out of sight of the house. When her house was visible, he braked and put the car in park. He'd stopped just before a bend, so anyone turning into the driveway couldn't see his car, but that meant he had a limited view. Before he left the car, he cranked the driver's window down to dangle a white rag from it. That way, anyone passing the car would assume the car had broken down. With his car being so ancient and rusty, no one passing would think twice about it.

Frigid air blasted him as he stepped from the car. Only the thought of Faithe in danger made him brave the cold. He crept along the property line hidden by the bushes and headed toward the house. All the windows were dark. Either the family hadn't returned yet or they were in bed. No sign of a man with a gun.

Crist breathed a sigh of relief. So far, she was safe.

A heavy coating of white still clung to the tree branches, and frigid winds whipped through the foliage, showering him with snow. Shivering, he pulled his hood strings tighter and crunched through icy snowdrifts that hadn't been trampled to slush the way they had been in the city. Crist hoped Burt hadn't sent him on a wild goose chase.

While Crist picked his way through the snow, horses' hooves clattered on the road, coming from the opposite direction. He ducked so he couldn't be seen in the buggy's battery-powered lights. The carriage turned into the driveway and circled to the barn beside the house. In the faint light from the buggy, Crist could identify Faithe.

She opened the barn door, unhitched her horse, and led it into a stall. With a small battery-powered lantern and a bucket of tools, she went into the stall. From the movement of shadows, she was currycombing her horse. After she finished and watered him, she pulled the buggy into a small room on the side of the barn with room for one more carriage. Her mother must not be home yet. So Faithe was alone.

She closed the barn door and went into the house. Soon a soft light moved around a room near the back door. That must be the kitchen. Crist stepped closer to the house until he was hidden in the front bushes. His teeth chattered as the circle of light moved up the stairs. Faithe was heading for bed. Maybe Burt had been mistaken. Crist should head for home. If Faithe looked out and saw him here, it would add to her suspicions.

Crist had turned to leave when a speeding car roared by. The car passed Faithe's house, but the driver screeched to a stop several yards down the road. In jerky motions, the car backed up until it careened unsteadily into Faithe's driveway. A man jumped out and slammed the door with such force the car rocked.

"Margaret Ann, get out here now!" the man bellowed from the front lawn, shattering the peacefulness of the night.

Crist's stomach twisted when Faithe opened the door and held up her lantern, throwing a tiny pool of light around her and illuminating her face. A small beam highlighted the furious lines of the man's face.

"Can I help you with something?" she asked in a gentle voice.

Although she spoke calmly, her posture revealed her wariness. Crist wanted to jump in front of her to protect her, but he'd been around enough angry men to know it would only provoke more rage. And a bully like this was likely to take it out on Faithe. As long as the man didn't touch her, he'd stay hidden and bide his time. Surprise would give him an advantage.

"Get my wife out here." The man let out a string of curses.

"Your wife? I don't know who you are."

"Don't play games with me." The man stomped up the steps. "I'll drag her out of there if I have to."

Faithe pulled back slightly from the doorway, but she stood strong, almost defiant. "I'm the only one here."

Crist cringed. She'd made a tactical error in letting the man know she was alone. Now he'd know she was at his mercy, and he was free to take advantage of her. Crist could barely restrain himself from rushing over to protect her.

"I know she's in there, and I'll find her if I have to rip the house apart." He bounded onto the porch and reached out to yank open the door.

Faithe forestalled him by opening the door wide. "You're welcome to search the house."

Her action threw him off balance. All set to muscle his way through the door, he almost pitched forward onto his face with the momentum. He grabbed at the doorjamb to steady himself and stared at Faithe uncomprehendingly for a moment. He blinked a few times, shook his head, and regained his blustering attitude. He lunged through the door into the dark kitchen.

He banged into something and swore. "Turn on the lights," he yelled.

"We're Amish. We don't have electricity." Faithe's words were quiet and controlled.

She must be praying. Crist wished he hadn't strayed so far from God that he had no business asking for anything. He crept closer to the house and positioned himself so he could see in the kitchen window.

"You liar. Give me that light."

Before he could snatch it from her, Faithe held it out to him, again throwing him off balance. To cover his miscalculation, he barked, "Hold that thing still so I can get it."

"Certainly." Faithe stood still and extended her arm all the way out.

Smart move, Faithe. Keep him as far away from you as possible. Crist admired her calmness. She seemed to know how to handle the bully.

The man grabbed the light and searched the walls. Crist ducked just before the light shone in his direction.

"Where are the light switches?"

Faithe answered patiently, "The Amish don't have electricity."

"Everybody has electricity unless it's cut off for missing payments." His tone seethed with frustration.

"I'm sorry, but the light you're holding is the only light we have, except for the kerosene lamp."

"Well, turn it on," he demanded.

"It's in the living room, so it won't be much help in here."

The beam from the small light the man was holding moved away from the window above Crist's head. He waited until it focused in a different direction before standing and peering into the window.

The man's back was to Crist, and he focused the light on Faithe's back as she moved through the doorway and lit a lamp on a stand.

The man coughed as the odor of burning kerosene filled the room. "That thing stinks."

"Should I turn it off?" She sounded as if she were entertaining company and seeing to their comfort.

Crist was amazed at her composure. It was as though the angry man hadn't rattled her at all.

"No. I need to see." The man tore through the downstairs, yanking open cupboards and doors.

Crist called 911 to report an armed intruder. Although he hadn't seen a weapon—only a bulge that might possibly be a gun—Crist suspected Burt was correct about that too. He should have called sooner, but with the back door standing open, he'd worried about being overheard. Now, all the banging and swearing going on inside covered Crist's low whisper on the phone.

He wished he could alert Faithe to his presence, so she'd know she wasn't alone and let her know the police were on their way, but he worried the man might see him and panic, taking Faithe as a hostage. He didn't want to alert the man to his presence or scare him into a rage against Faithe.

The man stomped down the basement steps, screaming, "Margaret Ann, get up here." He returned, panting and red-faced, and pounded up the stairs.

Faithe followed him up, and Crist slipped into the house. He peeked behind the open doors and chose the pantry. It had enough room for him to stand when he almost closed the door, and it was central to the kitchen so he could burst out if needed.

Overhead, swearing accompanied the banging and slamming of cupboards and doors. "Where are they?" he screamed.

"I can assure you, they aren't here." There was a firmness to Faithe's tone now, almost as though she was speaking to a petulant child.

She was an amazing woman. Was her lack of fear connected to her deep trust in God? When they'd talked at the restaurant, she'd indicated it was, but anyone could mouth those words about trusting God in all situations. Crist was getting to see the reality of her faith in a crisis.

As long as the banging continued, Crist could be assured the man wasn't hurting Faithe. He hoped the cops would arrive soon. The man was running out of rooms to check. When he didn't find his wife, would he turn his fury on Faithe?

For the first time, Crist wondered about the woman and children. They hadn't come home with Faithe. Had they arrived earlier? It didn't seem so, unless they were well hidden. He couldn't imagine Faithe calmly letting the man go upstairs to search if he'd find them.

Were they coming with her mother? He hadn't noticed them in the restaurant when he'd been eavesdropping.

The man flung open another door upstairs and crashed around the room directly above where Crist stood. Objects went flying and thumped on the floor.

"Please don't destroy my *mamm*'s things," Faithe begged. "You can see there's no one here."

Judging from the bumps and crashes, he ignored her plea. Finally, the noise stopped. "Where is she then?" he screamed.

"Where is who?" Faithe's words sounded teary now.

Crist wanted to charge upstairs to confront the intruder and comfort Faithe. She'd held it together so well until now. The man must have destroyed some things that were precious to her mother.

"Stop playing games. Tell me where Margaret is, or you'll regret it."

Crist almost jumped out of the closet and raced up the stairs, but Faithe's voice floated down to him, and it sounded as if she was descending the stairs.

The man thundered after her. "Is Margaret out in the barn?"

"I don't know anyone named Margaret, except for an *Englisch* neighbor who lives three houses away."

"Don't lie to me," he growled.

Faithe stepped into the kitchen where Crist could see her. The man grabbed Faithe's wrist and spun her around to face him. If he jumped out now, the intruder could grab her and use her as shield.

God, I know I don't deserve to have my prayers answered, but please, please keep Faithe safe. And if it's Your will, give me a chance to save her.

Lights flashed in the driveway, and the man swore. "Did you call the cops?" He kept hold of her wrist and pulled a gun from his pocket. Putting it against her back, he said in a low, threatening voice, "You tell them I'm a friend, here visiting. Get them out of here or you'll regret it."

Crist's heart thumped so loudly he was afraid it would give him away. He didn't want to make a sudden move and risk the man pulling the trigger. The man turned so his back was to Crist as he strong-armed Faithe to the door. Crist couldn't tackle him for fear the gun might go off.

Terror seized him. He'd been in this situation before and... He squeezed his eyes shut to stop the memories swirling up. The past paralyzed him, holding him hostage until he couldn't move or think. He had to save them. *Mamm. Daed. Ethan.* He'd failed before, and he'd fail again. The fear... the helplessness... the agony...

Please, God, he groaned inwardly. *If You give me the courage to save her, I'll forgive him, come back to the church... Please don't let Faithe die.*

With another whispered prayer, Crist, his legs so shaky he could barely stand, stepped from the pantry. "I know where Margaret is."

The man whirled and pointed the gun at Crist's heart. "So you're the scum she's been cheating with."

"No!" Faithe shrieked and tried to jump in front of the gun, jostling the man's arm.

The gun went off, but the shot went wild. A searing pain shot up Crist's arm, and he collapsed to the floor as officers burst through the door. Faithe broke from the man's grip, but instead of racing for the door, she rushed to Crist and knelt at his side.

"Go," he mumbled. "Get away. Don't let him kill you too."

The world around him grew hazy, and Crist could barely comprehend the movement surrounding him. The last thing he saw before everything went black was Faithe's concerned face hovering over him like an angel.

Chapter Nine

The minute the man's attention had been diverted, Faith had broken free from his grasp. She'd tried to get in front of Crist before the man shot him, but she hadn't made it. As the man readied to shoot again, Faithe hunched over Crist protectively, using her back as a shield. That way any bullets would hit her rather than Crist.

She vaguely heard feet pounding up the stairs, the door banging open behind her, and deep voices ordering, "Drop the gun. Hands in the air." Most of her attention was focused on the man lying on the floor. Blood poured from his arm.

"Crist!" she snapped, hoping to keep him from drifting off.

He glanced up at her as if he didn't recognize her. Then his eyes closed, and he faded into unconsciousness.

Faithe had to stop the flow of blood but didn't have time to look for cloth for a tourniquet. She yanked the pins from her apron and wrapped the strings tightly around his arm. Twisting the ends together, she did her best to keep it tight.

An ambulance siren wailed as it sped up the driveway, spitting gravel. Faithe had been so focused on Crist, she hadn't paid attention to the progress of the scuffling behind her. But from the corner of her eye, she could see the police handcuffing Molly's husband. At least that's who she assumed it was.

Two EMTs burst into the kitchen and hurried toward Crist, while Molly's husband kicked and screamed and threatened to sue. Faithe handed the apron ends to the first EMT as the police steered Molly's husband out the door.

"Good job," the EMT said as she knelt beside Crist.

Faithe stayed out of their way as they stabilized him. An officer took Faithe aside to question her about the incident. She tried to explain as best she could, but when the EMTs started pushing Crist to the ambulance, she hurried after them.

The policeman followed along behind. "We'll need a full statement."

"I need to stay with Crist," Faithe said, tears filling her eyes. "Please?"

The officer nodded. "I'll arrange to take your statement later."

"Can I ride along to the hospital?" she asked the EMTs before they shut the ambulance door.

"Next of kin?" one EMT asked.

Faithe shook her head. "I have no idea how to contact his family, but someone should be with him."

"He has no wallet, no ID on him. The only thing in his pocket is this notebook. Looks like dates, times, descriptions of people, and license numbers. Any idea what this is or what his name is?"

"I only know his first name is Crist. I think he lives on the streets near our restaurant. I've seen him writing in that book sometimes, but I don't know what it is." Faithe tried to recall if Crist had said anything else about himself. "Oh, he mentioned having a brother who wasn't quite right. They were both planning to come to our Thanksgiving dinner tomorrow at our restaurant."

"Where's the restaurant?"

For a second, Faithe couldn't remember the address. Worry for Crist blocked everything from her mind. She stumbled as she gave the street name, then the number.

The EMT looked up from the equipment he was monitoring. "You the ones who have that free dinner every year?"

Faithe could only nod. The Thanksgiving dinner seemed so distant, but preparations should begin tomorrow morning. She had prayed for God to give her a sign as to whether or not they should hold the meal. Was this her answer? If she stayed with Crist, she had no idea how long it would take. Maybe they wouldn't be able to have the dinner after all.

But the restaurant reminded Faithe of *Mamm*. She gasped. *Mamm* would worry if Faithe wasn't there when she got home. The house was a disaster, and many of *Mamm*'s precious things were strewn across the floor, broken or damaged.

The woman EMT looked up from monitoring Crist. "Are you all right? You weren't hurt, were you? We should have asked you that earlier."

"I'm fine. I'm just concerned about my mother getting home and finding the house a mess and me gone. She might panic."

"Officers will be at the house for a while, collecting evidence. They can let her know."

"I wish I could prevent her from going home from the restaurant. She could spend the night with *Mammi*—I mean, my grandmother."

The woman pulled a cell phone from her pocket. "This is my personal cell. Give her a call."

Faithe fumbled with the phone, uncertain how to use it, although some of her buddy bunch friends had cell phones. They had an old-fashioned landline in the office. *Mamm* had been reluctant to install that, but *Daed* had insisted.

The EMT helped Faithe punch in the number and hit the phone button.

Hearing *Mamm*'s voice made Faithe's eyes well with tears. So much had happened, she didn't know where to start.

"I'm on my way to the hospital"—at *Mamm*'s sharp indrawn breath, Faithe hastened to redirect her explanation—"not for me. I'm helping that man who comes into the restaurant sometimes."

"What is going on?" *Mamm* demanded.

"I don't have time to explain right now, but whatever you do, don't go home. Please go and stay at *Mammi*'s."

"Faithe Joy, I want to know what's happening."

"Please just trust me. I'll get to *Mammi*'s as soon as I can. I have to go. This isn't my phone."

Mamm was still sputtering when Faithe hung up the phone and handed it back.

An EMT radio crackled to life. Faithe tuned out all the chatter of channels and other words she didn't understand, but she paid close attention to the last part of the message. "Car registered to Crist Petersheim found nine hundred yards from the driveway."

"Patient's name confirmed as Crist. So last name Petersheim?"

Once again Faithe was struck by the fact that he had an Amish name. He didn't wear Amish clothes, and he drove a car, but had he once been Amish? Perhaps that was why he was antagonistic toward any mentions of God.

Crist's eyes fluttered. "Faithe?"

"I'm here, Crist."

"Stay with me," he begged before his eyes closed again. He murmured a slurred word that sounded like *angel*.

The ambulance pulled into the covered emergency entrance at the hospital, and Faithe hung back while the EMTs unloaded Crist. Then she followed them into the emergency waiting room. When she tried accompanying them down the hall, one of the nurses stopped her.

"Sit here, and we'll bring you news after he's been treated.

Faithe sat on one of the plastic chairs, waiting and praying. Her whole world had been turned upside down in one evening. She had a hard time seeing what good would come from the embezzlement, the gunshot wound, and Molly's husband finding her location, so she prayed God would help her accept His will.

As she usually did to calm her nerves, she listed all the blessings she was thankful for:

1) They had food to feed the people who would be coming tomorrow, if they held the Thanksgiving dinner. If not, the food could feed future restaurant patrons.

2) Crist's wound looked bad, but he was alive. If the bullet had hit him in the heart, he might have died.

3) The police had captured Molly's husband. Faithe had no idea how long they'd hold him, but she doubted he'd try to come after Molly tonight if they let him go.

4) She was grateful she hadn't known Molly's full name was Margaret, or she might have felt obliged to tell the truth. As it was, she felt guilty for misleading him when she knew his wife's whereabouts, but Molly's safety had been her primary concern.

5) God had answered their prayers for Molly's protection. If Molly had slept at their house, she might have been hurt or killed. Instead she was safe at *Mammi*'s and getting a restful sleep. She and the children had food and a roof over their heads.

6) Although the news about *Daed*'s restaurant partner embezzling all their funds had been devastating, if talking to Mamm hadn't delayed Faithe, she would have picked up Molly and her children, and they would have all been there when her husband arrived. Faithe didn't even want to imagine what would have happened if he'd found Molly hiding anywhere in the house. Hearing about their dire financial situation last evening benefitted three people, even if it hadn't been good news for her and *Mamm*.

Faithe continued listing all her blessings, not just tonight but over her lifetime. By the time she was done, she'd lost all track of time, and her heart was singing praises to God for His goodness, keeping her spirits up. If God had worked out all those things in her life, surely she could trust Him to work out the present situation.

She glanced up to see Crist walking toward her, his arm in a sling. The sleeves of his coat and shirt had been cut off. Her face heated, and she averted her eyes from the brawny muscles exposed above the cast. She rushed over. "Are you all right?" she asked. "They let you go already?"

"Gunshot wounds are nothing new for this hospital. Mine was only a flesh wound. I've lost the use of my arm until it heals, but it could have been much worse." He smiled at Faithe. "Thanks to you it wasn't."

Faithe imagined the outcome if the bullet had hit its intended mark. "I'm so sorry about your arm, but I'm glad you're alive."

"So am I." His gaze met hers, and sparks shot through her. Faithe broke the eye contact. First his muscles, now his eyes. She couldn't let herself fall for him. That was *verboten*.

∞ ∞ ∞

Crist was still slightly groggy from the pain killers they'd given him, but he hoped they hadn't made him so loopy he'd misread the look in her eyes, the connection between them. He'd experienced that electricity before, but this time she'd looked at him with more interest, with deeper caring. Or was it only his imagination?

When she glanced away, it was as if he were drawn from her by a swift current, drifting down a river alone. Crist shook his head to clear away the fanciful notions, though the sense of loneliness and isolation remained with him. He blamed these fantasies on the fogginess in his brain.

To banish the thoughts, he needed to concentrate on the practical. "I guess we need to find a way home." His car was parked at her house, so they needed to get there. A taxi would be expensive and cut into his savings, but he had to make sure she was safe.

"It's a little late to call a driver, although Irene always tells us to call anytime."

Crist reached his left arm across his body to get his cell phone from his right pocket. He'd have to set things up differently until his right arm healed. "Why don't you call her to see? If she can't come, I'll call a taxi."

Faithe awkwardly pushed the buttons and soon arranged for a ride. "I asked Irene to pick up *Mamm* at *Mammi*'s house. Irene lives close to *Mammi*, so it won't be a problem. They'll be here in about twenty minutes. She'll bring one of Josiah's coats for you. You can't go outside like that." Faithe gestured toward his bare arm and blushed.

Crist hid a smile. Maybe she wasn't as unaffected by him as she acted.

He reined in his thoughts. He had no right to be thinking about her like that. Yet he couldn't help enjoying fleeting memories of her leaning over him in the house before he plunged into the nightmares of the past. He'd also glimpsed her during his trip to the hospital. "You came in the ambulance with me, didn't you?"

"Yes, and you were unconscious." She gestured toward two chairs in a back corner, away from some of the noise and confusion. Once they were settled, she asked, "Do they need to monitor you?"

"No, they said I could go." He wasn't sure how much he wanted to share, but if he told the truth, she might not worry as much. It wasn't easy, though. He took a deep breath before admitting, "I didn't pass out only because of the wound."

Her eyes invited him to continue, but the story was so painful, so raw, it was hard to put into words. "I-I had a flashback." He forced himself to go on. "When I was twenty, my family went to the mall." He swallowed down the huge lump in his throat. "*Mamm*, *Daed*, Ethan, and me. Ethan was twelve."

As if sensing his distress, she laid her hand over his. Her touch both burned and comforted. He directed as much of a smile toward her as he could—a lukewarm, corners-of-lips-barely turned up—to thank her, but the weight of the past hung too heavily over him to manage more than that.

"A teen"—he squeezed his eyes shut, trying to block out the images rushing past—"with an assault rifle started shooting randomly, spraying bullets into the crowd." The darkness behind his eyes mirrored the darkness of the past. "He started near *Mamm*. My parents were Amish, so they believed in nonviolence. People screamed at *Daed* to tackle the kid. Instead, he stepped in front of *Mamm* to protect her."

The slight headache he'd had earlier increased until tight bands encircled his forehead, squeezing tighter and tighter until he could barely draw in a breath. Pain radiated from his temples and down through his clenched jaw. Describing the events made them come to life again.

"A bullet pierced his heart, and he crumpled forward, leaving *Mamm* exposed. She went down next before I could reach her. I tried to knock Ethan out of the way, and we both fell."

Crist's throat tightened, and he could barely choke out the words. "On the way down, while I had my arms wrapped around him, a bullet entered his skull."

The sound filled Crist's ears. Ethan's body jerked and was almost torn from his hands. His brother's body spasmed. Several more sharp blasts split the air around him, and Crist lay on the ground, shielding Ethan's body, as shrieks, wails, and groans echoed around them. He prayed like he had never prayed before. For his brother. His parents. The people bleeding around him. And most of all that the shooting would stop.

A group of men took down the shooter from behind. Other sounds faded into the background. All Crist focused on was the silence of the gun. No more bullets.

He so badly wanted to crawl to his parents to see if they were still alive, but he had to guard his brother. Not until hands lifted him to his feet did he let go.

"Crist?" Faithe's soft voice broke the spell of the past. "I'm so sorry," she said. "I can't even imagine how awful it must have been."

Nobody could ever know that darkness, that agony, unless they'd been through it. Crist's heart had been ripped from his body.

"The whole way to the hospital in the ambulance, I prayed, begging God to spare my parents and heal my brother. To keep all three of them alive. To save the others who'd been shot."

Crist's stomach twisted as he relived that ride. They'd made him sit up front because they were struggling to keep Ethan alive. Being separated from his brother, not knowing what was happening to him or to his parents had been unbearable.

"They didn't have enough ambulances for the victims. I didn't find that out until later from the newspaper. *Mamm* and *Daed* were some of the last seriously wounded to go." Would things have gone differently if they'd been taken immediately? "The police called for other emergency responders from even more distant counties to transport those with less traumatic wounds."

"Were your parents...?" Faithe's voice trailed off as he shook his head.

"*Daed* died on the way to the hospital. *Mamm* made it through the night, but she never woke." He'd held her hand while Ethan was in surgery, but she'd lain still and unresponsive.

Faithe sucked in a breath. "Oh, Crist."

"I lost my whole family that day. The bullet had lodged in Ethan's brain. They operated, but he was paralyzed, and with his brain injuries, they warned me that when he woke, he might be a vegetable the rest of his life."

Tears ran down Faithe's cheeks, and she squeezed his hand. He turned his hand over so he could entwine his fingers with hers, grateful for her touch.

"Ethan recovered a little more than they expected, but except for some hand, head, and slight shoulder movements, he's completely paralyzed. He's alert now, but he has memory issues and can barely speak. The worst of it is..." Crist pinched his lips together to hold back the agony and guilt.

Faithe set her other hand on his wrist, just above their entwined fingers. The light pressure penetrated his coat sleeve, comforting him. Warmth and caring flowed from her, encouraging him to continue.

"I keep reliving that day and wondering, if I hadn't tried to save him, would the bullet have whistled past him? Is it my fault? Every time I look at him, I ask if I'm to blame."

The teardrops sparkling in Faithe's eyes made Crist want to hug her, hold her close. Knowing she cared enough to shed tears for him touched him deeply.

When she spoke, her voice was barely above a whisper. "I'm sure it wasn't your fault, and I'm sorry you had to go through all this, but God must have a reason."

She'd just said the words he never wanted to hear. If he hadn't been drawing so much comfort from her touch, he might have withdrawn his hand and turned away. The bishop had conveyed the same exact message, one he'd found too hard to believe. Faithe might lose all respect for him if he told her the truth, but he felt compelled to be honest.

"I left the faith the day of my parents' funeral. Any God who would allow twenty innocent people, including my good, upright parents, to be killed and turn a twelve-year-old boy into a vegetable..."

Faithe sat silent a moment. Then, with compassion in her eyes, she said, "I can understand how you might feel that way after all you went through, but when you turned your back on God, you turned your back on His comfort too. I don't know how you made it through that tragedy without Him."

"I haven't gotten through it. It still haunts me." The bishop had urged him to do something else that day, something he'd never been able to do. "I also turned my back on the faith because I couldn't do what the church encouraged me to do—forgive the killer."

Crist had harbored that bitterness in his heart. He wanted revenge. He wanted to see that teen pay a price. He'd read the news, attended the trial, even sat in the witness box to condemn the boy.

"I don't know if I can ever forgive him. At the trial they said he'd been high on drugs that day. I've made it my mission to combat drugs in our area and our state. I don't want anything like this to happen to anyone else ever again."

Her eyes wide, Faithe studied him. "Are you with the police?"

Crist shook his head. "No, only an ordinary citizen who wants to do his part to stop the flow of drugs."

"Isn't that dangerous?"

"It could be. I'm not playing the hero or anything, though, just noting some information I hope will help."

Faithe ducked her head and said shyly, "Isn't that something good that's come out of your tragedy? God doesn't promise to make everything turn out the way we want. He sees the big picture."

"Are you saying that my family had to sacrifice their lives to save drug addicts?"

Faithe smoothed the fabric of his coat sleeve. "I didn't mean it that way. I just thought it was beautiful that you've done something to help others despite your pain."

He hadn't meant to be so sarcastic when she was only trying to be kind. "I'm sorry for jumping on you, but this whole situation has been so agonizing. You touched a tender spot."

"I've sometimes found tender spots are places I need to turn over to God for healing."

Crist blinked a few times to clear the moisture from his eyes. Her words kept hitting exposed nerves he didn't want to examine, and he certainly didn't want to hand any of them over to God.

Chapter Ten

"Oh, there you are." An *Englischer* with short, dark hair streaked with gray approached Faithe. "I've been looking all over for you."

After stealing a quick look at Crist to be sure he'd composed himself, Faithe rose. "Thanks for coming so late at night, Irene. I'm sorry we weren't waiting near the door for you. I lost track of time." She'd been so caught up in Crist's story, she hadn't even thought to glance at the clock.

Irene held out a dark coat. "I assume this is for you."

"Thank you," Crist said, his voice husky, and his words hesitant.

After hearing his story and that he'd left the Amish, Faithe wondered if wearing an Amish coat would make him uncomfortable. She wished she'd known his story before asking Irene to bring her *onkel*'s coat. Irene would have lent him one of her husband's.

Crist reached out awkwardly with his left arm, a reluctant expression on his face.

"Let me help you with that." Faithe took the coat from Irene and held it out for Crist to put his left arm in the sleeve, then she gently draped it over his right shoulder and brought it around to meet in the front. As she buttoned the coat, she faced away from Irene and whispered, "I'm sorry. I didn't know how you felt when I asked Irene to bring this coat."

"It's all right." His expression contradicted his words, but he added, "I appreciate your thoughtfulness."

Faithe shrugged into her coat and tied on her black bonnet. Her heart went out to Crist. After all he'd been through, she could understand why he felt angry at God, but she prayed he'd find his way back to forgiveness and faith.

When they reached the car, Faithe insisted on sitting in the back with *Mamm* so Crist had more room. She also hoped to speak to *Mamm* without the others overhearing. Often the engine noise made it difficult for people in the front seats to hear.

While Irene engaged Crist in conversation, Faithe whispered a condensed version of the evening's events, with the exception of what Crist had confided. He hadn't intended his confessions to be heard by anyone else. Repeating things he'd told her in private felt like gossip. Amid *Mamm*'s gasps, Faithe also explained the house was a mess. She wished there were a way to soften *Mamm*'s losses.

When Irene pulled into the driveway, Crist insisted on paying, but Irene assured him the bill had already been settled. Faithe shot *Mamm* a grateful glance for her thoughtfulness. Her mother must be aware of Crist's homeless status and had planned ahead to avoid discomfort.

"I assume my car's still around the bend, so I'll go get it. Thank you so much for the ride." He reached for the door handle. "I'd be happy to help clean up first."

"You can go and get your car, young man," *Mamm* said, "but you'll pull it in our driveway. The only place you're going tonight is to bed upstairs." Crist opened his mouth, but *Mamm* cut him off before he could say a word. "No arguments."

"Yes, ma'am."

Faithe wasn't sure if he'd said *ma'am* or *Mamm*, but either way, her mother beamed.

"I appreciate *youngie* who obey their elders," she said.

Crist was far from the age of the *youngie*, so Faithe hoped he'd appreciate *Mamm*'s teasing. He laughed, although it had a hollow sound, making Faithe wonder if it brought back memories of obeying his parents when he was younger. How hard that must be.

They thanked Irene, and Faithe and Crist pushed open their car doors. The wind almost snatched it from Faithe's hand. Crist, who'd already gotten out of the front seat, reached out and steadied her door with his good hand.

While Faithe and *Mamm* went inside, Crist walked off to get his car. A while later, he pulled it into the driveway and came to the door, his cheeks ruddy from the cold. *Mamm* let him in, and he stared at the downstairs.

"You've straightened everything already."

Faithe had scrubbed the blood stains, while *Mamm* tidied and returned things to the cupboards. She didn't want Crist to be reminded of what had happened. His gaze immediately went to the spot, though, and his face grew grim.

He looked away quickly and faced *Mamm*. "What can I do to help?" His left hand clawed at the button on the front of the coat.

Mamm hurried over and batted his hand away. "I'll do that." She unbuttoned the coat and helped him slip it off.

Faithe shouldn't be jealous of her own mother, but she wished she were the one undoing his coat. She'd enjoyed buttoning it over his broad chest. While Crist had his back to her and *Mamm* hung the coat on a hook, Faithe sneaked a look at the back of his arm exposed by the ripped-off sleeve. His muscles appeared hard and strong, as if he did farm work or manual labor. That couldn't be true because he was homeless and he'd mentioned finding information about drugs. His physique didn't seem like someone who sat around.

Mamm turned and caught her staring. Faithe's face heated, and she pretended to be worried about Crist's arm. She was, but it was partially a deception to cover her interest.

"We have a shirt Crist could put on, don't we? I expect he's probably chilly," Faithe said hastily. She was the youngest, so all her brothers had already left home, but there might be a shirt of *Daed*'s.

Mamm gave her a knowing look that made Faithe cringe. "Check the room at the top of the stairs. There should be a shirt or two in that closet." She explained to Crist, "That room belonged to my sons."

Crist winced at the word *sons*, and Faithe wished she could comfort him. She'd also need to tell *Mamm* Crist was an orphan, so she'd be careful not to hurt him inadvertently.

"I'll be right up to help you button it." *Mamm*'s no-nonsense voice forestalled any idea of Faithe going near Crist.

Faithe had intended to clean *Mamm*'s room but worried her *mamm* would misinterpret her eagerness to go upstairs, so she waited and followed *Mamm* up. *Mamm* stopped so suddenly at the top of the steep staircase, Faithe almost took a tumble. If she hadn't been holding the broom, she might have. Sucking in a breath, *Mamm* headed toward her bedroom rather than to help Crist. Faithe trailed after her, wishing she could ease some of *Mamm*'s heartache.

Mamm bent and picked up a piece of china, then sank onto her bed. "My *mamm* gave me this on my wedding day. It was passed down to every generation since we came over to America from Switzerland."

"Oh, *Mamm*."

Crist hurried into the room.

"Is everything all right?" His eyes widened at the mess on the floor.

"I wanted to give you this on your wedding day," *Mamm* said to Faithe, running a finger over the smooth glaze.

Crist bent and picked up several matching pieces. "If you can find all of these, I know someone who can glue it together. It won't be perfect, but he can make it look almost like new."

While Faithe and Crist picked up the pieces, *Mamm* laid a kerchief on the bed. They set the broken bits on it, and when they'd gathered all of them, *Mamm* tied the corners together and held it out to Crist.

"Thank you," she said, as Faithe swept the rest of the mess into a dust pan. "You haven't changed your shirt."

"It's time for bed," Crist pointed out. "I don't want to wrinkle a shirt."

Faithe wondered if he wanted to avoid dressing in Amish clothes. He was right about bedtime, though. It was way past time for them to be asleep, and they needed to be up even earlier than usual tomorrow.

∞ ∞ ∞

Crist lay awake, his mind whirling. It had been so long since he'd slept in an actual bed, he had trouble falling asleep. The softness closed around him, cushioning him, but his arm ached despite the painkiller he'd taken.

To distract himself, he pulled out his phone to check that his email had been received. After he'd been bandaged at the hospital, while he waited for his prescription and paperwork, he typed a firsthand account of the incident with Molly's husband, using one finger of his left hand, and sent it off, typos and all. He'd gotten a confirmation. He quickly powered the phone off because the battery was low. He couldn't chare it in an Amish home.

Being in this Amish home reminded him of the desperate promise he'd made when he'd prayed for Faithe's safety. His stomach churned. Had he really agreed to go back to the church? Did bargains made under duress count?

The painkiller kicked in, and Crist drifted off, still undecided about his vow. He woke with a start to clattering downstairs. Dawn hadn't even arrived, but Faithe and her *mamm* were already leaving for the restaurant. They'd told him to come whenever he wanted, and he'd promised to pick up the people on his list. If he was driving, he'd skip the painkillers, even though his arm was throbbing.

Crist managed to sleep for two more hours before he needed to visit Ethan. He washed up as best he could and tossed the coat over his shoulder. He managed to get his left arm in the sleeve, but couldn't button it. He held the coat closed with one hand as he went to the car. It took a while for the heater to kick on, and he shivered most of the way to the city.

When he entered, Sophie gasped. "What happened to you?"

"Just a little accident."

It proved almost impossible to feed his brother left-handed without slopping food down the front of Ethan's bib. When he was done, he struggled with dressing Ethan with only one hand. Joe came in, carrying a small pile of clothes over his arm.

"Sophie insisted I help you clean up and dress. She doesn't want you going to this special dinner looking like that." Joe pointed to the clothes Crist had slept in. "She thinks these clothes will fit."

Despite Crist's protests, Joe helped him shower without getting his bandages wet, assisted in dressing him, and then adjusted the arm and sling into place. "I do this every day for the boys here," Joe said. "It's no different."

Crist appreciated Joe's help, but it bothered him to take the houseparent's time when others needed him more. Joe only waved him off, saying it was the least he could do, with all Crist did for Ethan.

Ethan watched the whole procedure and even giggled twice. After Joe left, Crist sat down with Ethan, unsure how much his brother would understand.

"Do you remember we're invited for Thanksgiving dinner today?" After Ethan's head tip indicated he did, Crist continued, "I have a question for you."

He asked his brother the question, and Ethan responded, "Help."

He had Ethan's permission, but did his brother comprehend the consequences? Crist explained it would mean putting off their plans even longer, but he wanted to help Faithe.

Ethan again responded with "Help."

Crist set a hand on his brother's shoulder and squeezed it lightly. "You have a good heart, Ethan. Thank you for being willing to wait. Now I'm going to pick up some people and take them to the dinner, then I'll pick you up."

When Crist dropped off the first passengers, he followed them in. Faithe smiled at him, and he held out an envelope. "I'm supposed to give this to you."

"What is it?"

Crist shrugged, but waited while she opened the envelope. She slid out a rectangular piece of paper. Her eyes widened, then she pressed a hand to her mouth, while a tear trickled down her cheek. She turned the paper so Crist could see a check made out to the restaurant for five thousand dollars.

"God is so good," she said. "I need to go show *Mamm*."

Crist nodded. "You needed the money?"

"We certainly did." Keeping her voice low, she explained that her *Daed* had left the Amish four years ago and turned over his half of the restaurant to a friend and business partner.

That must be the Mr. Mason they'd been discussing last night. Crist wanted to find him and make him return the money he'd stolen.

Faithe explained that part of the story. "*Daed*'s partner emptied the bank account, so we had nothing to pay the bills that are due."

"That's so wrong."

"Well, God is taking care of us. Tomorrow I'll open a new account with this money so he can't touch it. This will cover the most pressing bills." Her heart overflowing with gratitude, she glanced up from the check. "Thank you so much for bringing it. Who is this Alexander Parker?"

Crist couldn't meet her eyes. Instead he mumbled something about not paying attention to the man. "I need to pick up the next group." He hurried off before she could ask more questions.

After he dropped the second load of passengers at the restaurant door, he drove to the group home to find Ethan staring out the window. His brother brightened as soon as Crist pulled into the curb. Sophie must have been waiting for him, too, because the second he buzzed, the door opened.

She greeted him with flushed cheeks and damp tendrils curling around her sweaty forehead. She wore a pretty dress rather than her usual sweatsuit or jeans.

"You look nice," Crist told her.

"So do you," she responded. "I'm glad Joe got you fixed up. Ethan's so excited. I hope you both have a good time today."

"Thanks. You too." Crist pushed Ethan down the front ramp and to the car. His brother insisted on wearing his black dress hat, even though it was several sizes too small.

Joe helped Crist by lifting Ethan into the car and collapsing and stowing the folding wheelchair. Crist thanked him and took off for the restaurant, Ethan bobbing his head and shoulders. It had been a long time since he'd taken Ethan out.

As soon as they arrived, Faithe squatted in front of the wheelchair and laid a hand on Ethan's.

He wriggled his fingers. A sign he was delighted.

Faithe looked up into Ethan's eyes. "Can you feel this?"

To Crist's surprise, his brother said *no* without hesitation.

"This?" She touched her fingertips to Ethan's. At his slight head bob, she slipped the fingers of her right hand under his. It looked as if she pressed her fingers against Ethan's. "Does this work for shaking hands?" she asked.

His brother's beaming face was answer enough. Crist's heart swelled. Most people, other than those from the group home, glanced at Ethan and then quickly looked away. A few nodded briefly, but he'd never seen anyone actively try to communicate with Ethan. She hadn't acted surprised at Ethan's Amish clothes either.

Before she stood, she motioned to the woman standing nearby. "This is Ada. She'll be marrying my *onkel* soon."

As Ada knelt and took her place, Faithe stood and said to Crist, "Ada teaches at the special school."

Ada repeated the same handshake Faithe had used. "Nice to meet you, Ethan." She gestured toward the table. "We have lots of food. Are you hungry?"

Ethan's head bob and shoulder shake were more pronounced than usual.

Instead of looking to Crist for permission as most people did, Ada asked Ethan, "Would you like me to push you, or would you prefer to do it yourself?"

After asserting his independence by saying, "Self," Ethan headed off with Ada, who introduced him to several people, leaving Crist alone with Faithe.

"He'll be fine," she said as if sensing his worries about his brother. "Ada will make sure he's a part of things."

Crist's eyes grew misty as a group of children surrounded Ada, some using sign language, and took turns shaking Ethan's hand. "He's never done anything on his own like this since..." He choked and couldn't continue speaking.

Faithe laid a hand on his arm. She may have meant to comfort him, but her touch sent electricity shooting through him.

∞ ∞ ∞

Faithe had made a mistake touching Crist. Her heart beat so loudly, she worried he could hear. She needed to get away.

The Thanksgiving Day newspaper bundles thumped against the restaurant door.

"They're late today," she said, uncertain of how to escape.

"Maybe the delivery person slept in," Crist said. "I'll get them." He retrieved the papers, but stopped to read an article in one of them. Then he headed straight toward her.

So much for getting away. The other part of her rejoiced.

"Here's a story about last night."

Faithe took the paper from him and read it. "They've arrested Molly's husband and will be taking him back to New Hampshire, where he's committed some crimes. He's locked up. At least for now. Wait until I tell Molly."

After she read the paper, a teary-eyed Molly hugged Faithe. "This is the first Thanksgiving in twelve years my heart is overflowing with gratitude. It's the only time I've been able to relax and enjoy a meal."

Faithe hugged her back. "I'm so glad."

"Even better," Molly added, "last night, before you told me Bill had been arrested, I prayed and asked God's forgiveness for straying so far from my faith. I feel so fresh and clean inside, ready for a new start."

Faithe thanked God for a day full of miracles. But she prayed for one more. That Crist would find his way back to God, too.

Chapter Eleven

Being around Faithe and the other Amish visitors brought back memories of the past.

Years ago he'd bent his knee and joined the church, dedicating his life to God. After Ethan's accident and his parents' deaths, bitterness had crept in. During his brother's recovery, he'd sold all that he had to pay for Ethan's care because they'd had no insurance. The church had offered to help, but once he'd left the faith, he refused their contributions.

Seeing Ethan enjoying the company of others, Crist wondered if his brother would like to go back to church. His brother seemed to have kept his simple faith. If only Crist could have that easy acceptance, that belief in God. He toyed with the idea of attending church this Sunday. Could he return? He'd made a promise, and he should keep it.

He sat across from Faithe at dinner. Her joyful, thankful heart made him long for a belief like hers and her simple acceptance of God's will in all circumstances. When she'd talked of her *daed*, it was without judgment. Last night when she'd heard the news of the embezzlement, she'd prayed and taken it in stride. No one here today would have known what this meal was costing her. He was grateful he'd been able to bring her that envelope, but he suspected she'd have been equally as joyful without it. She'd also been calm when she'd faced Molly's husband.

Her life had shown him he needed to get right with God. Tomorrow after he met with the police to give his statement, he'd talk to the bishop. As everyone circulated through the dessert lines, he sidled up to the bishop.

His throat dry and his stomach roiling, he asked if they could meet, and they set a time. As soon as the bishop walked away, Crist regretted it. He wanted to follow him and break the appointment. He wasn't ready to face this. He wasn't ready to face God.

On the way to the group home later that evening, he asked Ethan, "Would you like to go to church on Sunday?"

His brother bounced his shoulders and bobbed his head with enthusiasm. He said only one word, "God," but he said it with equal parts reverence and delight. Even his brother had a greater amount of faith.

Ethan had experienced the deaths of their parents and faced his own traumas without complaint. Only Crist harbored anger and resentment, and he didn't want to let it go.

After he'd taken everyone home, he returned to the restaurant to help with the dishes. Faith's *mamm* insisted he stay with them until his shoulder healed. Molly and her family were staying with Faith's *mammi*. No wonder Faithe was such a giving person. She'd seen it in action in her own family.

The word *family* ripped him apart inside. Other than Ethan, he had no family and never would. Could he ever reach the point where he accepted that as God's will?

That question kept him awake most of the night. He woke exhausted in the morning, did his best for Ethan with Joe's assistance, and acquiesced when Joe insisted on helping him shower and dress again. He disliked being helpless and dependent on others, but perhaps God was showing him he needed to be humble.

He drove Faithe to the police station that morning, so they could both give their statements, and drove her back to the restaurant. On the way, she faced him and said shyly, "You don't have to answer, but I wondered why you choose to live on the streets."

Crist hesitated. He'd told her some of the darker truths about his past, but was he ready to confess one of his major secrets? Faithe hadn't judged him, even when he told her he'd walked away from the Amish. He decided to be honest, hoping she'd understand.

He took a deep breath before saying, "I've been saving money to buy a home and make it handicap accessible for Ethan. He wants to live with me, and I want to do it as soon as possible. I figured if I slept in the car, I could save the rent money to make our dream come true sooner."

"You're doing it for your brother? I don't know many people who would sacrifice their comfort that way for someone else."

Crist brushed it off. It was no hardship for him. True, it wasn't easy being on the streets, but all he had to do was remind himself of his brother. It also made it easy to skip meals. Every penny added up. They'd had a setback, but that was something he and Ethan felt strongly about, so he'd have to work hard to replace it.

He didn't mention his afternoon plans to Faithe. After meeting with the bishop, Crist went back to Faithe's house while she and her *mamm* were at work and spent several hours wrestling with fury and resentment until he finally got down on his knees to ask for forgiveness. He rose feeling lighter, as if a heavy weight had been lifted. Then he sat at the kitchen table and wrote a letter to the shooter, letting him know he'd forgiven him. His eyes blurred as he wrote the words, and pictures of his parents intruded. Each time he went back to prayer until every word he wrote was true and heartfelt.

He looked up the address on the prison website and mailed the letter on the way to dinner with Ethan. As he crossed off the date before he and Joe put Ethan to bed, Crist pointed to the next day. "Tomorrow we'll go to church."

Joe's raised his eyebrows. "Church?"

"Yes. Oh, and I'll be picking up Ethan in a carriage." He'd talked to Faithe's mother, and she'd offered to lend him hers. She'd also told him to wear any of the clothes in the bedroom closet.

Joe appeared puzzled. "Baby carriage?"

"No, that's what the Amish call a buggy." After tomorrow, it would be his only mode of transportation. He'd talked to Burt, who'd found him a buyer for the car. He didn't know what the future would hold career-wise, but the bishop had agreed he could keep his cell phone temporarily to finish up his job. As usual, he'd left his phone charging in Joe and Sophie's front hall and picked it up on the way out of the group home.

When Crist arrived the next morning, Sophie and Joe stared out the window. "Wow, a real Amish buggy," Sophie said.

"Carriage," Joe corrected, and Crist smiled.

Joe helped Ethan into the buggy and stowed the wheelchair in the back. "Have fun," he said, as Crist flicked the reins to start the horse.

Crist had no plans for fun today, only serious business. Later, as he knelt before the church, he was so nervous, his voice shook, but he made his confession before God and the church.

∞ ∞ ∞

Faithe couldn't believe her eyes when Crist knelt in front of the congregation. She brushed away tears as he spoke. God had answered her prayers. *Thank you, Lord.*

He looked so handsome in Amish clothing. She struggled to keep her mind on the sermons because he was directly across from her. After the service, she stayed busy helping to serve the meal, but she sneaked peeks at Crist whenever she passed. She could hardly wait until it was time to go home, so she could talk to him.

Crist took Ethan home after the church service and stayed with him for dinner, so Faithe fixed supper, did the dishes, and then paced the living room and kitchen until he returned.

He looked exhausted, and the tight lines around his mouth indicated he was in pain, but his eyes lit up when he saw her, lifting Faithe's spirits.

Now she could respond to his smiles and his looks without guilt. But when she asked him to tell her about his change of heart, he pleaded exhaustion.

"I'm not used to riding in a buggy, and all the jostling has set my arm throbbing. I'd like to tell you all about it, but could we do it tomorrow evening?"

Faithe tried not to let her disappointment show. "That would be fine."

"I'm meeting Burt around seven to sell my car, but I could come to the restaurant after that to help you with cleanup. If you'd like, we could ride back to the house together. That would give us plenty of time to talk."

He wanted to spend time alone together? Did he mean what she thought he did? Usually when a man asked you to ride in his buggy, it meant he wanted to court you. Surely Crist knew that, didn't he?

Faithe hugged that secret to herself as she went to bed, and she woke early the next morning filled with hope.

The whole day, she almost burst with excitement. She'd never felt this way about anyone before. The joy inside bubbled out. Most of the customers remarked on her glowing face, and she practically danced from table to table, her skirt and apron swishing to her happy steps. *Mamm* encouraged her to be more serious, even a little somber, but all the excitement burst from her in rapid talk and smiles so wide her cheeks ached.

The day passed too slowly to suit her, but finally—finally!—seven came and went. Then eight. As the clock hands edged toward nine, the phone rang in the office. She rushed to it, but didn't make it in time.

Crist's deep voice filled the air as she raced across the kitchen. "I can't come. I'll explain later."

By the time she picked up the phone, only the dial tone greeted her. She sank into the desk chair and replayed the message, but it came across as even more cold and clipped than it had the first time. She sat with her head in her hands.

Had she scared him off by being overly eager? Had he gotten cold feet? Had she misread his intentions?

Whatever the answers to her questions, he'd rejected her.

∞ ∞ ∞

Burt had come through with a buyer, and Crist met them near the park. Before meeting Burt, Crist had packed all his belongings from the car into his duffle bag. He debated about offering Burt his *Englisch* clothes, but he might need them, so he stuffed them inside.

It was obvious the family had little money, so Crist took what they offered. He counted out the money and returned a twenty-dollar bill to the father. "You overpaid," he said because he wanted to leave them with some gas money. He'd filled the tank earlier, but the car guzzled gas pretty quickly.

As soon as the transaction had been completed, Crist thanked Burt and cut through the alleys, taking a shortcut to the restaurant. He'd told Faithe he'd be there at seven, but it was a bit after that. He screeched to a halt just before he dashed into the alley behind the pharmacy, and he slid back into the shadows.

The same van idled at the delivery entrance, and several men loaded boxes into the back. This time he was approaching from the opposite direction, so he could read the license plate. He noted that, then pulled out his phone and called 911. Then he videoed the activity.

One of the guards from the other night paced in Crist's direction. Had the man seen him? His heart pounding, Crist flattened himself against the brick wall of the building beside him.

Sirens screeched in the distance, coming closer.

"Let's get out of here," one man said. He slammed the back doors of the van and squeezed into the driver's seat.

The guard walking toward Crist turned around and hurried back. The other guard had already climbed into the van. A man holding an armload of boxes scurried into the back entrance and shut the door.

The sirens grew louder, but they wouldn't make it in time to catch these men. Crist heaved a chunk of broken asphalt so it crashed against the back of the truck. The guard rushed in that direction.

He examined the door and the area around the van. "Nothing here."

As soon as his back was turned, Crist lobbed another missile, startling the man. This time the guard didn't look at the door; he started toward Crist.

"Get in here," the driver called, "or we'll leave you behind."

The sirens seemed to be a few blocks away, but the van would be gone by the time they arrived. The driver lurched into reverse, executed a three-point turn, and stepped on the gas. Crist took a chance and staggered into the alley in front of them.

The driver braked so hard, the van rocked back and forth. The driver lowered his window and shouted, "Get out of the way." He added a string of curse words that Crist blocked out.

Instead of staggering across the street, Crist wove from side to side in the middle of the street. The van rocketed backwards into the parking lot, and the driver pulled hard to turn the vehicle in the opposite direction just as a cop car blocked that end of the alley. Another police car pulled into the alley from the other direction. Two more blockaded the cross streets at the opposite ends. Officers emerged from the vehicles, guns drawn.

The first officer grabbed Crist's arm, then he did a double-take. "You're Amish?"

"I joined yesterday." Crist held out his phone as the other officers headed for the van. "I have a video on here. Proof they were loading boxes onto the van."

"Great. Send it to us. Now get out of the way."

Crist stepped into the shadows and filmed the action.

"We're just here to do a delivery," the driver shouted.

"A witness says the opposite."

"Who's the witness? I know my rights, man."

Another officer went to the pharmacy service entrance and knocked. "No answer, and everything's dark."

One of the guards shrugged. "We got here a little early. So what? That's not a crime."

Crist kept filming, stopping from time to time to snap stills as the men were led away. He also snapped the interior of the cargo van when the police opened the back door.

After the police impounded the vehicle and the squad cars drove off with the guards and the driver, Crist clicked off his video. The time flashed on his screen: 9:03.

Faithe! He'd forgotten all about her. He looked up the restaurant number.

An officer approached. "Can you come downtown to give a statement?"

Crist nodded. "I don't have a car, though."

"Go get in mine." The officer pointed.

Crist dialed the restaurant number and left a brief message for Faithe. He'd have to explain once this was all over.

The rest of the night was a blur. Making statements at the police station, showing the video, typing up a story of his own and emailing it, reporters swarming the station for pictures and scoops.

He tried to stop them from taking pictures because he'd returned to the faith. He covered his face, but their insistence increased once they discovered there was a reward connected with the drug bust. A huge reward offered by a wealthy businessman whose son had overdosed on opioids.

The police asked him to stay while they took care of the reward paperwork, then the news stations wanted to interview him. TV cameras showed up, and Crist kept repeating he didn't want to be photographed.

"You're going undercover as Amish?" reporters kept asking.

Crist tried to explain, but soon gave up as the rumors spread. The only good thing was, once they thought he was going undercover, they only audiotaped his answers and kept the cameras focused on the officers who'd made the drug bust. When they did the stories about the reward, they interspersed his interview with cuts from the businessman's reaction to the drug bust. They also added information about his gunshot wound.

"Injured in the line of duty," one of them said, "taking down a criminal and wife abuser last week. Then stopping a drug bust this week, getting a reward of three hundred thousand dollars. You're going to be famous."

Crist tried to explain the truth, but none of them would listen. Once the media frenzy ended and the reporters left to file their stories, Crist turned his notebook over to the officer who'd been interviewing him. Together they went over the notes, and Crist fleshed out what he'd jotted in the book.

The sun was rising by the time he left the station. His arm ached like a toothache, and he needed sleep. One of the officers offered to drive him out to Faithe's house. Crist wanted to talk to her, but she'd be busy at the restaurant by now, and he needed a clear head for the conversation he wanted to have with her. He'd borrow her *Mamm*'s buggy to have breakfast with Ethan, then get cleaned up before he told her the truth about himself.

Chapter Twelve

Yesterday Faithe had barely been able to contain her joy, but Crist had never returned last night. Had he gone back to sleeping on the streets? That alone should be a warning sign.

She counted her blessings until her attitude changed to cheerful, and then she did the morning prep work before the restaurant opened. She pulled up the blinds, unlocked the front door, and picked up the small bundles of newspapers. Barely glancing at them, she arranged the national papers in the wire racks. Then she picked up the local papers and stopped dead.

Crist's picture was splashed on the front page of all three newspapers.

Ignoring the work she needed to do, Faithe sank into the nearest chair and began to read. The story described him as a master of disguise. He'd infiltrated different communities to get secret information. He'd masqueraded as elderly and later as wheelchair-bound to do an exposé on discrimination. He'd joined a white supremacist group to uncover their crimes. The list went on and on.

The more Faithe read, the sicker she became. Crist had said he wanted to eliminate drugs. He'd gotten his wish. He'd cancelled with her last night because he was busy with a drug raid. Now he was a hero with a huge reward.

But he'd deceived her. Had he faked becoming Amish as part of a new undercover assignment? One newspaper made it sound that way. Had he planned to court her as part of his cover?

According to the newspaper, his name wasn't Crist Petersheim. He was Alexander Parker, a well-known reporter. He'd even written one of the articles about the drug raid. That story had no picture of Crist. Or should she say Alexander Parker.

That name sounded familiar. Faithe leapt up from the table. A leftover copy of Thursday morning's paper should still be in the recycle bin. She went to pull it out. The story about Molly's husband was below the fold. At the bottom it read, *Alexander Parker and Carter Jamison contributed to this story.*

Then she remembered where else she'd seen that name before. On the check for five thousand dollars. He'd tricked her into believing he lived on the streets, when he was wealthy enough to run around donating money. The story about saving for a house for Ethan must have been a lie too. If she hadn't already deposited that check, she'd hand it back to him.

Faithe's eyes blurred with tears. *Alexander Parker.* She'd fallen for an *Englischer.*

∞ ∞ ∞

The bells jangled as Crist pushed open the restaurant door, and his heart plummeted. From the look on Faithe's face, she'd already seen the newspapers. In fact, the papers were spread out at the table where she was sitting. His mouth went dry. How would he explain this? Would she listen? Would she believe him?

"Faithe, we need to talk."

She shook her head. "I don't think so. Congratulations on the drug raid and the reward. I know how much it means to you, especially after what happened with your family." Her eyes narrowed. "Or was that story faked to get my sympathy?"

"No, it was real. All of it. You saw Ethan."

"The papers said you spent months in a wheelchair to get a story. How do I know Ethan wasn't one of your reporter friends posing as a—" Her voice broke.

Faithe's words ripped into him like a knife twisting in his chest. She believed he'd concocted everything he'd told her. *Please, God, help her to listen.*

"Your confession in front of the church on Sunday... Was that faked too? It came about so suddenly. Now you're disguising yourself as Amish. Was I supposed to be part of your cover?" She closed her eyes and wrapped her arms around herself. The pain on her face revealed how deeply he'd hurt her.

"Please let me explain."

Faithe stood. "What is there to explain? These newspapers did a fine job." She folded them neatly, turned her back, and arranged them in the wire racks. When she stood, she said wearily, "If Ethan is real, I'm glad you have the money to buy him a home." She headed for the kitchen doors.

"Wait, Faithe." He strode toward her and placed a hand on her arm, but she shook it off.

"Please don't touch me again." Her voice shook.

"Faithe!" he begged. But she walked through the swinging doors, letting them swing shut in his face.

∞ ∞ ∞

Mammi glanced up with alarm as Faithe burst through the kitchen door. "What's wrong?"

Faithe waved a hand to indicate she couldn't talk about it. Walking through those doors and leaving him behind was the hardest thing she'd ever done, but she had to get away before the tears fell. All her hopes and dreams dashed. She'd fallen for an *Englischer* and a liar.

She'd made some cruel accusations, and maybe some of them weren't true. She needed to ask his forgiveness for her attitude and for not listening to his side of the story, but not now. She couldn't do that without revealing her feelings for him. Perhaps later, after she'd composed herself. Much, much later. By then he'd have moved on to another reporting job, another life, another girl. An *Englisch* girl.

She pressed her fingers to her eyes to hold back the tears. "I'm going into the office for a few minutes. I'll be out to serve the tables when we open."

Behind the closed office door, she prayed until she had enough calmness in her soul to face the customers. Her heart had shattered into pieces, pieces too small for Crist—or anyone—to glue back together. But she still had her faith. She still had God, and that was the most important part of life.

She wiped her eyes, straightened her back, pasted on a smile, and headed out of the office. She owed her customers the best she had to give, despite her heartbreak. Her composure lasted until she walked through the kitchen doors to find Crist seated at his usual table, his face hidden by the menu.

The menu. She'd thought he was shy and seeking privacy, but he'd been hiding so customers wouldn't recognize him. Her gut twisted. So many lies.

She moved through her tables taking orders and saved Crist for last. Carrying a cup and saucer along with the coffee pot, she approached his table.

"Would you like some coffee?" She almost added sarcastically that it was free, but she held her tongue. When he nodded, she poured it and asked, "Would you like anything else?"

"Yes, I would." He looked her in the eye. "Time to talk with you."

"I'm sorry. As you can see, I'm quite busy."

"I'm going to sit here all day, every day, until you agree to talk to me."

"We need the booth for paying customers." The debt hanging over the restaurant had to be paid, or they'd lose it.

"I'll be a paying customer. I have enough money to order food every half hour, so I won't take away from your revenue."

"Please, Crist. I mean, Alexander. Just eat your meal and go."

"Not until you talk to me, Faithe."

"I-I can't."

"At least give me a chance to explain."

"Fine, we can go into the office on my twenty-minute break at 10:30."

Crist's disappointment was evident. "That's not much time, but I'll take whatever you give me."

Before she turned to go, he said, "I'll take the full breakfast platter. Fully paid for, of course."

Faithe scurried around taking care of customers. The ball of dread in her stomach grew as the clock hands inched closer and closer to 10:30.

One minute before her break, Crist stood and crossed the restaurant to stand by the kitchen door. "I don't want to waste a second of my precious time with you."

The way he said *precious* made her pulse flutter, until she reminded herself he wasn't Crist. He was a con man and an *Englischer*.

At 10:30 she pushed open the swinging doors and wove around cooks to reach the office door with Crist-Alexander on her heels. Once they entered the office, he closed the door behind him. Faithe wanted to tell him to leave it open, but she couldn't push the words past the tightness in her throat.

She averted her eyes because looking at him was too painful and her attraction to him was too strong.

"Faithe, I know you're probably not going to believe me, but my real name is Crist." He pulled out a driver's license with his picture on it.

"Alexander is a pen name I took when I started writing for the newspaper. I'm really Amish, and everything I told you about my family is true. So was my confession before the church. You helped point my way back to God."

Faithe struggled with doubt. If he was used to playing a role, he might be acting now. His words sounded so sincere, but could she trust him?

He rushed through an explanation about his life after his parents' death, getting Ethan into a home, and how one reporter who'd interviewed him after the shooting had taken him under his wing and taught him the trade.

He finished by saying, "I've explained to the paper that I can't do any more stories that call for disguising myself. I won't change my Amish clothes or tell half-truths or lies anymore. I'm not sure what that will mean for my assignments, but with the reward money, I plan to start fixing a house for Ethan and invest the rest."

Faithe sensed his sincerity, but part of her hesitated to trust.

"I'd like to invest in the restaurant, if you'd let me." Crist met her eyes and set sparks flying through her.

"I don't know."

"Would you pray about it with me? You said before God laid things on your heart. He laid it on your heart to feed me breakfast that morning when I only had coins in my pocket. I felt so guilty about that ten-cent tip."

"I thought it was the widow's mite."

"I suppose at the time it was."

"It couldn't have been. You—well, Alexander—wrote a check for five thousand dollars."

Crist ran his finger around in circles. "I have a checking account as Alexander to pay newspaper expenses and bills, but the money…" He swallowed hard. "That was from the money I'd been saving for Ethan. He agreed we should give it to you. Even after I told him it would mean putting off the house, he kept saying *Help*."

"You gave me your savings? But why? How did you know?"

Crist hung his head. "I have a confession to make. I eavesdropped the day your *Mamm* got the call about the embezzler. I didn't mean to. I walked into the restaurant to help you deliver the invitations. I didn't want you to be embarrassed, so I went back outside."

Faithe's cheeks colored. "I can't take that money now." She wasn't sure how she felt about him pretending not to overhear.

"I wasn't honest about the eavesdropping, but that was before my confession at church. I promise to always tell you the truth."

Faithe only knew one solution to her dilemma. "Let's both pray about this." When Crist nodded, she bowed her head and silently poured out her heart to God. Then she asked for guidance for the future. A deep sense of peace came over her. Perhaps God had allowed the embezzlement so Crist could invest in the restaurant.

When she lifted her head, she had a clear answer. "I need to talk to *Mamm*, but I think she'd be willing to take you on as a partner."

"Thank you," Crist said. "You don't know how happy that makes me. But"—he swallowed hard before meeting her eyes—"I don't only want to be a partner in the restaurant business." He reached for her hand. "I want a partner for life. Would you consider courting me?"

Faithe's joy bubbled over. God had given her more than she could have asked or thought. Her heart knew the answer the second he asked. Without hesitating, she said a resounding, "Yes."

He looked startled for a moment, then stood and swept her into his arms. She wound her arms around his neck, and he bent his head to place a tender kiss on her lips.

The door opened behind them, and *Mamm* cleared her throat. "Break's over, Faithe. You have customers waiting."

They broke apart, but Faithe glowed from head to toe. "I'll get back to work, but Crist can explain everything to you." She smiled at him. "And when he's done, I hope I'll see my favorite customer sitting in his booth for the rest of the day, and every day after that."

"I don't think so," Crist said, and Faithe's spirits plummeted until he added, "No more sitting for me. The only place I want to be is beside my favorite waitress. Now and forever."

Faithe agreed. That sounded perfect.

Thanksgiving Frolic

By Thomas Nye

Author's Note:

Surprisingly, Amish do not have a Dutch background. Almost all Amish people have German ancestry. The German word for Germany is Deutschland, and so, to be more correct, we should call the language Amish people speak, Pennsylvania Deutsch. Somewhere along the way, English speaking people began to refer to this German people group with a similar word, Dutch. The dialogue in this story would almost entirely have been spoken in this Pennsylvania form of German. However, the Amish dialect of German is not a written language.

Furthermore, if I wrote everything in Pennsylvania Dutch, very few readers would be able to understand what is being said (including me). Instead of blending English and Pennsylvania Dutch, I chose to write this novella in English. Try to think of this story as one that has been written in Dutch but translated into English. I only use one "Dutch" word in this story, "schput." This is a very common word used by Amish and Mennonites, including my wife's Mennonite family. To make schput, would be to make fun of. One form of "schputting" a person would be to say something complimentary in a facetious way. I used this word because it is such a natural part of English conversations in my area of Iowa.

Most Amish groups use a German Bible, which is written in a language they refer to as High German. This High German language would be comparable to King James English for a modern English-speaking person. When Amish families use an English Bible, they almost exclusively use The King James Bible. That is why the verses in this novella are quoted in King James English.

There are several scriptures quoted in The Thanksgiving Frolic. I didn't want to distract from the story by listing passage references in the story. Here are the scripture references in the order they appear in The Thanksgiving Frolic: 2 Corinthians 9:6, Galatians 6:7-9, Matthew 7:5, James 4:10, 1 John 1:8-9
Also, another footnote: It is common for Amish people to talk

about "standing up" in the morning rather than "getting up" as most English-speaking folks would say. Another Amishism would be to coin a phrase Monroe uses in this story. He says about Rosemary, "She is quite a Rosemary." This is usually an affectionate comment indicating that she is unique, and whatever it is that makes her unique, she has a lot of it. One more note: Amish people often work together on projects of all sizes, and some refer to these gatherings as frolics.

Chapter One

"I have something exciting to tell you!" Rosemary said, her voice ringing within the small confines of Monroe's buggy. Monroe clucked to his horse, Buster, and they pulled away from a Sunday evening youth gathering. Winds swirled, tossing leaves across the gravel driveway. Even though gusts pushed against the thin, black buggy-top, Monroe and Rosemary filled up the small interior, keeping it warm. With his head held high, Buster charged out onto Highway 61 at top speed.

"What were you going to tell me?" Monroe leaned back to make himself more comfortable and stole a glance at Rosemary. A semi-truck met them on the highway. Its headlights flooded the interior of his buggy, illuminating Rosemary's startled blue eyes as she turned her bonnet with the flash. Her hands firmly gripped the buggy seat's edge.

"What's the matter, Rosemary?"

"What's the matter?" she cried, her body jostling with the sway of Buster's gait. "That horse of yours is about ready to run off!"

Monroe shrugged. "He's not going anywhere. It's a cool night and he's feeling his oats, that's all." He leaned over to look out of the tiny back window.

Rosemary asked, "Why do you have to drive such a wild horse?"

A car followed shortly after the truck, and headlights revealed that Rosemary still hadn't let go of her grip on the edge of her seat. Monroe leaned forward so he could see around her bonnet. He smiled because her face looked a little more relaxed, and he liked the way a few stray curls were brushing against her cheek with the motion of the buggy. She always pulled her blond hair tightly under her Amish covering before she left home; however, as evenings wore on, a few curls usually peeked out around the edges. After the car whooshed past, he could still see movement as Rosemary struggled to pull her black shawl tighter.

Monroe chuckled, thinking about the flash image of her startled face in the headlights. "He's not wild, he's just fast. That's the kind of horse I like," he explained. "Now, tell me your exciting news."

Rosemary leaned back against the wall on her side of the small buggy seat, bracing herself as though expecting a crash at any moment. "I was going to tell
you—" She stopped talking as Buster surged close to a ditch-bank. Monroe pulled hard on his left line, drawing his horse back toward the center of the road.

"You were going to tell me..."

"I was going to tell you that my dad organized a Thanksgiving frolic." Her voice rose at the end of her sentence as the buggy wobbled near a ditch again.

Monroe grinned at how nervous she seemed. He made a point to ask in a casual way, "Thanksgiving frolic?"

"Dad hired a driver to take a load of people up to Charles City the week of Thanksgiving." The words tumbled out of Rosemary's mouth in rhythm with Buster's quick hoofbeats.

Monroe chuckled at her jiggly words. "What are *they* going to do up there?"

"*We* are going to help two Amish families that have come onto hard times," she explained. "One family has several children with special needs, and the other family's dad has been sick. Both of their farms need a lot of work."

Monroe nudged Rosemary's elbow. "It sounds like you're planning to go along?"

"Yes," she said turning to face him and leaning forward. "This is the best part: My dad said that I could ask you to come along."

"Yeah, you and your family are always wanting to help someone," Monroe mumbled and looked out the tiny back window of his buggy. Again.

Rosemary elbowed him. "What are you looking at?"

"Another horse is coming up behind us. I think it's Vernon."

"You *are not* going to race him with me in this buggy!" she scolded. "And if it *is* Vernon, then Dorothy is with him."

"We can't let my *little* brother and your older sister pass us!" Monroe said through clenched teeth. "Buster doesn't want a horse to pass us any more than I do!"

Buster's hoofbeats clapped loudly as his shoes hit the pavement in rapid succession ahead of them, and the motion caused the little vehicle to sway as he sped down the highway. A rumbling of steel-rimmed wooden wheels echoed under the buggy-seat.

"Monroe, please! Slow down!"

"I'm already holding Buster back!" he assured her. "If I wasn't, there's no way Vernon's horse could be gaining on us."

She didn't seem too convinced as she gripped the dashboard with one hand and the back of the buggy seat with her other.

"Ha, ha! Vernon thinks he's gaining on us," Monroe said, his laugh filling the inside of the small buggy.

In the glow of Monroe's buggy lights, another horse's head came into view right beside them. Vernon's horse was snorting as he paced quickly, trying to pass Buster.

"I thought you said King couldn't pass Buster?"

"He can't," Monroe insisted.

"It looks like he is." Rosemary pointed as the horse moved forward and Dorothy came into sight beside them. "And, she's laughing!" Rosemary shouted.

"We're going to get the last laugh," Monroe announced. "I'm holding Buster at the same speed that King is going. When I let Buster go, we'll leave them behind."

Both horses continued their high-speed race, side-by-side, until another set of headlights appeared, coming toward them on the highway.

Rosemary threw her hands in the air. "Monroe, look out! A car is coming!"

Monroe loosened his driving lines, and Buster picked up speed. Vernon flailed his driving lines at King in a last-ditch effort to pass Buster.

"Monroe—Monroe!" Rosemary cried with her hands on her cheeks, "Please stop Buster before that car gets any closer!"

Monroe ignored Rosemary's plea, making a kissing sound to his horse. Buster surged ahead as the car veered onto the opposite shoulder of the road, kicking up dust and rocks.

Monroe laughed and looked out the little window behind him. "I guess Vernon gave up. King is behind us now!"

Rosemary folded her arms in a huff and leaned against her side of the buggy. Monroe couldn't see her face in the dark buggy, but he smiled, knowing exactly what her expression would be: her full lips pursed tightly and her eyes narrowed to slits. He knew silence meant that she was mad at him, but he liked it that she was pretty even when angry.

Rosemary didn't utter a word as they climbed out of the buggy and stood near the hitching rack at her home farm. She fidgeted with her covering strings while Monroe tied Buster.

Rosemary finally broke her silence, and muttered, "Do you want to go to the Thanksgiving frolic with us, or not?"

"I doubt my dad will let me go," Monroe said.

"You're of age." She put her hands on her hips. "You should be able to decide for yourself."

"I can, but I work for my dad." Monroe raised his hands. "We helped my older sister and her husband build a house this summer and got behind on our own work. We have corn to pick, Dad's fencing business to keep up with, and besides, we're putting up a new loafing shed for our cattle. It's just too busy a time for me to go to some frolic."

Even in the dim light he could see her wrinkling her nose. "What's a loafing shed?"

"You don't know what a loafing shed is?" Monroe poked her side to tease her. "It's a long building that is open on one end. That way our cattle can come and go as they please to get out of bad weather."

Suddenly, a man's deep voice interrupted their conversation. "It's time to sow the seed if you want to yield a crop."

"Grandpa, what are you doing out here this time of night?" Rosemary exclaimed, more with a tone of concern than surprise. The old man didn't have a coat or hat despite the biting November chill. Faint lantern-light that shimmered through a kitchen window not far from the hitching rack glowed in his snowy-white hair and beard.

"I was just checking on my horse." A few strands of white hair were tossed about on his balding head as he spoke.

Rosemary hurried over to her grandfather's side and took his hand in hers. "Come inside, Grandpa. It's too cold for you to be outside like this."

The old man walked with his granddaughter toward the smaller house behind her family's large home and repeated his mysterious words. "It's time to sow good seed."

Monroe followed along. "It's fall, Mose, not planting season."

The old man stopped following Rosemary and turned to face Monroe. "He which soweth sparingly shall reap also sparingly; and he which soweth bountifully shall reap also bountifully."

Rosemary gently pulled on her grandpa's arm. "Let's go inside and get warmed up." She looped her arm in her grandfather's, then gave Monroe a squinty eye glare. Monroe caught up with them and took Mose's other arm, helping Rosemary to direct her grandpa into his house. Once they got him through the doorway, they found Rosemary's grandmother quietly rocking back and forth in a bent hickory rocker.

"I found Grandpa outside without any shoes, hat, or coat," Rosemary told her grandma.

Grandma pulled her shawl tightly around her frail shoulders, and her voice crackled out, "He never did mind the cold much."

Rosemary looked directly at her grandma. "Did you know he went outside?"

Wrinkles on the old woman's face showed her years, but her kind smile made her look young for a moment. "Yes. He said he was going to throw a flake of hay to his horse. Did you feed your horse, Mose?"

"Yes." The old man nodded. Even his once blue eyes seemed to have grayed with age.

Rosemary helped her grandpa take a seat at the table. She raised her eyebrows at Monroe as she stepped over to kneel beside her grandmother's rocking chair. The two women began to talk in hushed tones. Monroe assumed that Rosemary didn't want her grandpa to hear her words. He concluded that her raised eyebrows were a signal for him to occupy Grandpa's time. So, he sat at the table with Mose and struck up a conversation.

"It's not a season for planting. This is harvest time," Monroe ventured to say.

"Whatever a man soweth, that shall he also reap." Mose paused as if to give Monroe a chance to soak in the words. The old man placed one hand on a Bible and continued his mini-sermon. "He that soweth to the Spirit shall of the Spirit reap life everlasting. And let us not be weary in well doing: for in due season we shall reap, if we faint not." Mose looked across the table at Monroe and raised his bushy, white eyebrows. Suddenly, the old man's blue eyes looked clear. "Do you know how to rid yourself of pride?"

Monroe's eyebrows rose. After a moment, he said, "I guess by acting more humble?"

"That seems like the right answer," Mose said with a smile. "But if a man is *acting* humble, he will only become proud of how humble he is."

Monroe eyed the elderly man, uncertain if Mose's words were lucid or part of his dementia. He tried again. "Then I guess it's by becoming a Christian?"

"There are many Christians who are caught up in false humility," Mose challenged. The old man's gaze intensified, almost willing Monroe to read the answer in them.

It was too late at night for riddles. Monroe shrugged. "What's the answer?"

Mose shook his head. "I want you to think about it as you go about your harvest," he said. "When you're done with fall fieldwork, come back and tell me what you've discovered."

Rosemary had finished her conversation with her grandmother and stepped near Monroe and tapped his shoulder. "Come on. Let's go. It's time for my grandparents to turn in for the night."

She led the way out through the door, chiding Monroe as soon as they got outside. "Why do you egg on my grandpa? You know that he's getting old and forgetful. He doesn't need you younger men asking him questions to make *schput* of him."

"We're not making *schput*. Mose is interesting. I ask him questions to hear what he will say."

Rosemary marched on ahead of Monroe to the barn opposite the house, her fists brushing against the folds of her dress.

Monroe started after her, switching on a headlamp that he had strapped onto his black broad-brimmed Sunday hat. "Where are you going, Rosemary?"

"I'm going in to check on Grandpa's horse. I want to know if he actually did feed it."

Rosemary didn't thank Monroe for the light, but she obviously benefitted from his help as she walked toward the dark barn. When the headlamp revealed a broken-down fence with patched-together sections, Monroe winced at how messy everything looked. A few large, round bales of hay sagged near an unpainted barn, brown and obviously no good anymore. The barn door creaked on its hinges as they stepped inside, and Rosemary struggled to walk over deep straw that had been heaped up to cover manure instead of cleaning it out.

Monroe's headlamp lit up a box-stall, and Mose's buggy horse came into view, contentedly munching on hay. Rosemary didn't say a word. She turned and headed for the house with Monroe following and lighting her way. He smiled at the determined set of her shoulders and the way she stomped through the house door. Monroe noticed his brother's horse tied next to Buster at the hitching rack. He liked that his younger brother dated Rosemary's sister, and they had fun hanging out together as couples, but sometimes he wished Rosemary could be a little more lighthearted, like her older sister.

Chapter Two

Monroe followed Rosemary inside, where a gas lantern lit up the warm farmhouse, accompanied by a gentle hissing sound. He took off his black coat and hat and hung them on a set of hooks next to Rosemary's shawl and bonnet. Monroe's younger brother, Vernon, had already taken a seat in the living room. They eyed each other as Monroe walked in. Vernon had always been shorter, but also a little stronger than Monroe. His reddish hair looked matted down where his broad-brimmed hat had been pressed on until he came into the house. Monroe wondered if his own hair needed attention. He looked into a tiny mirror near a china hutch and ran a comb through his bowl-cut brown hair. He met eyes with Vernon's reflection in the mirror, and the brothers smirked, obviously both thinking about their buggy race and near disaster. Though neither of them spoke, Monroe seated himself on the couch beside his brother and waited.

Rosemary joined her sister in the kitchen, the hushed tones of their conversation mixing with a clamor of kitchen sounds. A tinkle of a spoon in a dish, cupboard doors opening and then closing, and a fridge door suctioned open and then sealed shut. Monroe glanced at his brother again. With images of a horse and buggy race still fresh in their minds, they both struggled to hold back laughter, knowing the girl's parents were already sleeping.

Rosemary and Dorothy came through the kitchen doorway, crossed the hardwood floors carrying plates laden with goodies, setting them on a coffee table in front of Monroe and Vernon before taking seats near their boyfriends. Monroe began by snatching up a few of Rosemary's specialty, chocolate cupcakes. Vernon sorted out a couple of cookies. Rosemary heaped bowls with salty popcorn while Dorothy filled glasses with chocolate goat milk.

As they grazed on snacks, Rosemary looked at her sister. "So, Dorothy, did you tell Vernon about the Thanksgiving frolic?"

Dorothy nodded, her usual carefree smile in place. "Yes, Vernon is planning to go with us."

Monroe looked at Rosemary, who raised her eyebrows and pursed her lips. He smiled, noticing yet again how pretty she was. Both sisters were blond, and their eyes equally blue, but Monroe liked the faint freckles that decorated Rosemary's dainty nose. That was why he'd sent his best friend, Elrose, to talk to her and set up their first date three years ago. Other boys had teased him because he dated the younger of Simon Miller's daughters and left the older sister for his younger brother, Vernon. Dorothy was fairly pretty and more lighthearted than her sister, but Monroe was certain he had chosen the prettier of the two.

Rosemary looked directly at Monroe. "Well, what do you have to say about Vernon going on the Frolic?"

"I'd say he hasn't asked our dad yet," Monroe shot back.

"Oh, we'll think up some story to tell Dad," Vernon said. "He'll complain that we're shirking our duty, but after a while, he'll quit scolding us."

Dorothy laughed at Vernon's comment, but Rosemary's face contorted. "Why can't you just tell your dad the truth? Wouldn't he be happy that his sons want to help someone in need?"

Monroe couldn't help sneering. "I've told you how our dad is. All he thinks about is keeping our place spotless. His farm and buildings *have* to be the best. He doesn't have any time for people with a messy—" He stopped mid-sentence. "... farm," he finished, despite the insult his words would cause.

Rosemary set down the spoon she had lifted to her mouth. "I suppose he says that about us?"

"I don't know," Monroe said. "We haven't mentioned you girls to him." He immediately regretted saying that as well.

Even carefree Dorothy looked at Vernon with a piercing glare. "You *have* mentioned me around your house before I hope?"

Vernon shrugged. "I'm sure I have." He glared at his brother out of the corner of his eyes. "Some time, anyhow."

"You girls should know about our dad by now." Monroe took the heat off his younger brother. "Everyone in the community knows Dad as a man of his word. He keeps all the rules of the church and keeps his farm spotless, but he's not as quick to help as some."

Rosemary nodded. "I guess our dad *is* too quick to help others when our own farm needs to be cleaned up a bit," she confessed.

"Maybe if he had sons still at home, he could push them like our dad does us," Vernon muttered. Dorothy laughed, but Vernon's gaze remained serious. "And then his sons would be thinking about jumping the fence, like we are."

Rosemary immediately sat up straight in her chair and questioned Monroe with her eyes.

Monroe returned her gaze and shook his head. "Speak for yourself, Vernon. I never said that I was gonna do that." He sighed and stood up. "We probably better get going now. Dad will be cracking the whip at first light."

"You go ahead and leave if you want," Vernon said with a laugh. "I'll worry about tomorrow when it gets here."

"It may never get here for you if you drive your horse like you did tonight," Monroe teased. Vernon gave Monroe an eye squint, but his ears turned red, a dead giveaway that he was embarrassed.

Rosemary followed Monroe into an enclosed porch as he put on his coat and hat. She fiddled with her covering strings for a moment and then said quietly, "Will you ask your dad about going to the Thanksgiving frolic with us?"

"Okay, I'll ask him." Monroe gazed down at Rosemary until she smiled up at him. "Are you still planning to go with me to the horse sale this Thursday?"

She nodded. "Yes."

"I'll pick you up at the bakery when you get off work. Around noon, right?"

She nodded again and grinned at him. He returned her smile, then headed out to his waiting horse.

Buster nickered as Monroe stepped close and untied him. "That Rosemary is quite the Rosemary," he whispered to Buster. "I'd ask her to marry me if I hadn't opened my big mouth and challenged my best friend to a contest." Monroe let out a sigh. "I thought I was smart when I promised that I wouldn't get married until after he did."

As Buster headed down the dark road toward home, Monroe's thoughts drifted back to his younger days. He and Elrose spent most of their evening hours fishing along Quale Creek. Their friendship hinged on outdoing each other. They often made a contest of who could catch the most fish, or the biggest fish. If they talked about making hay, they contended about who could put up more bales, or who could throw a bale further. It had always been in good fun, but when they started going to Singings, Elrose schputted Monroe about how neatly he combed his hair, "For the girls."

"You'll be married long before me!" Monroe's memory was so vivid he could almost hear his own voice echoing within the buggy.

Elrose had one-upped him next. "If you get married first, I'll schput you until we're old and gray."

Monroe recalled his own words, "You'll get old and gray before I give you a reason to schput me!"

A set of headlights appeared as a car rounded a curve up ahead. The light flooded onto where Rosemary had been sitting earlier. He looked at the empty spot, wishing that he had the courage to end the contest with his friend. Monroe recalled how the flash of light had shone on Rosemary's sweet face earlier in the evening. He could almost hear her excited voice, "We are going to help two Amish families that have come onto hard times." A slight prick stung his heart for a moment.

Monroe didn't have a chance to consider where that feeling came from because he had to rein in his powerful horse. Buster's years on the racetrack conditioned him with a sense of urgency and made him a perfect horse for Monroe. His high-stepping front legs reached greedily for the road ahead while his back legs powered the motion and propelled him forward at top speed. As Monroe listened to the rhythmic beat of Buster's hooves on the highway, his mind went back to the question Rosemary's grandpa had asked. "*Do you know how to rid yourself of pride*?"

Monroe shook it off. He didn't struggle with pride anyway.

Chapter Three

Monroe's dad called up the steps just as the first glint of light hinted at sunrise. "We're wasting daylight boys! It's time to stand up and get our work done!"

Monroe got out of bed and pulled on his work clothes. He slapped Vernon's foot hanging out from beneath the covers. "It's time to stand up, Vernon! Dad called up here five minutes ago. Don't make him mad this early in the day."

Vernon groaned, but didn't move until Monroe slapped at his bare foot again.

"Quit it, I'm getting up," he moaned from under the covers.

Monroe had already milked the cow by the time Vernon stumbled out to feed the steers. The brothers met up in the horse barn and worked together to brush and harness a team of sorrel Belgian horses with cream-colored manes and tails.

"How are we going to ask Dad about that frolic?" Vernon looked to his older brother for wisdom.

Monroe shrugged. "I'm not sure. I think I'll just say that Elrose is going and he wants me to come along."

"Thanks a lot." Vernon stopped snapping the harness into place and glared at his brother. "Then I'll have to come up with a reason that I want to go."

"Don't worry. I'll mention you going along when I bring it up."

Breakfast foods sizzled on the Hostetlers' oak table when the brothers came inside. Monroe and Vernon's mother, Esther, hurried about her kitchen. Her plum Amish dress was the only object of color to be seen, other than food. Their dad, Joe, sat in his usual spot nearest the door. His salt and pepper chin-beard matched his bushy eyebrows and balding head. After a short, silent prayer, Joe never looked up at the family again. He began his methodical spoon to mouth routine like it was another chore he had to do. Esther began her daily work of trying to cheer up the mood with small talk.

Monroe appreciated his mother's effort to improve the atmosphere and decided to try easing into conversation with his dad before bringing up the Thanksgiving frolic. "Dad, we harnessed up some horses this morning. Vernon and I plan to shock corn again today."

Joe grunted a wordless response.

Monroe hesitated while he gathered his courage, and then spoke again. "Elrose, is going along on a work frolic with Simon Miller and family during the week of Thanksgiving."

"That sounds nice," Esther commented, her smile warm.

Monroe reached his goal in a final rush of words. "Simon invited Vernon and me to go along."

His dad looked up from his plate for the first time all breakfast. "Simon Miller? He needs to have a frolic at his place and catch up on his own work before heading off to help someone else. The Bible even says, "'... first cast out the beam out of thine own eye; and then shalt thou see clearly to cast out the mote out of thy brother's eye.'"

Vernon met Monroe's gaze, his brow scrunched. Monroe gave a slight shrug in return before Joe continued.

"I don't want you boys going with the Simon Miller family anywhere. If a son of mine married one of that man's daughters, I wouldn't help them get a start farming, that's for sure."

Esther set down her fork and asked in a gentle way, "Why would you say that?"

"Because I'm not going to waste money on a failing business," Joe said with a scowl. "A farmer can't make any money when everything is a mess like his place."

Monroe and Vernon looked at each other, but they didn't dare flinch. Their mother smiled slightly. "Simon's daughters are hard workers. They always keep up their family's large garden and share produce with neighbors and friends. Just because their dad doesn't have a neat farm doesn't mean that his daughters wouldn't be good homemakers."

Joe scoffed, "It seems unlikely."

"Well, Elrose is going along to help with the frolic," Monroe repeated. "He wants my help and Vernon's. And there would be a lot of other people there besides Simon Miller and his family."

"You can put it out of your mind." Joe met eyes with each son in turn. "You know how far behind we are on our own work. When our corn is all shocked, we need to put our new building up before bad weather sets in, and for sure before Thanksgiving. If we get that all done, your older sisters' families can use your help on their farms. If you want a chance to help someone, you can help them."

Monroe and Vernon didn't say another word about it until they were alone out in the cornfield. They hacked at corn stalks with their machetes, taking out their frustrations on the lifeless stems. Cold November winds began to pick up as the day went on.

Eventually, Vernon rehashed the topic. "I told you we would have to come up with a better story if we want to go along on that Thanksgiving frolic."

"I'm not even worried about the frolic anymore," Monroe looked at his younger brother. "I'm more worried about telling Dad that I want to marry one of Simon Miller's daughters. What would he say if he knew we both want to?"

Vernon shook his head. "C'mon, don't be silly. You know that Dad already knows we are dating them. He just pretends he doesn't because he's hoping that we'll move on to other girls before we decide to get married. He said all of that to make us change our minds about them."

Monroe took off his hat and scratched the back of his neck. "You might be right."

"It shouldn't matter as much to you, anyway," Vernon reminded Monroe. "You and Elrose have that little contest about who will be married last. But, I'm not part of any silly contest, and I want to ask Dorothy to marry me soon."

Monroe kicked a corn stalk. "I wish I never would have opened my big mouth to Elrose. I'd like to ask Rosemary to marry me, but, I can't let Elrose win now. His girlfriend is putting a ton of pressure on him to get married and if I can just hold out a little longer, I'll win. I'll be able to schput Elrose for life."

Vernon laughed. "That would almost be worth it. Elrose deserves it, after all the schupting he dishes out to the rest of us boys."

Monroe grimaced as he began chopping stalks again. "Besides, Dad won't let me marry her anyway."

Cold autumn winds whisked over trees near the creek, where only few leaves remained, stubbornly holding on to bare limbs. The old wind shook the trees furiously until a few more leaves lost their grip and fell to the ground, where they were tossed end over end across the field toward Monroe and Vernon. The young men struggled against the wind as well. They gathered their cornstalks into piles and then raised them into teepee shaped shocks. Monroe held stalks upright while his younger brother added more. Once enough stalks accumulated, the weight of the shock held up against the wind.

As they worked, Monroe's mind continually returned to what his dad had said about Simon Miller's daughters. It bothered him that his dad didn't want him dating Rosemary. It pained him that his dad had scoffed at her whole family because of their messy farm, especially after Rosemary asked if he said that about them.

He held another set of cornstalks for Vernon to tie and asked, "How do you think a person rids himself of pride?"

Never willing to miss a chance to tease his brother, Vernon asked. "Why? Are you proud of our corn shocks?"

Monroe tossed a small ear of corn at Vernon. "Just answer with the first thing that comes to mind."

"Well, the Bible says, 'Humble yourselves in the sight of the Lord, and he shall lift you up.' It must be that you point out your own faults." Vernon glanced at Monroe to see if he had answered correctly.

"Huh. It does say to humble yourself. So, I guess it is possible to get rid of pride?" Monroe stood and looked at their corn shock and tried to think of bad things he could say about himself. "I sure was mean last night when I refused to let you and King pass me and Buster!"

The brothers laughed, and the wind whipped the sound across the field.

"I don't think you feel too sorry about that," Vernon called over the howling winds.

His brother meant to tease—of that, he had no doubt. Still, Monroe suspected that pride had also played a part in his refusal to allow Vernon to pass him. The next time Monroe and his brother tied shocks, Vernon continued their conversation, still shouting over the wind. "What makes you ask about pride like that?"

"Old Mose asked me if I knew how to get rid of pride, and I didn't know the answer," Monroe struggled to explain over the wind's howl.

"I wouldn't worry too much about anything Mose says," Vernon shouted back. "He's been a little confused lately. Dorothy told me that he embarrassed their whole family in town a few weeks ago."

Monroe leaned closer to his brother. "What happened?"

"He told some worldly people that it was time to till up the soil and plant good seed." Vernon laughed and then continued. "Here it is—November—and he's telling people it's planting time."

"Yeah, but sometimes I think he comes to himself and makes sense," Monroe said.

"You're as loopy as he is, if you think that."

Monroe smiled at his brother's joke, but he didn't feel like laughing about it. Something about the old man seemed special.

Chapter Four

Thursday, right at noon, Buster clip-clopped at top speed toward the Morning Delight Bakery where Rosemary worked every Tuesday and Thursday until 12:00. Rosemary waited for him at the hitching rack with a black jacket over her bright-blue dress, holding two large twist doughnuts. She jumped into Monroe's buggy, and they headed out for the horse sale.

"I sure am glad you work at this bakery," Monroe said as she handed him a doughnut.

Her blue eyes sparkled as she carefully untwisted her twist doughnut and broke off a piece. "Is that because it's close to your home farm and you can stop in and see me?"

He took a large bite of sugary-sweet doughnut. "Well, that, too."

Rosemary elbowed Monroe and laughed as she popped the piece of doughnut she had torn off into her mouth. They only made it a few hundred feet before Rosemary leaned forward and held up one hand. "Wait, Monroe, did you hear that?"

Monroe faced her and wrinkled up his brow, trying to listen.

"Whoa," Rosemary called to Buster as she reached over and pulled on the lines Monroe held. "Listen, there's a kitten crying."

Monroe scoffed, "Who cares, we have a barn full of kittens."

Rosemary slid open the door and started to climb out.

"Wait a second," he chided, "where are you going?"

Rosemary rushed down the steep ditch bank and called, "Oh, look, Monroe, a poor little kitty is caught by its tail in some weeds." Her bright-blue dress wriggled about in tall grasses that had turned brown under a November-gray sky.

Monroe worked hard to hold Buster in place while he watched her wrestle the kitten loose. She climbed the steep ditch-bank holding a little yellow fuzz-ball in her arms. The kitten's bright-blue eyes matched Rosemary's as she pushed out her lower lip and crooned, "Isn't it cute?"

Buster pawed at the road and shook his mane. "Yes, it's cute, but Buster and I want to get going!"

She set down the kitten and nudged it toward an Amish farmhouse that stood a short distance from the road, then ran and jumped in with Monroe and said, "Okay, quick go!"

Monroe gave Buster slack and his horse surged ahead. "Did you really need to help that cat? There's no shortage of kittens in the world."

Rosemary cocked her head. "What if you needed help and The Lord said, 'Do I really need to help this person? There's no shortage of people in the world.'"

Monroe laughed. "You are *quite* the Rosemary."

Buster's merry gait caused the buggy to sway gently as they rode over rolling hills toward the horse sale. Harvested fields around them lay dormant under a November chill. Another buggy came into view when they rounded the top of one rather steep hill. Monroe's horse effortlessly blew past the slow-moving buggy.

"That Henry J. has about the slowest horse of any boy I know." Monroe laughed until he noticed she didn't.

Rosemary gave him a glare. "Don't say anything bad about Henry J. He's my cousin."

"I would have thought he'd be embarrassed by that old nag he drives." Monroe shook his head. "How can he show his face at a horse sale after we blew past him like we did? I've never had anyone pass me. Not since I bought Buster."

Rosemary sat quietly for a short time. Monroe glanced at her as she continued untwisting her doughnut and breaking off small bites. Her breath puffed out like smoke inside the cold buggy, and she chewed slowly, gazing out of the buggy's window.

"Rosemary, what are you thinking about? Just tell me."

"I feel like you have an issue with pride," she blurted out.

Monroe raised his eyebrows. "Pride? Just because I have a fast horse, you think I'm proud?"

"You're becoming more like your dad all the time," she muttered.

"What? How is having a fast horse anything like my dad?"

"He has to have everything perfect on his farm, and he judges those who don't. Just like you have to have the fastest horse and judge those who don't."

Monroe didn't answer her accusation, but slumped on his buggy seat, watching Buster's swift gait. They didn't speak another word until they were inside the sale barn. The scent of hamburgers and french-fries floated through the warm stands around the auction ring. A rhythmic chant of numbers rang out in a soothing way and helped him forget about his awkward conversation with Rosemary.

One horse after another passed through the sale ring while Monroe and Rosemary sat side-by-side and watched.

Rosemary nudged Monroe with her shoulder. "What kind of horse do you like best?"

"Dutch-cross is my favorite. I like how they hold their heads high," Monroe said. He looked at Rosemary, and their eyes met for a moment. He wondered if high-headed horses seemed prideful to her. "What do you like best?" he asked.

"I like Percherons. They're so huge and gentle, and I've always preferred black work horses."

"Me too," he agreed. "Although my dad has Belgian work horses, I think I'll have Percherons when I get my own farm someday."

Rosemary didn't say anything, but her eyes sparkled as she glanced at him. He hoped she took his comment to suggest that someday, when they were married, they would own Percherons.

After watching horses sell for about an hour, Monroe suggested they get hamburgers. "That smell is making me hungry."

She gave him a shy smile. "Me too."

They squeezed through the crowd. About half of the men there were Amish, with long chin-beards and black broad-brimmed hats. The other half were non-Amish farmers with feed caps and hooded sweatshirts. Young Amish men preferred to wear stocking caps pulled up to a point on top like Monroe did with his. Amish women pulled their black shawls around themselves tightly to keep out the cold. Very few English women or young people could be seen in the crowd.

Monroe and Rosemary found the end of the line at the concession stand and stood quietly, waiting for their turn to order hamburgers. An Englisher in front of them turned around and gave Monroe a friendly smile.

"Well, if it isn't one of Joe Hostetler's boys!"

"Hello, Bill," Monroe replied. "Are you buying any good horses today?"

"None as good as that Mr. Buster I sold you!" Bill said. "I never should have let that horse go. I bet nobody has passed that buggy of yours since you bought him."

Rosemary scrunched up her brow. "Mr. Buster?"

Bill's face broke into a huge grin. "Didn't Monroe tell you? His real name is Mr. Record Buster, but at the racetrack we just called him Mr. Buster."

Monroe pushed his stocking cap up enough to scratch the high part of his neck and glanced at Rosemary. "I didn't think you'd like that name."

Bill looked from him to Rosemary, and his lips curled into a sly smile. He slapped Monroe on the back. "Is this your girlfriend?"

Monroe nodded and felt his ears heat up, and he pulled his stocking cap back down far enough to cover them.

"You own the fastest horse *and* have the prettiest girl around." Bill gave Monroe a friendly shove. "You're a chip off the old block!"

Monroe looked at Bill sideways. "What does that mean?"

"It means you're just like your old man," Bill said, and laughed. "He always has to have the best of everything."

Monroe choked out a short chuckle to be polite. An Amish girl behind the counter interrupted their conversation.

"Who's next in line?"

Monroe couldn't make himself look in Rosemary's direction while Bill placed his order. Suddenly the Amish girl behind the counter said, "Monroe and Rosemary, are you two here shopping for a family horse?" Her eyes twinkled as she teased them.

"We're hungry for hamburgers not horses—" Monroe righted his tongue after stumbling over his words. "— wanting to buy hamburgers."

The girl behind the counter laughed as if Monroe had been trying to be funny.

Rosemary turned her eyes to the ground. "I'm not really hungry after all."

Monroe ordered two hamburgers. "I'll eat them both if you really don't want one."

They wound their way down through the crowd into the area where horses were kept in stalls, taking their time so Monroe could eat his hamburgers. Rosemary studied the horses with more fascination than usual, avoiding any eye contact or conversation with Monroe. As they rounded a corner they saw Rosemary's dad and grandpa standing with a couple of Englishers.

"Hello, Simon. Hello, Mose," Monroe said, as politely as he could with a bite of hamburger still in his mouth.

“Rosemary told me she was going to be at this sale,” her dad said with a smile.

Rosemary remained silent, her lips pursed.

Old Mose reached out and shook Monroe’s hand. “Are you buying horses for spring fieldwork?” he asked.

Monroe didn’t know how to answer. He glanced at Rosemary, and her face flushed red. “I’m just looking at horses today,” he said. “We have plenty of Belgians at home right now, and we’ll have more colts in the spring.” He immediately wished he hadn’t used the word spring.

“It’s time to sow good seed,” Mose said.

The other men laughed, and Rosemary took her grandpa’s hand and pulled him away. “Let’s go look at some horses, Grandpa.”

Monroe looked at the other men awkwardly. They fit the description of lumberjacks, with flannel shirts and work boots. The bigger fellow with a huge mustache and a seed-cap spoke up.

“That Mose is an interesting man,” he said. “He has his calendar a little mixed up, but he always has interesting ideas about life.”

The smaller man with shaggy hair and a scruffy chin nodded. “Yeah, Mose was just giving me advice about my boss.”

“Oh, really, what was that?” As soon as the words left his mouth, Monroe winced, worrying that he might have been better off to let the topic drop.

“Well, I’m a hired man on a farm, and my boss is a cheapskate. He works me long hours and doesn’t pay worth a darn. Then he came down with pneumonia and expects me to help his family until he can get back on his feet.” The man worked a toothpick in the corner of his mouth and squinted his eyes at Monroe.

Monroe thought it all seemed awkward and didn’t know what to say, but the man continued staring at him as though expecting a reply. “What did Mose suggest?” Monroe asked, curious in spite of himself.

"He says that I should do the right thing, because it's the right thing to do," the man said. "Mose also told me that I should act on what I believe, not react to how others treat me."

"Huh." Monroe nodded thoughtfully. "That sounds like pretty good advice to me."

"I guess you're right, but I don't know if I'm that good of a man," the stranger said.

Rosemary's dad smiled. "Ask God for help to do the right thing."

The men nodded in agreement. Monroe turned to see what Rosemary and her grandpa thought and realized they were a few box stalls away, looking at a team of massive black Percherons. Simon and the strangers continued their conversation while Monroe joined Rosemary and Mose.

Monroe asked, "Are those the kind of horses you like?"

"We always had Belgians," Mose answered, "but this team looks like they could get a lot of work done."

Monroe intended for Rosemary to answer his question, but she seemed upset and didn't make any attempt to look in Monroe's direction. Rosemary's dad joined them and said, "Grandpa, we should go sit near the sale ring and watch some horses sell."

Old Mose headed off in the direction of the sale ring, but Rosemary leaned toward Simon and whispered, "Dad, don't let Grandpa get into conversations with people. He gets too confused."

Simon nodded that he understood, and the two men headed into the auction area.

Rosemary pulled her black jacket shut and then folded her arms. "I want to go home now."

"We haven't been here that long." Monroe turned to Rosemary and saw a tear forming in the corner of her eye. "Okay, let's go," he agreed.

While Buster clip-clopped toward Rosemary's house, Monroe thought about Mose and the advice he had given the strangers.

"I don't think you should try to keep your grandpa from talking to people," Monroe said.

"They just laugh at him." Her voice sounded thick, drawing Monroe to glance at her in time to see a tear streaming down her cheek.

"Most people understand that old folks get confused. I don't think you should let that bother you." Monroe glanced again to see what she thought of his opinion.

"You don't understand." She dabbed at the corner of her eye with a hanky. "My grandpa was always so kind to us grandchildren. He always took time to answer all of my questions." She unfolded the hanky and blew her nose. "It pains me to see him like this, and it's worse if someone's laughing at him."

Monroe kept quiet after that. They rode along listening to the sound of buggy wheels grinding on the road. Monroe's mind went back to Bill and his words. "*You're a chip off the old block.*" He hated it that the man had said the words at all, but it was ten times worse that he had said them in front of Rosemary. "*You're just like your old man—he always has to have the best.*"

Those words kept ringing in his ears, until Rosemary blurted out, "Is that how you think of me?"

Monroe snapped his head back. "Is what how I think of you?"

"Like that man said." Rosemary looked out the side window and began to sniffle again. "Do you think of me like a horse? Did you go to the singing and shop around until you found a girl with the right hair color, who was put together the way you wanted?"

"No, Rosemary. Listen, I think you are pretty, but it's more than that." Monroe grappled for words.

"What more? What is it that makes you want to date me?" She sat hunched on the buggy seat as far from him as she could get, refusing to look in his direction. "For all I know you aren't even going to ask me to marry you. Every time I bring it up you change the subject."

"Now, listen, Rosemary, I've always treated you right, and you know that I've never paid attention to any other girl. Why would you say something like that?"

"It's just that we've been dating for a long time, and other couples our age are already married. Maybe you started dating me for the wrong reasons, and now your dad doesn't want you to marry me and you don't know how to end it."

Monroe scratched at his collar that suddenly felt too tight. "Rosemary—that's not it."

She continued looking out the side window as they rode in silence. When they pulled up at Morning Delight Bakery, Monroe helped her fetch her horse from the barn and hitch it to her buggy.

"I don't think I can go to the Thanksgiving frolic with your family." Monroe forced out the words, knowing he had to tell her even though it didn't seem like a good time for it.

She looked him straight in the eyes. "Did you ask your dad?"

"Yes, I asked him; check with Vernon. Dad gave us a lecture about all the work we have to finish on our own farm before winter hits. And then he told us that if we want to help other people, we should help our brothers-in-law on their farms."

"Why do I have the feeling you aren't telling me everything he said?" Her face paled and the sparkle disappeared from her eyes. "Is that why you haven't asked me to marry you—because your dad doesn't like my family?"

"Rosemary, why would you say that?" Monroe averted his gaze and focused on dirt that he smoothed with his foot, afraid that she would see the truth in his eyes.

She turned away from him and said, "Never mind about the Thanksgiving frolic. I wouldn't want you to help others who aren't as good as your family." She climbed into her buggy and shook her driving lines, sending her horse clip-clopping down the lane.

Chapter Five

The following morning started out much like any other day on Joe Hochstetler's farm. Chores were done on time, as usual. Breakfast sat on the table exactly at 8:00am. Joe's family took a few moments for devotions, and then the day's work began. Joe charged out of the kitchen as soon as they finished praying and scolded his sons. "We have to get this building started today, or it'll never be completed before bad weather hits. Next week we'll have one less day to work because of Thanksgiving." He said it as though Thanksgiving would be nothing more than a nuisance.

An angry wind gusted from the northwest and made working conditions bad. Joe's temper flared when he couldn't get his tape-measure to hold still long enough to make an accurate mark. Monroe and Vernon did whatever they were told, but only halfheartedly. Monroe kept thinking about the Thanksgiving frolic scheduled for the following Monday. He imagined riding in a warm van with Rosemary and her family. They were always happy and loved to tell funny stories of days-gone-by. He couldn't help but think that it would be much more fun to work with a group of happy people on a project together than to be stuck with his grouchy dad and brother at home.

By noon, Joe and his sons had put up part of one wall, though the wind fought against them all morning. Shortly after lunch, Joe climbed a ladder and drove nails into a brace that would hold the second wall in place until the structure took shape. Just as he leaned out to drive in his final nail, he slipped. Monroe surged forward, instinctively trying to catch his father, but Joe hit the ground with a sickening thud. Monroe's and Vernon's eyes met in horror for an instant, before Vernon took off running as fast as his legs could carry him. Monroe knew his brother would sprint the half mile to a phone shed and call 911.

Monroe hovered over the silent body of his father as the winds howled. He tried to lay his head on his dad's chest to listen for a heartbeat or the sound of breathing. The wind refused to quiet down long enough for either to be audible. Monroe looked up toward the house and wondered whether he should run and get his mother or stay beside his dad and try to comfort him.

All at once, he thought, *I should pray*, so he laid a hand on his father's chest. "Dear God, please help my dad. Don't let him die."

Monroe's thoughts swirled as he waited for help to come. *Would his dad live? Would he ever be the same if he did survive?* As much as his thoughts raced, time seemed to drag because he couldn't think of anything he could do to help. He found himself remembering the kitten Rosemary had rescued, and how he had chided her, *"Did you really need to help that cat? There's no shortage of kittens in the world."*

Her words of admonition came to him clearly. *"What if you needed help, and God said, 'There's no shortage of people in the world.'"*

Monroe prayed again. "Oh, Lord, please help my dad, and my family—make us more like Rosemary's family."

He looked in the direction of the phone booth and saw Vernon running toward him. Monroe hoped that by some miracle his brother would be bringing good news.

Vernon panted out, "An ambulance...is on its way."

Suddenly, a pickup truck came barreling into their lane. Monroe recognized the vehicle as one owned by Jim Door. As one of the local volunteers trained as "first responders" and a near neighbor, Jim had come to help until an ambulance arrived.

Jim hurried over and knelt beside Joe, placing two fingers against his neck. "What happened?"

"Dad fell from that ladder and landed on his side," Monroe said, his voice quavering. "He hasn't moved or let out a sound since."

"He has a good pulse," Jim said, straightening up again. He spoke with such confidence Monroe felt himself exhale fully for the first time since his dad fell.

Vernon searched Joe's face. "He's still alive?"

"Yes, he's alive, but we'd better not move him. It's always best to be sure that there are no broken vertebrae. Get a blanket and we'll cover him up where he is, to keep him from suffering from shock."

Monroe jumped up and ran toward the house, bursting through the door. He found his mother in the back room sewing. "Mom, we need an old blanket! Dad fell from a ladder, and an ambulance is on its way."

Monroe's mother gasped. "How badly is he hurt?" She grabbed a quilt that lay neatly folded beside her and flung it to her son.

"I don't know," Monroe shot out as he ran back outside with Esther close behind. He outran his mother and quickly laid out the quilt to cover his dad. Jim was talking to Joe and getting some slight response.

Vernon's attention went to his mother, who had come up wringing her hands. "Dad is conscious now," he said. "He's mumbling something, but it's hard to understand him."

Jim spoke to Joe quietly, but confidently. "You're going to be fine, Joe. Don't try to move. We have an ambulance coming, and it'll be here any minute. It's best if you stay as still as possible."

As Jim spoke, the whine of a siren could be heard in the distance, growing louder as the ambulance came into view. It roared up their lane, and Vernon raced out to meet them. Paramedics rushed over with a bodyboard and began the slow process of moving Joe onto it. Monroe stood with his mother and brother, watching helplessly. He wanted the paramedics to hurry and get his dad to the hospital, but they seemed to take forever to strap him onto their stiff stretcher. When they finally had Joe strapped firmly onto the board, they hoisted him into the back of the ambulance and suggested that Monroe's mother ride along. The ambulance slowly made its way out of the Hostetler lane and disappeared.

"Why aren't they going faster?" Vernon said the words Monroe had been thinking.

"They're concerned that he may have a back injury," Jim answered. "We thought about having a helicopter come and get him, but his vital signs seemed good, so they'll take it slow and get him to the hospital without jostling his spine too much."

"Is he going to be okay?" Monroe searched Jim's face for some sign of hope.

"I think so," Jim's face showed little emotion. "You boys can catch a ride to the hospital with me if you want."

Monroe looked at his brother and answered for them both. "I think we'll take a buggy. That way we'll have a way home when it's chore time."

Half an hour later, Monroe and Vernon entered their dad's hospital room quietly, their broad-brimmed black hats held in their hands as they moved toward his bed. A machine beeped rhythmically while their father slept.

Esther stood from a chair that had been pushed next to the bed. She held a bunched-up hankie near her mouth and folded the other arm to her waist. Her eyes glistened as she forced a smile and whispered, "The doctor says that your dad is going to be fine. He has a concussion and some broken ribs. He fell on his side and has bruises all the way down to his hip and leg." She looked down at her husband and shook her head before speaking to her sons again. "We are very blessed. The doctor told me that if your dad had landed on concrete, he probably would have died. And he said that we should be thankful the ground isn't frozen yet. The soft ground in the cattle lot saved him."

"It was the Lord that saved me," Joe said, his voice hoarse.

Both Monroe and Vernon jumped, surprised to hear their father speak.

Esther stepped closer to her husband. "Shsh—you shouldn't try to talk, Joe," she said. "The doctor says that you shouldn't try to do too much."

"You boys might as well go on your Thanksgiving frolic," Joe said, his voice a raspy whisper. Neither Monroe nor Vernon spoke. Joe took a few long, slow breaths and then continued. "There's no way we can finish the loafing shed now anyway."

"We'll get it done somehow, Dad," Vernon said.

Esther gave her sons a soft smile. "Let's not worry about that now."

They sat for at least an hour in the dark hospital room, listening to the constant beeping of a contraption that monitored Joe's vital signs. Occasionally, a nurse stepped into the room, spoke softly to Joe and checked his IV bag.

"You boys better get home and start your chores," Joe said hoarsely.

"Don't worry, Dad," Monroe assured him. "We'll take care of everything at home."

Esther stood up and smoothed out her apron again. "On your way home, you boys should stop and let your sisters know what is going on. They'll want to visit their dad this evening."

Monroe stood up as well, nodding. "Will you come home tonight?"

She shook her head. "The nurse told me that I could sleep on this recliner."

The brother's footsteps echoed down the long hallway as they walked through the hospital. A cold gust of wind met them at the door and shocked them back to reality. They pulled their hats down snuggly and shut their coats tight.

"Well, I guess we can go to the frolic," Vernon said as Monroe untied Buster and climbed into his buggy.

"I don't think I'll go," Monroe answered. "I got an idea while we were sitting in Dad's hospital room."

"What are you talking about?" Vernon looked at Monroe as if his brother wasn't making sense.

"I'm going to try and organize my own Thanksgiving frolic right here," Monroe said.

Vernon raised his eyebrows. "Who are you going to help?"

"Our dad," Monroe exclaimed. "He needs our help as much as anyone."

"Suit yourself," Vernon scoffed. "I'm going with Dorothy's family now that Dad has given us permission."

Chapter Six

A few days later, Monroe and his best friend, Elrose, met at Yoder's Auction Barn. Elrose never missed a household auction, and he always expected Monroe to join him. Yoder's Auction sold anything from used furniture to old tools. A crowd of people milled about inside a huge building. Rows and rows of items waited for their moment in the spotlight. The auctioneer wore pointy-toed boots and a cowboy hat. His handle-bar mustache stood out on either side of the microphone through which he rattled out a chant like a yodeling cowboy. He spoke with a drawl when he wasn't chanting, and threw in a few jokes to keep the audience entertained.

Several Amish boys worked at the Auction Barn and took turns holding each of the smaller items up in the air as the auctioneer sold it. The black and gray beards of Amish men could be seen on every side. Amish women wore black bonnets that matched their shawls. Little Amish children stood near their parents with sheepish faces, gawking at the few Englishers in the crowd. Monroe and Elrose walked the rows of merchandise looking closely at each item.

Elrose stopped in front of a tableful of tools. "How is your dad doing?"

"He's getting better every day," Monroe answered. "He may be able to come home soon." Monroe picked up an old hammer that would soon be auctioned off and examined it, then turned to his friend. "Elrose, I want to try and organize a work day at our place before my dad comes home. I'd really like to finish our loafing shed before Dad gets out of the hospital."

Elrose raised his eyebrows, which moved his stocking hat. "Wouldn't that take several days?"

"Yeah, maybe," Monroe said. "But if we could get about ten guys our age to come over next Tuesday we could get most of the hard part finished. Then Vernon and I could finish things up when we get time."

Elrose took off his dark stocking hat, scratched the back of his neck, and straightened his hat before putting it back on his head. "How did you come up with this idea?"

"I was mad at my dad because he told me I couldn't go with Simon Miller's family to the Thanksgiving frolic," Monroe said. "But then I was talking to a man at the horse sale who said old Mose gave him advice about how to deal with a mean boss—that a person should do what is right because it's right."

Elrose smirked, but nodded, so Monroe continued. "After thinking about what old Mose said, I feel like I should try to organize my own frolic to help my dad."

Elrose nodded his agreement. A few young men that they both knew walked past and Elrose stopped them. "Hello Myron, Duane. What do you boys have going on next Tuesday?"

The young men glanced at each other, then Myron shrugged. "Nothing that I know of," he said.

"Well, you guys heard about Monroe's dad falling off a ladder a few days ago, didn't ya?"

They both nodded.

"We're going to organize a work day," Elrose explained. "We're going to try to finish the building he was working on. If you guys could come to Monroe's on Tuesday that would really help!"

They both nodded again. Duane said, "I think I could bring my three younger brothers with me, too!"

Monroe gave them each a handshake and grin. "That would be great!"

The boys both nodded as they moved on, and Elrose called after them, "If you think of anyone else to invite, go ahead!"

Monroe nudged his buddy. "Thanks, Elrose. I really appreciate your help getting my frolic going."

Elrose shrugged. "Somebody needed to get it started."

"Now you're making schput!" Monroe said.

Elrose smiled and put a hand on Monroe's shoulder. "I think it sounds fun! I'll try to get my younger brother and some of his friends to come and help too."

They walked along a row of tall dressers that were waiting to be sold, and Elrose nudged Monroe with his elbow. "I am surprised you aren't going along with Simon's family, though," he teased. "Rosemary won't be too happy if her future husband isn't on *her* Thanksgiving frolic."

"We don't have any wedding plans," Monroe teased back.

"I still think I'm gonna be married last," Elrose said. "There's no way Rosemary will let you wait another year to marry her."

"All I've gotta do is get her to wait longer than your Linda!" They both laughed as they stepped around the last dresser in the row. Monroe stopped short when he realized a young woman was right in front of him.

"Oh, R-Rosemary, I d-didn't know you were here."

Rosemary stared at him, her blue eyes wide and her mouth hanging open, then turned and hurried for the door. Monroe ran and caught up with her as she climbed into her buggy.

"Wait, Rosemary; I want to talk to you." Monroe took hold of Rosemary's horse so she couldn't leave.

Her eyes flashed with anger. "Tell me that what I just heard in there isn't true."

"Don't take it so bad; you know how guys are."

Rosemary leaned forward on her buggy seat. "No, maybe I don't; how are they?"

"You know..." Monroe looked Rosemary's horse in the eye before he mumbled, "We don't want everyone to think we're like a tamed bull, being led around by a nose ring. Our buddies would make *schput* of us our whole lives if we were like that." Monroe held her horse even though it shook its mane and tried to break free of his grip.

"Don't worry, nobody will ever be able to make *schput* of you on account of me," she said. "You can forget about the Thanksgiving frolic *and me*! Now, let go of my horse." She cracked her buggy whip without hitting anything, and her horse pulled loose from Monroe's hands, and charged out through the parking lot and onto the highway. Monroe stood and watched her buggy's flashing lights disappear into the sunset.

Monroe hung his head and kicked at a rock as he headed back inside to where Elrose was watching the auction.

"Did Rosemary hear what I said?" Elrose asked. The auctioneer's loud chant covered up most of their words, keeping the crowd around them from hearing their conversation.

Monroe nodded slowly. "Yes." He didn't even try to hide his disappointment. "If I were you, I'd go see Linda before she has a chance to talk with Rosemary. Go ahead and ask Linda to marry you—I promise I won't schput ya."

"What about Rosemary? Are you gonna ask her to marry you?"

"I think I've lost my chance."

The rattling of the auctioneer's chant usually seemed warm and friendly, but at that moment it annoyed Monroe and churned up his racing thoughts. Although he usually enjoyed hanging around a warm auction barn on a cold evening, he left a few minutes after Rosemary drove away.

Chapter Seven

The following Tuesday morning, Monroe and Elrose examined lumber lying in a neat stack near the building site, covered by a dusting of snow.

Elrose brushed some of it off and asked, "Do you think we can do this?"

Monroe shrugged. "I want to try, for my dad."

They started at one corner and began to frame up the top edge along the posts that had been set earlier. Only a few minutes later, the first of their friends arrived.

Monroe lifted a hand in greeting. "Myron, Duane, thanks for coming over. We really need your help here."

"My younger brothers are going to round up some more help and bring them yet this morning," Duane said with a smile, obviously pleased to bring such good news.

The four young men had one corner of the frame in place when Duane's younger brothers arrived. They brought a whole group of teenage boys with them, just as Duane had promised. They'd all been to many barn raisings in their short lives and knew what to do.

Monroe found himself so busy organizing the workers that he didn't have a chance to swing a hammer during the next hour. They had completely finished one side when a van pulled into the lane.

"Who could that be?" Elrose and Monroe met eyes and they both shrugged.

"Maybe some family from out of state?" Monroe guessed. "They might be here to visit my dad, after hearing about his accident."

The van drove past the house and came to a stop near the new building. A large crew of workers emerged, including Vernon and Dorothy. Simon Miller opened the passenger door and helped old Mose climb out.

"We finished our work up north sooner than we expected," Simon explained. "We heard you had a Thanksgiving frolic going on here and decided to come join you."

"That would be great," Monroe choked out, his emotions overwhelming him. He studied the new faces, and his heart sank as he noted that Rosemary hadn't come with the group. Maybe she had asked to be dropped off at her home, not wanting to come around so soon. Still, Monroe felt warmed by Simon's willingness to help. The sight of old Mose swinging a hammer almost brought a tear to his eye, and the ache that had been growing inside his heart doubled when he saw Dorothy and Vernon working together.

Rosemary's grandpa and a few other old men wore black broad-brimmed hats, despite a cold wind that whipped through the work area. The sight of them made Monroe feel like pulling his stocking hat on tighter.

Simon looked over the project and called Monroe aside. "I'm very impressed that you and your friends made so much progress here."

"They're all good workers," Monroe said.

Simon nodded in agreement. "However, I see a problem in one corner of the structure."

He led Monroe to the corner that he and Elrose had started with earlier that morning. Simon pointed to the top edge. "It's not far off, but I can see from here that it's a little crooked."

A few older men had come along in the van with Simon. They gathered around the crooked corner to discuss whether they needed to dismantle that section.

"We could fudge a little and make it come out pretty close," Simon told them.

"It's just a loafing shed for cattle, isn't it?" one of the other older men asked.

Monroe checked the men's faces. "Yeah, it probably wouldn't matter if it's not perfect."

"Yes, it does matter!"

Everyone turned to see who spoke. Mose stood looking up at the crooked corner. As soon as the others saw Mose, they dismissed his comment and continued their conversation.

"We could run another board along that edge, over the top of the crooked part," Simon suggested. "That way the rest of the structure would come out straight. It may look a little odd but who would bother to notice in a loafing shed?"

Mose spoke up again. "The Bible says, '*And whether one member suffer, all the members suffer with it; or one member be honored, all the members rejoice with it.*'"

By this time, most of the younger men and boys had stopped working, gathering around to listen to the older men debating about how to move forward with the project. Some of them snickered at Mose's words. They all knew that old Mose was going senile and often said things that didn't make sense. He was well-known for quoting scripture verses throughout his life. It seemed sad to everyone that he continued rehearsing scripture even when it didn't fit well with the moment.

"I know what my dad is trying to tell us," Simon said. "He used to tell a story about something that happened when he was a young man. He worked for a carpenter back in those days. One time he was assigned a project on his own, building a porch for a family he didn't know. He made a mistake and instead of taking it apart and starting over, he tried to work around his mistake and cover it up."

All the workers gathered close, hanging on every word and quite interested in how the story would end. Simon's voice cracked as he continued. "During that project, he met one of the girls that lived in the house he was working on. That girl is my mother." He paused for a moment, visibly moved—almost to tears. "Dad ended up moving into that house when they married. Every time we sit on our porch, Dad looks up at that place with his half-covered mistake and says, 'Simon, if you make a mistake, don't try to cover it up. Do whatever you can do to fix it.'"

No one spoke. Monroe picked up a crowbar and climbed a ladder. He started yanking the boards loose, the nails creaking as they were pulled free. The others watched silently for a moment before returning to their own work. Simon helped Monroe measure the corner and rebuild that section, correctly. Monroe used a level to be sure everything was plumb before he drove in another nail.

"Who knows?" Simon said with a slight smile. "One of my daughters may live on this farm someday."

Monroe knew that Simon meant his words to be encouraging, but they drove a surge of pain into Monroe's heart as he thought about the mistake he had made, failing to ask Rosemary to marry him.

Around noon, Monroe was working on the roof of the half-constructed loafing shed. He saw a buggy coming up the road, and his heart skipped a beat when he recognized Rosemary's horse as it turned into the lane. By the time he got down off the roof and made his way to the hitching rack, Rosemary had tied her horse and begun unloading plates of food out of her buggy.

"Where should I set up the food table?" Rosemary didn't look at Monroe.

"We should take everything inside our buggy shed, to get the workers out of the cold," he answered. He gazed at Rosemary, wishing he knew how to undo the mistakes he had made with her. "I'll help you carry everything in," he offered.

They unloaded boxes of food out of her buggy. Rosemary had put together a feast of egg-salad sandwiches, chips and potato salad—things she knew were Monroe's favorites. She began arranging everything on a large piece of plywood that Monroe had placed on two sawhorses as a makeshift table.

"Call everyone in for lunch," Rosemary instructed Monroe, still refusing eye contact.

Monroe didn't move, willing her to look in his direction. "Thank you for bringing this meal," he said. "It means more to me than I can say."

Rosemary shrugged. "I would have done it for anyone."

Monroe knew it was true. Rosemary and her family were always finding ways to help anyone in need, and she had made many a meal for others. It cut him to the heart that she made a point of telling him that he was just another person in need, no one special in her life.

A few moments later workers gathered for prayer. Everyone chit-chatted while they ate sandwiches inside the warm buggy shed, catching up on local news or telling stories about days-gone-by. Monroe stood near Mose, who was sitting in one of the few chairs available. He wanted to ask about the riddle of pride, but he didn't think it would be wise to bring it up in front of everyone. As Monroe thought about the old man's words, Mose spoke. "If one part of a building is crooked, the whole building is not right."

He knew that Mose was talking about the project and the mistake they had fixed; however, as the old man said the words, Monroe knew that it was true of a man as well. If one part of his heart was not right, all of his other strengths would be made useless.

Everyone headed right back to work after they finished eating. Monroe knew he belonged outside working—after all, he'd organized the frolic, and everyone needed his direction about how his dad wanted things done. However, he also felt it was his place to help Rosemary gather all the lunch leftovers and supplies and load them back into her buggy.

"I want to thank you again for bringing lunch for everyone," Monroe said to Rosemary when he passed plates to her. "My parents don't know about the frolic. Mom and Dad are still at the hospital, and I didn't think about getting everyone food."

"You're welcome," she answered, without emotion.

"Rosemary..." he started.

"I'm not ready to talk yet," she whispered.

Monroe swallowed his disappointment. "Okay, I understand," he said, shoving his hands into his pockets as he walked back toward the building project.

In the next few hours, a building began to take shape. With older men directing the work, and younger men eager to swing hammers and push saws, everything fell into place quickly. Monroe could almost imagine that the loafing shed might possibly be finished before dark—all but the final touches, anyway.

Vernon came close to where Monroe worked to hang tin. "Dad and Mom could come home today," he worried his lip as he spoke.

"Yeah, I'm not sure how Dad will take it," Monroe answered. "I'd like to think he'll be happy. He should be, anyway. He's been worrying about getting this project done for months."

"It looks like we are going to find out in a few minutes," Vernon said, pointing to a van pulling into their lane. They both recognized the vehicle as the one their Dad hired when he needed to go further than a buggy could take him.

The van drove right past the house and around the barn, pulling into sight of the work project. A few of the workers glanced at the vehicle, but most of them stayed busy with whatever part of the project they were assigned. Monroe and Vernon stayed busy as well, fearing how their father might react. Monroe stole a glance toward the van as his dad climbed out of the back sliding door and used a walker to maneuver toward the work site. Monroe and Vernon hid themselves behind other workers.

Suddenly, Monroe heard a loud shout.

"Stop, stop!"

Everyone stopped what they were doing and looked at Joe. Monroe's ears grew hot, despite the biting cold. They all knew that Joe Hostetler was a man set in his ways and strongly opinionated. Yet, Monroe was sure that they all expected him to be pleased to see his building taking shape.

"Stop working," Joe called out. "You all should head home now."

Every person there froze in place. Nobody knew what to do next. Monroe glanced at Vernon and then Elrose. They both had the same look of shock on their faces. Monroe's eyes went to Rosemary's dad next. Simon didn't look rattled, and was the only person who didn't stop working at Joe's command.

Joe raised one hand off his walker and motioned to the crowd. "Please, go home. I'm not worthy to have your help."

Those words stunned Monroe more than anything he had ever heard in his life. A few of the older men gathered around Joe.

"Please," Joe continued, "I'm ashamed to have you help me. I've been selfish and failed to help others when I should have. I don't deserve to have you all help me."

Many of the older men disagreed with him. "That's not true," one said.

"You are a good man." another tried to encourage him.

Then old Mose stepped forward. He raised his hands as though ready to preach a sermon, and everyone gave him their attention. "No, Joe is right. He is not worthy of our help."

There was a gasp—from Dorothy or Simon, Monroe guessed; perhaps both, judging by the look of horror on their faces. No other person moved or dared speak. The silent tension felt colder than the November breeze, hanging in the air like a blanket of ice.

And then Mose continued. "It is true that Joe has not always been willing to help others when he should."

Monroe watched his dad's face. Joe's chin began to quiver, which made his graying beard shake against his black winter coat. For the first time in Monroe's life, he pitied his dad. There was movement in the crowd as Simon finally stopped working and made his way over toward Mose—undoubtedly to take him by the hand and lead him away.

Before Simon got close enough to stop Mose's madness, the old man spoke again. "All of you who have always helped others should leave like Joe says." Mose looked from man to man, meeting eyes with all of them. "All of those here who are worthy, go on home. Those of us who have failed to help others from time to time and those of us who are not worthy, we should get back to work." At that, the old man reached over, picked up a hammer, and started driving a nail into a board.

For a moment, everyone watched old Mose driving nails into the wood. Then, one by one, as if his words, like nails, had been driven into their hearts and the point had sunk in, they joined Mose, returning to their work.

Monroe couldn't move. He had never heard a common man speaking such wisdom. He watched the scene before him in disbelief, as every man, woman, and boy, humbly acknowledged their own guilt by getting back to work. None of them could stand up and say that they were worthy. They had all failed in some way at some point in their life.

Joe took a hanky out of his pocket, then wiped his eyes and blew his nose. He watched as everyone put a strong effort into completing his project. Though Monroe was twenty yards away from his dad, he was sure he could see tears streaming down his father's cheeks.

Suddenly, Monroe realized he had tears on his own face. He'd been locked in place, so shocked at everything that had just transpired. When he realized that tears were falling from his own eyes, it was as if he was released to move again, and he wiped the tears off his cheeks with the sleeve of his jacket.

Monroe got back to work. At first, everyone worked at a silent, steady pace. Gradually, people began to talk and their pace picked up. After a few more minutes had gone by, the Thanksgiving frolic had advanced to a fever pitch. The workers talked among themselves with cheerful voices. Laughter rang out, accompanied by blows of the hammers and the singing of the saws. All the while, Joe watched from a chair that Simon had brought out of the buggy shed. Tears continued to stream down his cheeks as he watched his friends and neighbors doing his work. Monroe himself had to continually wipe his face with his sleeve, but nobody seemed to notice.

Chapter Eight

On Thanksgiving Day, Monroe could only think of Rosemary. He listened to the sounds of his mom and sisters toiling in the kitchen as they prepared a Thanksgiving feast of turkey, stuffing, sweet potatoes, mashed potatoes, gravy, dinner rolls, scalloped corn, and multiple side dishes—too many to count. The house was warm and moist because of all the simmering pots on the stove. So much so, the windows fogged over and dripped condensation. The aroma of baking turkey seeped into every room, tantalizing the entire family.

Monroe's older sisters and their husbands weren't that much older than he and Vernon, but they already had large families. Children played with toys at the feet of Monroe's brothers-in-law while they visited cheerfully. Even Vernon set aside his ornery ways and played on the floor with his nieces and nephews.

Monroe smiled as he looked around the room. The happy sounds and warm conversations were contagious, yet not enough to take his mind off Rosemary. He found himself trying to think of a reason to go see her. Instead of talking with his family, he pored over ideas of what he would say if he did talk to her. Nothing seemed quite right.

Finally, Esther called everyone to the table for the late afternoon meal. The whole family chatted and laughed as they gathered around, squeezing together closely in an effort to fit every member in. When they were finally seated, the talking hushed until the room became filled with silence. Even the smallest children sensed that it was time for prayer. Instead of saying *let's pray*, as he usually did, Joe cleared his voice and began to speak.

"You know, this accident of mine has proven to be one of the best things that ever happened to me." A tear rolled down his cheek as he spoke. "I had lost track of what is most important in life." He took a moment to compose himself, then continued. "At first, I was actually angry with God. I thought, 'Why would God allow me to suffer an injury that will keep me from being a good steward of the possessions He has entrusted to me?' I didn't understand that I was failing to be a good steward of something more important than possessions. I was failing to be a good steward of the relationships God has given me. Relationships with my wife and children, my grandchildren, my brothers and sisters in Christ, and even my neighbors and friends." He stopped and shook his hanky, then blew his nose into it.

Everyone around the table sniffled, and Esther passed around napkins for them to wipe their eyes and blow their noses. The children watched in amazement at the unusual display of emotion.

"What opened my eyes," Joe said, "was Monroe's kind act. Monroe asked his friends to help him as a surprise for me. When I saw my neighbors doing my work, I was humbled. At that moment, when I felt the power of their kindness towards me, I realized what it means to help others." Joe looked at Monroe and their eyes met. "Monroe thought to be kind to me, even though I had been harsh with him. That was an example of true Christian love. Let us pray with thankful hearts."

Everyone bowed and prayed within their hearts. Monroe prayed silently, *Dear Lord, thank you for Mose. Mose is the one who taught us all what it means to show true Christian love. Please Lord, bless Mose and his family.*

Monroe loaded his plate with everything his mother and sisters had fixed. He poured gravy over a mound of turkey, mashed potatoes and stuffing, letting the steam rise under his nose. Esther's table fell silent except for the tinkling of spoons and forks as everyone fellowshipped in the abundance of God's provision. Everything in the world seemed perfect, except for one thing.

Just as the meal came to an end, a knock sounded on the door. Monroe stood up before anyone else could move.

"I'll see who's here," he announced. He didn't know if the others suspected what was on his mind. He didn't care. His heart swelled with hope, expecting to see Rosemary's sweet face. He pulled open the door, and there stood Rosemary's sister, Dorothy.

"I stopped by to tell you that my grandpa had another stroke," she said. "We took him to the hospital, but we don't expect he will live through the night."

Monroe stared at her, speechless.

Vernon brushed past Monroe, grabbed his coat, and stepped outside with Dorothy, shutting the door behind them. If any of his family had not known that Vernon cared for Dorothy before, they were no longer left to wonder. Monroe felt all the hope go out of his heart. He slowly slid his chair up to the table again and stared at his empty plate. He could feel the eyes of his whole family resting on him.

"You can go see Mose's family if you feel you should," Mom said.

"Yes, please go and tell them that we are all praying," Dad agreed.

Monroe didn't say a word. He rushed to gather his coat and hat, then ran to the barn. He harnessed Buster so quickly, he later worried he might not have buckled everything into place correctly. Buster didn't seem to mind Monroe's encouragement to go fast. The sun sank low, due to the short days of late November, as Buster charged out of the lane and covered the miles between Joe's family farm and the hospital in record time.

Chapter Nine

Monroe found Simon Miller's family easily, as they were the only Amish family in the lobby. Vernon stood with Dorothy at his side. Rosemary looked Monroe in the eyes for the first time since they had broken up. She had clearly been crying. Her eyes were swollen and red. However, Monroe's face must have given away his inner turmoil because she touched his arm and asked, "Are you okay?" Her blue eyes filled with compassion and kindness.

"Can I see Mose?" Monroe pleaded.

"Yes, we've been taking turns going in," she answered. "We'll let you go in next."

Monroe nodded. He stood near Rosemary, but they didn't speak. He felt cold, as though his own blood was not flowing as it should. His head swam and his thoughts swirled. He had just prayed and asked for a blessing on Mose and his family. *How could God answer his prayer like this*?

"You can see Grandpa now," Rosemary said, her voice pulling Monroe out of his dark thoughts. She led him down the hall until she reached the doorway to Mose's room, then she pointed to a chair beside Mose's hospital bed and walked away.

Monroe stepped into the dimly lit room and took a seat. A monitor beeped steadily as Monroe took in the sight of Mose's lifeless body and sunken cheeks, then the electronic gadgets with flashing lights, pulsing sounds, and beeps.

"I need you to get well again, Mose," Monroe said. "I need you to tell me how to get rid of pride."

Old Mose didn't move. Hot tears streamed down Monroe's cheeks and dripped onto his hand. He didn't try to wipe them away, but let them fall freely.

After a moment, he continued. "Thank you for what you did for my dad. Your wisdom was a gift to our whole community, and especially to our family. I'm so thankful for the years God gave you. You have been a blessing to our whole community." He took hold of Mose's hand and squeezed it. Still, Mose didn't move.

Monroe felt numb and didn't know what to do next. He suddenly had a strong urge to breath in fresh air. He stood up and walked back through the lobby. He didn't stop to say anything to Rosemary or her parents, though he could see his tears had drawn their attention. When he stepped outside, he heard another set of footsteps and realized that Rosemary was right behind him.

"Wait, Monroe, I want to talk to you," she said. She looked at his face and wiped the tears off his cheeks with her fingers. "I didn't know you cared so much about Grandpa," she said, her lips trembling. "I thought you only talked to him to make fun of him."

Monroe forced his words through his tightening throat. "Your grandpa was about the best man I've ever known."

Rosemary's voice quivered as she murmured, "I heard about what he did at your Thanksgiving frolic."

"Yes. Thanks to Mose, our family will never be the same."

"I know what he would say to you." Rosemary laughed through her tears. "'I didn't do anything. God gave me the right words at the right moment. The Lord is always faithful.'"

"But I really needed to talk to Mose one more time." Monroe covered his face and turned away from Rosemary. "I needed Mose to answer a question he asked me."

Rosemary touched Monroe's back. "What question?"

"Mose asked me, 'How does a man get rid of pride?' He told me to come back after we were done with our harvest and he would tell me the answer if I didn't know it by then."

"By acting more humble I would guess," she answered.

Monroe shook his head. "That's what I told him, but he said that's false humility and leads people to be proud of how humble they are."

She tried again. "Well, I guess when a person asks Christ into his heart he becomes humble?"

"I tried that answer, too, and he said that many Christians struggle with pride even after asking Christ into their heart." Monroe's voice couldn't hide how discouraged he felt. For days, he had gone over all the things he wanted to tell Rosemary and yet, at this moment he couldn't remember any of it. He reached out and took her warm hand and gave it a slight squeeze. "Please tell your family that our family is praying for Mose, and all of you." He walked away and left Rosemary standing in the light of the hospital entryway.

Monroe headed back to his buggy as dusk began to be swallowed by darkness. Buster stood next to Dorothy's horse, which had brought her and Vernon to the hospital. Monroe slowly untied his horse and climbed into his buggy. Buster's hoofbeats echoed off buildings as they passed through empty streets and exited the small town.

Once Buster got onto the highway he tried to pick up speed as usual, but Monroe kept a tight rein, as the thought of going fast didn't seem to hold its former pleasure. A set of lights showed through the little window on the back of Monroe's buggy, indicating that another horse and buggy followed on the road behind them. Buster apparently heard the hoofbeats too, because he shook his mane and attempted to loosen Monroe's hold on his bit.

Monroe held tight on his driving lines and spoke to his horse. "What will it matter if another horse passes us?"

Suddenly Monroe had an urge to pray. He pulled off his hat and blurted out, "Dear Lord, please forgive me for the pride I have in my heart. Please Lord, forgive me for the way I treated Rosemary. I've looked down on others because my horse was better than theirs. I see where that is going to end up—with me living a life of pride in all that I possess. Please, Lord Jesus, give me a chance to make things right with Rosemary."

The other horse continued to gain on Buster, and it was all Monroe could do to hold his horse in check. He wanted to let another horse pass his, just to prove a point to himself and his horse. He finally pulled Buster over and made him stop in a farm lane, allowing the other horse to pass by. However, the other horse pulled into the lane and stopped beside them. A woman got out and appeared to be tying her horse to a nearby fence, so Monroe stepped out of his buggy and tied Buster.

"Monroe?"

Monroe squinted his eyes attempting to peer through the darkness. "Is that you, Rosemary?"

"Yes," she said. "I didn't think that could be you and Buster because I was able to catch up and almost passed you." She stepped around her buggy and moved toward Monroe. "Why don't you have a hat on?"

"Because I was praying," he said and swallowed a lump in his throat. He licked his lips to make them wet enough to talk. "What are you doing here?"

Rosemary stopped about five steps away from Monroe, her breath puffing out like smoke in the cold November air. "After you left, I thought about what you said. Well, I guess it was about what my grandpa told you—that people can become proud of how humble they are."

Monroe stared at her outline, barely visible under an inky-black sky. A host of stars twinkled in the crisp November night.

"I realized that *I am* that person," she said. "I judged you and thought that I was humbler than you. Please forgive me, Monroe."

Monroe didn't know what to say. Those words were the last thing he expected to hear.

"Also"—she took a step toward him, her voice rising as she became more animated— "I remembered what Grandpa used to say about how to get rid of pride!"

Monroe moved one step closer to Rosemary in anticipation. "What is it?"

"After you left, I could almost hear Grandpa's voice quoting this verse. 'If we say that we have no sin, we deceive ourselves, and the truth is not in us. If we confess our sins, He is faithful and just to forgive us our sins and to cleanse us from all unrighteousness.'"

Monroe's eyebrows raised in surprise as he nodded his head. "I should have thought of that verse."

Rosemary took another step toward Monroe. "What were you praying about?"

Monroe's heart pounded in his chest. He could feel her presence so close, yet, just out of reach. He leaned toward her. "While Buster trotted on the highway, I couldn't stop thinking about how proud I've been," Monroe confessed. "I asked God to forgive me and take away my pride in my horse and other possessions."

Rosemary's hands went to her cheeks in astonishment.

"I also asked The Lord to forgive me for the pride that kept me from asking you to marry me," he said. "I asked Jesus for a chance to make things right with you."

Rosemary took the final step that remained between them and took Monroe's hand. "I forgive you," she whispered and dabbed at the corner of her eye with her free hand.

He squeezed her smooth hand in his. "Rosemary, will you marry me?"

He could see her black bonnet nodding in the starlight.

"I'm sorry that I think you're the prettiest girl I've ever seen, but that's not why I want to marry you," he said.

She giggled.

"I want to marry you because of how kind you are. You're always finding ways to reach out and help others. You are quite the Rosemary and that's the type of wife I want."

They closed the final few inches between them and renewed their relationship with a kiss.

"Come back with me to the hospital," she said. "Please be part of my family's vigil for Grandpa. After all, my family will become your family now."

As Rosemary untied her horse, she ducked under its neck. "Oh, and by the way, you should call him Mr. Buster—I like that a lot!"

He could hear her giggle as she climbed into her buggy. Her horse trotted onto the road before Monroe could get his horse untied. He jumped into his buggy and took the lines. "Come on Mr. Buster we're gonna have our hands full trying to keep up with that Rosemary."

The sound of hoofbeats rang out on the highway as flashing buggy lights disappeared into the dark November night.

About the Authors

Laura V. Hilton

Laura V. Hilton is an award-winning, sought-after author with almost twenty Amish, contemporary, and historical romances. When she's not writing, she reviews books for her blogs, and writes devotionals for blog posts for Seriously Write and Putting on the New.

Laura and her pastor-husband have five children and a hyper dog named Skye. They currently live in Arkansas. One son is in the U.S. Coast Guard. She is a pastor's wife, and homeschools her two youngest children.

When she's not writing, Laura enjoys reading, and visiting lighthouses and waterfalls. Her favorite season is winter, her favorite holiday is Christmas.

Rachel J. Good

Rachel J. Good grew up near Lancaster, PA, the setting for many of her Amish novels. Striving to be as authentic as possible, she spends special time with her Amish friends, doing chores on their farm and attending family events. Rachel is the author of several Amish series, including Sisters & Friends (Charisma), Love & Promises (Grand Central), and two books in the Hearts of Amish Country series (Annie's Book Club). In addition, she has two *Amish Quilts Coloring Books* as well as stories in several anthologies, including *Springs of Love* (CelebrateLit).

Thomas Nye

Thomas Nye writes novels about horses and Amish life, with a touch of romance, and a foundation of faith in Christ. He and his wife, Shari, live on her family farm where they raised five children. Their six grandchildren love to visit Karma and Karla, a team of draft horses which Thomas purchased from an Amish friend. Walking a mail route for the U.S. Postal Service keeps Thomas close to nature and affords him many quiet hours which he uses to dream up novels. Over three decades of friendships with Amish neighbors has revealed a simple wisdom that he weaves into his writing. To find out more, visit: amishhorses.blogspot.com

A Note from the Publisher

We at Celebrate Lit Publishing just want to take a moment to thank you for reading our collection *Love's Thankful Heart*. We are so grateful that you chose to pick up this book and read it. If you enjoyed this collection, please check out our previous collections and keep an eye out for our future releases.

Celebrate Lit Publishing Collections

Let Love Spring by Jodie Wolfe, Sandy Faye Mauck, and Linda Shenton Matchett
A Spring of Weddings by Toni Shiloh and Melissa Wardwell
Springs of Love by Laura V. Hilton, Rachel J. Good, and Thomas Nye

80685357R00138

Made in the USA
Columbia, SC
20 November 2017